CAUGHT IN THE ORGAN DRAFT

CAUGHT IN THE ORGAN DRAFT

BIOLOGY IN SCIENCE FICTION

Edited by Isaac Asimov,
Martin H. Greenberg,
& Charles G. Waugh

Farrar · Straus · Giroux
New York

First edition, 1983

Printed in the United States of America
Published simultaneously in Canada by
McGraw-Hill Ryerson Ltd., Toronto
Designed by Charlotte Staub

Library of Congress Cataloging in Publication Data
Main entry under title: Caught in the organ draft.
  Includes bibliographical references.
  Summary: An anthology of twelve science fiction
stories with biological themes.
  1. Science fiction, American. 2. Children's stories,
American. [1. Science fiction. 2. Short stories]
I. Asimov, Isaac. II. Greenberg, Martin.
III. Waugh, Charles.
PZ5.C19 1983 [Fic] 82–15756 ISBN 0–374–31228–1

CONTENTS

INTRODUCTION

The term *Biology* comes from two Greek words, *bios* and *logos*. The former means "life"; the latter means "word," or, more abstractly, "rational discourse," or, translated into modern terms, "scientific thought." *Biology*, then, is, as the very name tells us, "the science of life."

Nothing can be more important to us, since we ourselves are examples of life.

Nor is the importance of biology merely a matter of selfish preoccupation. Consider that in a vast universe consisting of 100 billion galaxies, each built up of an average of 50 billion stars, there is but one world we know of—our own—that possesses life.

It seems unlikely that in so large a universe only one spot can be found with life, and it can be (and *is*) argued that in actual fact there are numerous places, many millions of them per galaxy, perhaps, in which life exists. Nevertheless, that remains speculation as yet, and we have no direct evidence for the existence of life anywhere—except here on Earth.

Furthermore, if we confine ourselves to Earth, life is a phenomenon of the planetary surface only. It is a fragile thing, dependent upon a narrow range of environmental conditions. These conditions threaten always to shift to the point of wiping out many bits of life. Freezes, fires, droughts, floods, volcanic eruptions, predators, parasites . . .

There are even current suggestions that periodically (on at least six different occasions) collisions of Earth with small asteroids have succeeded in nearly destroying life on the planet. The most recent occasion may have been only 65 million years ago.

We must picture life, then, as existing on only one planet and that just barely, by the merest hair.

But doesn't that show that life is extremely unimportant in the universe as a whole? An evanescent phenomenon? A trifling and temporary disease of matter? A tiny pimple flawing the mighty scheme of things?

Wait!

Of all the substances we know, only living things seem to display any sign of "consciousness," of awareness of their surroundings, of the ability to show adaptive response, that is, to react to those surroundings in such a way as to maximize their security and ensure their survival.

This is surely a unique property. All non-living objects endure whatever the environment has in store for them. All non-living objects face disaster precisely as they would face prosperity. Only living objects "know enough to come in out of the rain," to speak metaphorically. Even trees, which cannot move to avoid the ax, send out roots to find water and spread out leaves to bask in sunshine.

Such uniqueness of behavior produces a quality of life that far more than makes up for the insignificance of its quantity and for its terrifying fragility.

One might argue that in estimating the relative importance of the quality of adaptive response of life as compared with such disadvantages as its small quantity and great fragility, we are ourselves making the judgment, and that we, as examples of life, can scarcely be considered impartial.

True! But that is the very point! Only *life* can possibly make the judgment, because only life has the awareness to see that a question of judgment arises. Life is supremely important for the very reason that only life can question and decide the matter of importance.

In fact, we are now talking not merely about adaptive response, but about abstract thought, and that is something even more restricted. There are perhaps 2 million species of living things now alive, and in the entire 3-billion-year history of life on Earth, there may have been 20 million species altogether. And of them all, only one species, *Homo sapiens*, has given overwhelming evidence of capacity for abstract thought.

That may be our vanity, of course. It is possible that chimpanzees, gorillas, elephants, dolphins, whales, crows, octopi, and who knows what other species can engage in something that can be defined, by more or less liberal interpretation, as abstract thought. There is no question, though, that even if this be so, human beings have so far exceeded all other species in the ability to think that what we possess lifts us to a plateau so much higher than that on which other species rest that the quantitative superiority produces what is virtually a qualitative difference.

We can express this in actual deeds. *Homo erectus*, a

smaller-brained predecessor of ourselves, was the first species in the history of the Earth to make deliberate use of fire. *Homo sapiens* inherited that. No other species of life on Earth, however intelligent, uses or has ever used fire.

Nor is *Homo sapiens* the mere passive beneficiary of the inventive and innovative genius of *Homo erectus*. *Homo sapiens* has introduced, in a mere moment of time (geologically speaking), all the vast paraphernalia of what we call technological civilization. There is no question but that only *Homo sapiens* has, or (on Earth) has ever had, the capacity to develop a complex technology.

This means that only human beings, of all the life we know, have the capacity for developing instruments to extend their senses; to see the unseeable, hear the unhearable; to accumulate and record data; to weigh their significance; to reach conclusions.

So it is not merely life, but one species out of 20 million, we, who are aware of the universe more or less as it is, and who labor to understand it.

There may be other living beings elsewhere in the universe who are as aware and as toilful and as ardent in the pursuit as we. There may be many millions of them. Some may be far more advanced in the process than we are. —But we have no evidence of their existence.

As far as we know, therefore, we are the only beings in the entire vast universe who turn questioning eyes on stars, on atoms, on ourselves, and seek answers.

Is it not terrible, then, that our gathered knowledge, put to the service of our passions, has brought us to the edge of self-destruction? And if we destroy ourselves, is it not plain that we destroy something that may be utterly unique in the universe and that may never be replaced? Should we not labor to keep ourselves and our civilization alive out of self-love and vanity, if no nobler emotion will do?

If we do choose the path of adaptive response to the destructive aspects of our technology, if we do survive, human beings will undoubtedly continue to question and to learn and to advance in knowledge.

And it is characteristic of the restlessness of the human mind, that however rapid that advance may be, and however startling its findings, success can never be fast enough to satisfy our curiosity. We always move in advance of the findings, doing so in the form of speculation.

Science fiction is that branch of literature which is, among other things, specifically devoted to such speculation; and where can the speculation assume more fascinating guises than in the study of life itself, that most amazing and most nearly impenetrable aspect of the universe?

Here, then, are a dozen superb examples of biologically oriented science fiction chosen from the half-century of modern production.

Isaac Asimov

CAUGHT IN THE ORGAN DRAFT

ORIGIN

KEEP OUT
Fredric Brown

Daptine is the secret of it. Adaptine, they called it first;
then it got shortened to daptine. It let us adapt.

They explained it all to us when we were ten years old; I
guess they thought we were too young to understand before
then, although we knew a lot of it already. They told us just
after we landed on Mars.

"You're *home*, children," the Head Teacher told us after
we had gone into the glassite dome they'd built for us there.
And he told us there'd be a special lecture for us that evening, an important one that we must all attend.

And that evening he told us the whole story and the
whys and wherefores. He stood up before us. He had to

3

wear a heated space suit and helmet, of course, because the temperature in the dome was comfortable for us but already freezing cold for him and the air was already too thin for him to breathe. His voice came to us by radio from inside his helmet.

"Children," he said, "you are home. This is Mars, the planet on which you will spend the rest of your lives. You are Martians, the first Martians. You have lived five years on Earth and another five in space. Now you will spend ten years, until you are adults, in this dome, although toward the end of that time you will be allowed to spend increasingly long periods outdoors.

"Then you will go forth and make your own homes, live your own lives, as Martians. You will intermarry and your children will breed true. They, too, will be Martians.

"It is time you were told the history of this great experiment of which each of you is a part."

Then he told us.

Man, he said, had first reached Mars in 1985. It had been uninhabited by intelligent life (there is plenty of plant life and a few varieties of nonflying insects) and he had found it by terrestrial standards uninhabitable. Man could survive on Mars only by living inside glassite domes and wearing space suits when he went outside of them. Except by day in the warmer seasons it was too cold for him. The air was too thin for him to breathe and long exposure to sunlight—less filtered of rays harmful to him than on Earth because of the lesser atmosphere—could kill him. The plants were chemically alien to him and he could not eat them; he had to bring all his food from Earth or grow it in hydroponic tanks.

For fifty years he had tried to colonize Mars and all his efforts had failed. Besides this dome which had been built for us there was only one other outpost, another glassite dome much smaller and less than a mile away.

It had looked as though mankind could never spread to the planets of the solar system other than Earth, for of all of them Mars was the least inhospitable; if he couldn't live here there was no use even trying to colonize the others.

And then, in 2034, thirty years ago, a brilliant biochemist named Waymoth had discovered daptine, a miracle drug that worked not on the animal or person to whom it was given but on the progeny he conceived during a limited period of time after inoculation.

It gave his progeny almost limitless adaptability to changing conditions, provided the changes were made gradually.

Dr. Waymoth had inoculated and then mated a pair of guinea pigs; they had borne a litter of five, and by placing each member of the litter under different and gradually changing conditions, he had obtained amazing results. When they attained maturity one of those guinea pigs was living comfortably at a temperature of forty degrees below zero Fahrenheit, another was quite happy at a hundred and fifty above. A third was thriving on a diet that would have been deadly poison for an ordinary animal and a fourth was contented under a constant X-ray bombardment that would have killed one of its parents within minutes.

Subsequent experiments with many litters showed that animals who had been adapted to similar conditions bred true and their progeny was conditioned from birth to live under those conditions.

"Ten years later, ten years ago," the Head Teacher told us, "you children were born. Born of parents carefully selected from those who volunteered for the experiment. And from birth you have been brought up under carefully controlled and gradually changing conditions.

"From the time you were born the air you have breathed has been very gradually thinned and its oxygen content reduced. Your lungs have compensated by becoming much greater in capacity, which is why your chests are so much larger than those of your teachers and attendants; when you are fully mature and are breathing air like that of Mars, the difference will be even greater.

"Your bodies are growing fur to enable you to stand the increasing cold. You are comfortable now under conditions which would kill ordinary people quickly. Since you were four years old your nurses and teachers have had to wear special protection to survive conditions that seem normal to you.

"In another ten years, at maturity, you will be completely acclimated to Mars. Its air will be your air; its food plants your food. Its extremes of temperature will be easy for you to endure and its median temperatures pleasant to you. Already, because of the five years we spent in space under gradually decreased gravitational pull, the gravity of Mars seems normal to you.

"It will be your planet, to live on and to populate. You are the children of Earth but you are the first Martians."

Of course, we had known a lot of those things already.

The last year was the best. By then the air inside the dome —except for the pressurized parts where our teachers and attendants lived—was almost like that outside, and we were allowed out for increasingly long periods. It is good to be in the open.

The last few months they relaxed segregation of the sexes so we could begin choosing mates, although they told us there is to be no marriage until after the final day, after our full clearance. Choosing was not difficult in my case. I had made my choice long since and I'd felt sure that she felt the same way; I was right.

Tomorrow is the day of our freedom. Tomorrow we will be Martians, *the* Martians. Tomorrow we shall take over the planet.

Some among us are impatient, have been impatient for weeks now, but wiser counsel prevailed and we are waiting. We have waited twenty years and we can wait until the final day.

And tomorrow is the final day.

Tomorrow, at a signal, we will kill the teachers and the other Earthmen among us before we go forth. They do not suspect, so it will be easy.

We have dissimulated for years now, and they do not know how we hate them. They do not know how disgusting and hideous we find them, with their ugly, misshapen bodies, so narrow shouldered and tiny chested, their weak, sibilant voices that need amplification to carry in our Martian air, and above all their white, pasty, hairless skins.

We shall kill them and then we shall go and smash the other dome so all the Earthmen there will die, too.

If more Earthmen ever come to punish us, we can live and hide in the hills where they'll never find us. And if they try to build more domes here we'll smash them. We want no more to do with Earth.

This is our planet and we want no aliens. Keep out!

Fredric Brown (1906–72)
The late Fredric Brown was a writer who was equally talented in the mystery and science fiction fields, winning the Edgar Award of the Mystery Writers of America in 1948. As a science fiction writer he is best remembered for his short-short stories, many of which are only a few hundred words in length. He was also one

of science fiction's premier humorists, and his wonderfully funny books such as What Mad Universe (1949) and Martians, Go Home! (1955) are still entertaining thousands of readers today. Mr. Brown worked for the Milwaukee Journal for many years. An outstanding sampling of his work can be found in The Best of Fredric Brown (1977).

EVOLUTION

STUDENT BODY
Floyd L. Wallace

The first morning that they were fully committed to the planet, the executive officer stepped out of the ship. It was not quite dawn. Executive Hafner squinted in the early light; his eyes opened wider, and he promptly went back inside. Three minutes later, he reappeared with the biologist in tow.

"Last night you said there was nothing dangerous," said the executive. "Do you still think it's so?"

Dano Marin stared. "I do." What his voice lacked in conviction, it made up in embarrassment. He laughed uncertainly.

"This is no laughing matter. I'll talk to you later."

9

The biologist stood by the ship and watched as the executive walked to the row of sleeping colonists.

"Mrs. Athyl," said the executive as he stopped beside the sleeping figure.

She yawned, rubbed her eyes, rolled over, and stood up. The covering that should have been there, however, wasn't. Neither was the garment she had on when she had gone to sleep. She assumed the conventional position of a woman who is astonished to find herself unclad without her knowledge or consent.

"It's all right, Mrs. Athyl. I'm not a voyeur myself. Still, I think you should get some clothing on." Most of the colonists were awake now. Executive Hafner turned to them. "If you haven't any suitable clothing in the ship, the commissary will issue you some. Explanations will be given later."

The colonists scattered. There was no compulsive modesty among them, for it couldn't have survived a year and a half in crowded spaceships. Nevertheless, it was a shock to awaken with no clothing on and not know who or what had removed it during the night. It was surprise more than anything else that disconcerted them.

On his way back to the spaceship, Executive Hafner paused. "Any ideas about it?"

Dano Marin shrugged. "How could I have? The planet is as new to me as it is to you."

"Sure. But you're the biologist."

As the only scientist in a crew of rough-and-ready colonists and builders, Marin was going to be called on to answer a lot of questions that weren't in his field.

"Nocturnal insects, most likely," he suggested. That was pretty weak, though he knew that in ancient times locusts had stripped fields in a matter of hours. Could they do the same with the clothing of humans and not awaken them?

"I'll look into the matter. As soon as I find anything, I'll let you know."

"Good." Hafner nodded and went into the spaceship.

Dano Marin walked to the grove in which the colonists had been sleeping. It had been a mistake to let them bed down there, but at the time the request had been made, there had seemed no reason not to grant it. After eighteen months in crowded ships everyone naturally wanted fresh air and the rustle of leaves overhead.

Marin looked out through the grove. It was empty now; the colonists, both men and women, had disappeared inside the ship, dressing, probably.

The trees were not tall and the leaves were dark bottle-green. Occasional huge white flowers caught sunlight that made them seem larger than they were. It wasn't Earth and therefore the trees couldn't be magnolias. But they reminded Marin of magnolia trees and thereafter he always thought of them as that.

The problem of the missing clothing was ironic. Biological Survey never made a mistake—yet obviously they had. They listed the planet as the most suitable for Man of any so far discovered. Few insects, no dangerous animals, a most equitable climate. They had named it Glade because that was the word which fitted best. The whole land mass seemed to be one vast and pleasant meadow.

Evidently there were things about the planet that Biological Survey had missed.

Marin dropped to his knees and began to look for clues. If insects had been responsible, there ought to be a few dead ones, crushed, perhaps, as the colonists rolled over in their sleep. There were no insects, either live or dead.

He stood up in disappointment and walked slowly through the grove. It might be the trees. At night they could exude a vapor which was capable of dissolving the material from which the clothing had been made. Far-fetched, but not impossible. He crumbled a leaf in his hand and rubbed it against his sleeve. A pungent smell, but nothing happened. That didn't disprove the theory, of course.

He looked out through the trees at the blue sun. It was bigger than Sol, but farther away. At Glade, it was about equal to the Sun on Earth.

He almost missed the bright eyes that regarded him from the underbrush. Almost, but didn't—the domain of biology begins at the edge of the atmosphere; it includes the brush and the small creatures that live in it.

He swooped down on it. The creature fled squealing. He ran it down in the grass outside the grove. It collapsed into quaking flesh as he picked it up. He talked to it gently and the terror subsided.

It nibbled contentedly on his jacket as he carried it back to the ship.

Executive Hafner stared unhappily into the cage. It was an undistinguished animal, small and something like an undeveloped rodent. Its fur was sparse and stringy, unglamorous; it would never be an item in the fur export trade.

"Can we exterminate it?" asked Hafner. "Locally, that is."

"Hardly. It's ecologically basic."

The executive looked blank. Dano Marin added the explanation: "You know how Biological Controls works. As soon as a planet has been discovered that looks suitable, they send out a survey ship loaded with equipment. The ship flies low over a good part of the planet and the instruments in the ship record the neural currents of the animals below. The instruments can distinguish the characteristic neural patterns of anything that has a brain, including insects.

"Anyway, they have a pretty good idea of the kinds of

animals on the planet and their relative distribution. Naturally, the survey party takes a few specimens. They have to in order to correlate the pattern with the actual animal, otherwise the neural pattern would be merely a meaningless squiggle on a microfilm.

"The survey shows that this animal is one of only four species of mammals on the planet. It is also the most numerous."

Hafner grunted. "So if we kill them off here, others will swarm in from surrounding areas?"

"That's about it. There are probably millions of them on this peninsula. Of course, if you want to put a barrier across the narrow connection to the mainland, you might be able to wipe them out locally."

The executive scowled. A barrier was possible, but it would involve more work than he cared to expend.

"What do they eat?" he asked truculently.

"A little bit of everything, apparently. Insects, fruits, berries, nuts, succulents, and grain." Dano Marin smiled. "I guess it could be called an omnivore—now that our clothing is handy, it eats that, too."

Hafner didn't smile. "I thought our clothing was supposed to be verminproof."

Marin shrugged. "It is, on twenty-seven planets. On the twenty-eighth, we meet up with a little fella that has better digestive fluids, that's all."

Hafner looked pained. "Are they likely to bother the crops we plant?"

"Offhand, I would say they aren't. But then I would have said the same about our clothing."

Hafner made up his mind. "All right. You worry about the crops. Find some way to keep them out of the fields. Meanwhile, everyone sleeps in the ship until we can build dormitories."

Individual dwelling units would have been more appropriate in the colony at this stage, thought Marin. But it wasn't for him to decide. The executive was a man who regarded a schedule as something to be exceeded.

"The omnivore—" began Marin.

Hafner nodded impatiently. "Work on it," he said, and walked away.

The biologist sighed. The omnivore really was a queer little creature, but it was by no means the most important thing on Glade. For instance, why were there so few species of land animals on the planet? No reptiles, numerous birds, and only four kinds of mammals.

Every comparable planet teemed with a wild variety of life. Glade, in spite of seemingly ideal conditions, hadn't developed. Why?

He had asked Biological Controls for this assignment because it had seemed an interesting problem. Now, apparently, he was being pressed into service as an exterminator.

He reached in the cage and picked up the omnivore. Mammals on Glade were not unexpected. Parallel development took care of that. Given roughly the same kind of environment, similar animals would usually evolve.

In the Late Carboniferous forest on Earth, there had been creatures like the omnivore, the primitive mammal from which all others had evolved. On Glade, that kind of evolution just hadn't taken place. What had kept nature from exploiting its evolutionary potentialities? There was the real problem, not how to wipe them out.

Marin stuck a needle in the omnivore. It squealed and then relaxed. He drew out the blood and set it back in the cage. He could learn a lot about the animal from trying to kill it.

The quartermaster was shouting, though his normal voice carried quite well.

"How do you know it's mice?" the biologist asked him.

"Look," said the quartermaster angrily.

Marin looked. The evidence did indicate mice.

Before he could speak, the quartermaster snapped, "Don't tell me they're only micelike creatures. I know that. The question is: how can I get rid of them?"

"Have you tried poison?"

"Tell me what poison to use and I'll use it."

It wasn't the easiest question to answer. What was poisonous to an animal he had never seen and knew nothing about? According to Biological Survey, the animal didn't exist.

It was unexpectedly serious. The colony could live off the land, and was expected to. But another group of colonists was due in three years. The colony was supposed to accumulate a surplus of food to feed the increased numbers. If they couldn't store the food they grew any better than the concentrates, that surplus was going to be scanty.

Marin went over the warehouse thoroughly. It was the usual early construction on a colonial world. Not esthetic, it was sturdy enough. Fused dirt floor, reinforced foot-thick walls, a ceiling slab of the same. The whole was bound together with a molecular cement that made it practically airtight. It had no windows; there were two doors. Certainly it should keep out rodents.

A closer examination revealed an unexpected flaw. The floor was as hard as glass; no animal could gnaw through it, but, like glass, it was also brittle. The crew that had built the warehouse had evidently been in such a hurry to get back to Earth that they hadn't been as careful as they should have been, for here and there the floor was thin. Somewhere under the heavy equipment piled on it, the floor had cracked. There a burrowing animal had means of entry.

Short of building another warehouse, it was too late to do anything about that. Micelike animals were inside and had to be controlled where they were.

The biologist straightened up. "Catch me a few of them alive and I'll see what I can do."

In the morning, a dozen live specimens were delivered to the lab. They actually did resemble mice.

Their reactions were puzzling. No two of them were affected by the same poison. A compound that stiffened one in a matter of minutes left the others hale and hearty, and the poison he had developed to control the omnivores was completely ineffective.

The depredations in the warehouse went on. Black mice, white ones, gray and brown, short-tailed and long-eared, or the reverse, they continued to eat the concentrates and spoil what they didn't eat.

Marin conferred with the executive, outlined the problem as he saw it and his ideas on what could be done to combat the nuisance.

"But we can't build another warehouse," argued Hafner. "Not until the atomic generator is set up, at any rate. And then we'll have other uses for the power." The executive rested his head in his hands. "I like the other solution better. Build one and see how it works."

"I was thinking of three," said the biologist.

"One," Hafner insisted. "We can't spare the equipment until we know how it works."

At that he was probably right. They had equipment, as much as three ships could bring. But the more they brought, the more was expected of the colony. The net effect was that equipment was always in short supply.

Marin took the authorization to the engineer. On the way, he privately revised his specifications upward. If he couldn't get as many as he wanted, he might as well get a better one.

In two days, the machine was ready.

It was delivered in a small crate to the warehouse. The

crate was opened and the machine leaped out and stood there, poised.

"A cat!" exclaimed the quartermaster, pleased. He stretched out his hand toward the black fuzzy robot.

"If you've touched anything a mouse may have, get your hand away," warned the biologist. "It reacts to smell as well as sight and sound."

Hastily, the quartermaster withdrew his hand. The robot disappeared silently into the maze of stored material.

In one week, though there were still some mice in the warehouse, they were no longer a danger.

The executive called Marin into his office, a small sturdy building located in the center of the settlement. The colony was growing, assuming an aspect of permanency. Hafner sat in his chair and looked out over that growth with satisfaction.

"A good job on the mouse plague," he said.

The biologist nodded. "Not bad, except there shouldn't be any mice here. Biological Survey—"

"Forget it," said the exec. "Everybody makes mistakes, even B.S." He leaned back and looked seriously at the biologist. "I have a job I need done. Just now I'm short of men. If you have no objections . . ."

The exec was always short of men, would be until the planet was overcrowded, and he would try to find someone to do the work his own men should have done. Dano Marin was not directly responsible to Hafner; he was on loan to the expedition from Biological Controls. Still, it was a good idea to cooperate with the executive. He sighed.

"It's not as bad as you think," said Hafner, interpreting the sound correctly. He smiled. "We've got the digger together. I want you to run it."

Since it tied right in with his investigations, Dano Marin looked relieved and showed it.

"Except for food, we have to import most of our supplies," Hafner explained. "It's a long haul, and we've got to make use of everything on the planet we can. We need oil. There are going to be a lot of wheels turning, and every one of them will have to have oil. In time we'll set up a synthetic plant, but if we can locate a productive field now, it's to our advantage."

"You're assuming the geology of Glade is similar to Earth's?"

Hafner waggled his hand. "Why not? It's a nicer twin of Earth."

Why not? Because you couldn't always tell from the surface, thought Marin. It seemed like Earth, but was it? Here was a good chance to find out the history of Glade.

Hafner stood up. "Any time you're ready, a technician will check you out on the digger. Let me know before you go."

Actually, the digger wasn't a digger. It didn't move or otherwise displace a gram of dirt or rock. It was a means of looking down below the surface, to any practical depth. A large crawler, it was big enough for a man to live in without discomfort for a week.

It carried an outsize ultrasonic generator and a device for directing the beam into the planet. That was the sending apparatus. The receiving end began with a large sonic lens which picked up sound beams reflected from any desired depth, converted them into electrical energy and thence into an image which was flashed onto a screen.

At the depth of ten miles, the image was fuzzy, though good enough to distinguish the main features of the strata. At three miles, it was better. It could pick up the sound reflection of a buried coin and convert it into a picture on which the date could be seen.

It was to a geologist as a microscope is to a biologist.

Being a biologist, Dano Marin could appreciate the analogy.

He started at the tip of the peninsula and zigzagged across, heading toward the isthmus. Methodically, he covered the territory, sleeping at night in the digger. On the morning of the third day, he discovered oil traces, and by that afternoon he had located the main field.

He should probably have turned back at once, but now that he had found oil, he investigated more deliberately. Starting at the top, he let the image range downward below the top strata.

It was the reverse of what it should have been. In the top few feet, there were plentiful fossil remains, mostly of the four species of mammals. The squirrel-like creature and the far larger grazing animal were the forest dwellers. Of the plains animals, there were only two, in size fitting neatly between the extremes of the forest dwellers.

After the first few feet, which correspond to approximately twenty thousand years, he found virtually no fossils. Not until he reached a depth which he could correlate to the Late Carboniferous age on Earth did fossils reappear. Then they were of animals appropriate to the epoch. At that depth and below, the history of Glade was quite similar to Earth's.

Puzzled, he checked again in a dozen widely scattered localities. The results were always the same—fossil history for the first twenty thousand years, then none for roughly a hundred million. Beyond that, it was easy to trace the thread of biological development.

In that period of approximately one hundred million years, something unique had happened to Glade. What was it?

On the fifth day his investigations were interrupted by the sound of the keyed-on radio.

"Marin."

"Yes?" He flipped on the sending switch.

"How soon can you get back?"

He looked at the photo-map. "Three hours. Two if I hurry."

"Make it two. Never mind the oil."

"I've found oil. But what's the matter?"

"You can see it better than I can describe it. We'll discuss it when you get back."

Reluctantly, Marin retracted the instruments into the digger. He turned it around and, with not too much regard for the terrain, let it roar. The treads tossed dirt high in the air. Animals fled squealing from in front of him. If the grove was small enough, he went around it, otherwise he went through and left matchsticks behind.

He skidded the crawler ponderously to halt near the edge of the settlement. The center of activity was the warehouse. Pickups wheeled in and out, transferring supplies to a cleared area outside. He found Hafner in a corner of the warehouse, talking to the engineer.

Hafner turned around when he came up. "Your mice have grown, Marin."

Marin looked down. The robot cat lay on the floor. He knelt and examined it. The steel skeleton hadn't broken; it had been bent, badly. The tough plastic skin had been torn off and, inside, the delicate mechanism had been chewed into an unrecognizable mass.

Around the cat were rats, twenty or thirty of them, huge by any standards. The cat had fought; the dead animals were headless or disemboweled, unbelievably battered. But the robot had been outnumbered.

Biological Survey had said there weren't any rats on Glade. They had also said that about mice. What was the key to their errors?

The biologist stood up. "What are you going to do about it?"

"Build another warehouse, two-foot-thick fused dirt floors, monolithic construction. Transfer all perishables to it."

Marin nodded. That would do it. It would take time, of course, and power, all they could draw out of the recently set up atomic generator. All other construction would have to be suspended. No wonder Hafner was disturbed.

"Why not build more cats?" Marin suggested.

The executive smiled nastily. "You weren't here when we opened the doors. The warehouse was swarming with rats. How many robot cats would we need—five, fifteen? I don't know. Anyway the engineer tells me we have enough parts to build three more cats. The one lying there can't be salvaged."

It didn't take an engineer to see that, thought Marin.

Hafner continued, "If we need more, we'll have to rob the computer in the spaceship. I refuse to permit that."

Obviously he would. The spaceship was the only link with Earth until the next expedition brought more colonists. No exec in his right mind would permit the ship to be crippled.

But why had Hafner called him back? Merely to keep him informed of the situation?

Hafner seemed to guess his thoughts. "At night we'll floodlight the supplies we remove from the warehouse. We'll post a guard armed with decharged rifles until we can move the food into the new warehouse. That'll take about ten days. Meanwhile, our fast crops are ripening. It's my guess the rats will turn to them for food. In order to protect our future food supply, you'll have to activate your animals."

The biologist started. "But it's against regulations to

loose any animal on a planet until a complete investigation of the possible ill effects is made."

"That takes ten or twenty years. This is an emergency and I'll be responsible—in writing, if you want."

The biologist was effectively countermanded. Another rabbit-infested Australia or the planet that the snails took over might be in the making, but there was nothing he could do about it.

"I hardly think they'll be of any use against rats this size," he protested.

"You've got hormones. Apply them." The executive turned and began discussing construction with the engineer.

Marin had the dead rats gathered up and placed in the freezer for further study.

After that, he retired to the laboratory and worked out a course of treatment for the domesticated animals that the colonists had brought with them. He gave them the first injections and watched them carefully until they were safely through the initial shock phase of growth. As soon as he saw they were going to survive, he bred them.

Next he turned to the rats. Of note was the wide variation in size. Internally, the same thing was true. They had the usual organs, but the proportions of each varied greatly, more than is normal. Nor were their teeth uniform. Some carried huge fangs set in delicate jaws; others had tiny teeth that didn't match the massive bone structure. As a species, they were the most scrambled the biologist had ever encountered.

He turned the microscope on their tissues and tabulated the results. There was less difference here between individual specimens, but it was enough to set him pondering. The reproductive cells were especially baffling.

Late in the day, he felt rather than heard the soundless

whoosh of the construction machinery. He looked out of the laboratory and saw smoke rolling upward. As soon as the vegetation was charred, the smoke ceased and heat waves danced into the sky.

They were building on a hill. The little creatures that crept and crawled in the brush attacked in the most vulnerable spot, the food supply. There was no brush, not a blade of grass, on the hill when the colonists finished.

Terriers. In the past, they were the hunting dogs of the agricultural era. What they lacked in size they made up in ferocity toward rodents. They had earned their keep originally in granaries and fields, and, for a brief time, they were doing it again on colonial worlds where conditions were repeated.

The dogs the colonists brought had been terriers. They were still as fast, still with the same anti-rodent disposition, but they were no longer small. It had been a difficult job, yet Marin had done it well, for the dogs had lost none of their skill and speed in growing to the size of a great dane.

The rats moved in on the fields of fast crops. Fast crops were made to order for a colonial world. They could be planted, grown, and harvested in a matter of weeks. After four such plantings, the fertility of the soil was destroyed, but that meant nothing in the early years of a colonial planet, for land was plentiful.

The rat tide grew in the fast crops, and the dogs were loosed on the rats. They ranged through the fields, hunting. A rush, a snap of their jaws, the shake of a head, and the rat was tossed aside, its back broken. The dogs went on to the next.

Until they could not see, the dogs prowled and slaughtered. At night they came in bloody, most of it not their own, and exhausted. Marin pumped them full of antibiotics, bandaged their wounds, fed them through their veins, and shot them into sleep. In the morning he awakened them with an injection of stimulant and sent them tingling into battle.

It took the rats two days to learn they could not feed during the day. Not so numerous, they came at night. They climbed on the vines and nibbled the fruit. They gnawed growing grain and ravaged vegetables.

The next day the colonists set up lights. The dogs were with them, discouraging the few rats who were still foolish enough to forage while the sun was overhead.

An hour before dusk, Marin called the dogs in and gave them an enforced rest. He brought them out of it after dark and took them to the fields, staggering. The scent of rats revived them; they were as eager as ever, if not quite so fast.

The rats came from the surrounding meadows, not singly, or in twos and threes, as they did before; this time they came together. Squealing and rustling the grass, they moved toward the fields. It was dark, and though he could not see them, Marin could hear them. He ordered the great lights turned on in the area of the fields.

The rats stopped under the glare, milling around uneasily. The dogs quivered and whined. Marin held them back. The rats resumed their march, and Marin released the dogs.

The dogs charged in to attack, but didn't dare brave the main mass. They picked off the stragglers and forced the rats into a tighter formation. After that the rats were virtually unassailable.

The colonists could have burned the bunched-up rats with the right equipment, but they didn't have it and couldn't get it for years. Even if they'd had it, the use of such equipment would endanger the crops, which they had to save if they could. It was up to the dogs.

The rat formation came to the edge of the fields, and

broke. They could face a common enemy and remain united, but in the presence of food, they forgot that unity and scattered—hunger was the great divisor. The dogs leaped joyously in pursuit. They hunted down the starved rodents, one by one, and killed them as they ate.

When daylight came, the rat menace had ended.

The next week the colonists harvested and processed the food for storage and immediately planted another crop.

Marin sat in the lab and tried to analyze the situation. The colony was moving from crisis to crisis, all of them involving food. In itself, each critical situation was minor, but lumped together they could add up to failure. No matter how he looked at it, they just didn't have the equipment they needed to colonize Glade.

The fault seemed to lie with Biological Survey; they hadn't reported the presence of pests that were endangering the food supply. Regardless of what the exec thought about them, Survey knew their business. If they said there were no mice or rats on Glade, then there hadn't been any— *when the survey was made.*

The question was: when did they come and how did they get here?

Marin sat and stared at the wall, turning over hypotheses in his mind, discarding them when they failed to make sense.

His gaze shifted from the wall to the cage of the omnivore, the squirrel-size forest creature. The most numerous animal on Glade, it was a commonplace sight to the colonists.

And yet it was a remarkable animal, more than he had realized. Plain, insignificant in appearance, it might be the most important of any animal Man had encountered on the many worlds he had settled on. The longer he watched, the more Marin became convinced of it.

He sat silent, observing the creature, not daring to move. He sat until it was dark and the omnivore resumed its normal activity.

Normal? The word didn't apply on Glade.

The interlude with the omnivore provided him with one answer. He needed another one; he thought he knew what it was, but he had to have more data, additional observations.

He set up his equipment carefully on the fringes of the settlement. There and in no other place existed the information he wanted.

He spent time in the digger, checking his original investigations. It added up to a complete picture.

When he was certain of his facts, he called on Hafner.

The executive was congenial; it was a reflection of the smoothness with which the objectives of the colony were being achieved.

"Sit down," he said affably. "Smoke?"

The biologist sat down and took a cigarette.

"I thought you'd like to know where the mice came from," he began.

Hafner smiled. "They don't bother us any more."

"I've also determined the origin of the rats."

"They're under control. We're doing nicely."

On the contrary, thought Marin. He searched for the proper beginning.

"Glade has an Earth-type climate and topography," he said. "Has had for the past twenty thousand years. Before that, about a hundred million years ago, it was also like Earth of the comparable period."

He watched the look of polite interest settle on the executive's face as he stated the obvious. Well, it *was* obvious, up to a point. The conclusions weren't, though.

"Between a hundred million years and twenty thousand

years ago, something happened to Glade," Marin went on. "I don't know the cause; it belongs to cosmic history and we may never find out. Anyway, whatever the cause—fluctuations in the sun, unstable equilibrium of forces within the planet, or perhaps an encounter with an interstellar dust cloud of variable density—the climate on Glade changed.

"It changed with inconceivable violence and it kept on changing. A hundred million years ago, plus or minus, there was carboniferous forest on Glade. Giant reptiles resembling dinosaurs and tiny mammals roamed through it. The first great change wiped out the dinosaurs, as it did on Earth. It didn't wipe out the still more primitive ancestor of the omnivore, because it could adapt to changing conditions.

"Let me give you an idea how the conditions changed. For a few years a given area would be a desert; after that it would turn into a jungle. Still later a glacier would begin to form. And then the cycle would be repeated, with wild variations. All this might happen—did happen—within a span covered by the lifetime of a single omnivore. This occurred many times. For roughly a hundred million years, it was the norm of existence on Glade. This condition was hardly conducive to the preservation of fossils."

Hafner saw the significance and was concerned. "You mean these climatic fluctuations suddenly stopped, twenty thousand years ago? Are they likely to begin again?"

"I don't know," confessed the biologist. "We can probably determine it if we're interested."

The exec nodded grimly. "We're interested, all right."

Maybe we are, thought the biologist. He said, "The point is that survival was difficult. Birds could and did fly to more suitable climates; quite a few of them survived. Only one species of mammals managed to come through."

"Your facts are not straight," observed Hafner. "There are four species, ranging in size from a squirrel to a water buffalo."

"One species," Marin repeated doggedly. "They're the same. If the food supply for the largest animal increases, some of the smaller so-called species grow up. Conversely, if food becomes scarce in any category, the next generation, which apparently can be produced almost instantly, switches to a form which does have an adequate food supply."

"The mice," Hafner said slowly.

Marin finished the thought for him. "The mice weren't here when we got here. They were born of the squirrel-size omnivore."

Hafner nodded. "And the rats?"

"Born of the next larger size. After all, we're environment, too—perhaps the harshest the beasts have yet faced."

Hafner was a practical man, trained to administer a colony. Concepts were not his familiar ground. "Mutations, then? But I thought—"

The biologist smiled. It was thin and cracked at the edges of his mouth. "On Earth, it would be mutation. Here it is merely normal evolutionary adaptation." He shook his head. "I never told you, but omnivores, though they could be mistaken for an animal from Earth, have no genes or chromosomes. Obviously they do have heredity, but how it is passed down, I don't know. However it functions, it responds to external conditions far faster than anything we've ever encountered."

Hafner nodded to himself. "Then we'll never be free from pests." He clasped and unclasped his hands. "Unless, of course, we rid the planet of all animal life."

"Radioactive dust?" asked the biologist. "They have survived worse."

The exec considered alternatives. "Maybe we should leave the planet and leave it to the animals."

"Too late," said the biologist. "They'll be on Earth, too, and all the planets we've settled on."

Hafner looked at him. The same pictures formed in his mind that Marin had thought of. Three ships had been sent to colonize Glade. One had remained with the colonists, survival insurance in case anything unforseen happened. Two had gone back to Earth to carry the report that all was well and that more supplies were needed. They had also carried specimens from the planet.

The cages those creatures were kept in were secure. But a smaller species could get out, must already be free, inhabiting, undetected, the cargo spaces of the ships.

There was nothing they could do to intercept those ships. And once they reached Earth, would the biologists suspect? Not for a long time. First a new kind of rat would appear. A mutation could account for that. Without specific knowledge, there would be nothing to connect it with the specimens picked up from Glade.

"We have to stay," said the biologist. "We have to study them and we can do it best here."

He thought of the vast complex of buildings on Earth. There was too much invested to tear them down and make them verminproof. Billions of people could not be moved off the planet while the work was being done.

They were committed to Glade, not as a colony, but as a gigantic laboratory. They had gained one planet and lost the equivalent of ten, perhaps more when the destructive properties of the omnivores were finally assessed.

A rasping animal cough interrupted the biologist's thoughts. Hafner jerked his head and glanced at the window. Lips tight, he grabbed a rifle off the wall and ran out. Marin followed him.

The exec headed toward the fields where the second fast crop was maturing. On top of a knoll, he stopped and knelt. He flipped the dial to extreme charge, aimed, and fired. It was high; he missed the animal in the field. A neat strip of smoking brown appeared in the green vegetation.

He aimed more carefully and fired again. The charge screamed out of the muzzle. It struck the animal on the forepaw. The beast leaped high in the air and fell down, dead and broiled.

They stood over the animal Hafner had killed. Except for the lack of markings, it was a good imitation of a tiger. The exec prodded it with his toe.

"We chase the rats out of the warehouse and they go to the fields," he muttered. "We hunt them down in the fields with dogs and they breed tigers."

"Easier than rats," said Marin. "We can shoot tigers." He bent down over the slain dog near which they had surprised the big cat.

The other dog came whining from the far corner of the field to which he had fled in terror. He was a courageous dog, but he could not face the great carnivore. He whimpered and licked the face of his mate.

The biologist picked up the mangled dog and headed toward the laboratory.

"You can't save her," said Hafner morosely. "She's dead."

"But the pups aren't. We'll need them. The rats won't disappear merely because tigers have showed up."

The head drooped limply over his arm and blood seeped into his clothing as Hafner followed him up the hill.

"We've been here three months," the exec said suddenly. "The dogs have been in the fields only two. And yet the tiger was mature. How do you account for something like that?"

Marin bent under the weight of the dog. Hafner never would understand his bewilderment. As a biologist, all his categories were upset. What did evolution explain? It was a history of organic life on a particular world. Beyond that world, it might not apply.

Even about himself there were many things Man didn't know, dark patches in his knowledge which theory simply had to pass over. About other creatures, his ignorance was sometimes limitless.

Birth was simple; it occurred on countless planets. Meek grazing creatures, fierce carnivores—the most unlikely animals gave birth to their young. It happened all the time. And the young grew up, became mature, and mated.

He remembered that evening in the laboratory. It was accidental—what if he had been elsewhere and not witnessed it? They would not know what little they did.

He explained it carefully to Hafner. "If the survival factor is high and there's a great disparity in size, the young need not ever be young. They may be born as fully functioning adults!"

Although not at the rate it had initially set, the colony progressed. The fast crops were slowed down and a more diversified selection was planted. New buildings were constructed and the supplies that were stored in them were spread out thin, for easy inspection.

The pups survived and within a year shot up to maturity. After proper training, they were released to the fields where they joined the older dogs. The battle against the rats went on; they were held in check, though the damage they caused was considerable.

The original animal, unchanged in form, developed an appetite for electrical insulation. There was no protection except to keep the power on at all times. Even then there

were unwelcome interruptions until the short was located
and the charred carcass was removed. Vehicles were kept
tightly closed or parked only in verminproof buildings.
While the plague didn't increase in numbers, it couldn't be
eliminated, either.

There was a flurry of tigers, but they were larger animals
and were promptly shot down. They prowled at night, so
the colonists were assigned to guard the settlement around
the clock. Where lights failed to reach, the infra-red 'scope
did. As fast as they came, the tigers died. Except for the
first one, not a single dog was lost.

The tigers changed, though not in form. Externally, they
were all big and powerful killers. But as the slaughter went
on, Marin noticed one astonishing fact—the internal organic structure became progressively more immature.

The last one that was brought to him for examination
was the equivalent of a newly born cub. That tiny stomach
was suited more for the digestion of milk than meat. How it
had furnished energy to drive those great muscles was
something of a miracle. But drive it had, for a murderous
fifteen minutes before the animal was brought down. No
lives were lost, though sick bay was kept busy for a while.

That was the last tiger they shot. After that, the attacks
ceased.

The seasons passed and nothing new occurred. A spaceship civilization or even that fragment of it represented by
the colony was too much for the creature, which Marin by
now had come to think of as the "omnimal." It had evolved
out of a cataclysmic past, but it could not meet the chal-
lenge of the harshest environment.

Or so it seemed.

Three months before the next colonists were due, a new
animal was detected. Food was missing from the fields. It
was not another tiger; they were carnivorous. Nor rats, for

vines were stripped in a manner that no rodent could manage.

The food was not important. The colony had enough in storage. But if the new animal signaled another plague, it was necessary to know how to meet it. The sooner they knew what the animal was, the better defense they could set up against it.

Dogs were useless. The animal roamed the field they were loose in, and they did not attack or even seem to know it was there.

The colonists were called upon for guard duty again, but it evaded them. They patrolled for a week and they still did not catch sight of it.

Hafner called them in and rigged up an alarm system in the field most frequented by the animal. It detected that, too, and moved its sphere of operations to a field in which the alarm system had not been installed.

Hafner conferred with the engineer, who devised an alarm that would react to body radiation. It was buried in the original field and the old alarm was moved to another.

Two nights later, just before dawn, the alarm rang.

Marin met Hafner at the edge of the settlement. Both carried rifles. They walked; the noise of any vehicle was likely to frighten the animal. They circled around and approached the field from the rear. The men in the camp had been alerted. If they needed help, it was ready.

They crept silently through the underbrush. It was feeding in the field, not noisily, yet they could hear it. The dogs hadn't barked.

They inched nearer. The blue sun of Glade came up and shone full on their quarry. The gun dropped in Hafner's hand. He clenched his teeth and raised it again.

Marin put out a restraining arm. "Don't shoot," he whispered.

"I'm the exec here. I say it's dangerous."

"Dangerous," agreed Marin, still in a whisper. "That's why you can't shoot. It's more dangerous than you know."

Hafner hesitated and Marin went on. "The omnimal couldn't compete in the changed environment and so it evolved mice. We stopped the mice and it countered with rats. We turned back the rat and it provided the tiger.

"The tiger was easiest of all for us and so it was apparently stopped for a while. But it didn't really stop. Another animal was being formed, the one you see there. It took the omnimal two years to create it—how, I don't know. A million years were required to evolve it on Earth."

Hafner hadn't lowered the rifle and he showed no signs of doing so. He looked lovingly into the sights.

"Can't you see?" urged Marin. "We can't destroy the omnimal. It's on Earth now, and on the other planets, down in the storage areas of our big cities, masquerading as rats. And we've never been able to root out even our own terrestrial rats, so how can we exterminate the omnimal?"

"All the more reason to start now." Hafner's voice was flat.

Marin struck the rifle down. "Are their rats better than ours?" he asked wearily. "Will their pests win or ours be stronger? Or will the two make peace, unite and interbreed, make war on us? It's not impossible; the omnimal could do it if interbreeding had a high survival factor.

"Don't you still see? There is a progression. After the tiger, it bred this. If this evolution fails, if we shoot it down, what will it create next? This creature I think we can compete with. *It's the one after this that I do not want to face.*"

It heard them. It raised its head and looked around. Slowly it edged away and backed toward a nearby grove.

The biologist stood up and called softly. The creature scurried to the trees and stopped just inside the shadows among them.

The two men laid down their rifles. Together they approached the grove, hands spread open to show they carried no weapons.

It came out to meet them. Naked, it had had no time to learn about clothing. Neither did it have weapons. It plucked a large white flower from the tree and extended this mutely as a sign of peace.

"I wonder what it's like," said Marin. "It seems adult, but can it be, all the way through? What's inside that body?"

"I wonder what's in his head," Hafner said worriedly.

It looked very much like a man.

Floyd L. Wallace (? –)
Floyd Wallace's first science fiction story appeared in 1951; between that year and the mid-1960's he wrote some two dozen stories for science fiction magazines. Unfortunately, he has never had a collection of his stories published, although one novel, Address: Centauri (1955), has appeared. In addition to "Student Body," his "Mezzerow Loves Company," and "Delay in Transit" are particularly noteworthy.

EVOLUTION

A SOUND OF THUNDER

Ray Bradbury

The sign on the wall seemed to quaver under a film of sliding warm water. Eckels felt his eyelids blink over his stare, and the sign burned in this momentary darkness:

TIME SAFARI, INC.

SAFARIS TO ANY YEAR IN THE PAST.

YOU NAME THE ANIMAL.

WE TAKE YOU THERE.

YOU SHOOT IT.

A warm phlegm gathered in Eckels' throat; he swallowed and pushed it down. The muscles around his mouth

37

formed a smile as he put his hand slowly out upon the air, and in that hand waved a check for ten thousand dollars to the man behind the desk.

"Does this safari guarantee I come back alive?"

"We guarantee nothing," said the official, "except the dinosaurs." He turned. "This is Mr. Travis, your Safari Guide in the Past. He'll tell you what and where to shoot. If he says no shooting, no shooting. If you disobey instructions, there's a stiff penalty of another ten thousand dollars, plus possible government action, on your return."

Eckels glanced across the vast office at a mass and tangle, a snaking and humming of wires and steel boxes, at an aurora that flickered now orange, now silver, now blue. There was a sound like a gigantic bonfire burning all of Time, all the years and all the parchment calendars, all the hours piled high and set aflame.

A touch of the hand and this burning would, on the instant, beautifully reverse itself. Eckels remembered the wording in the advertisements to the letter. Out of chars and ashes, out of dust and coals, like golden salamanders, the old years, the green years, might leap; roses sweeten the air, white hair turn Irish-black, wrinkles vanish; all, everything fly back to seed, flee death, rush down to their beginnings, suns rise in western skies and set in glorious easts, moons eat themselves opposite to the custom, all and everything cupping one in another like Chinese boxes, rabbits into hats, all and everything returning to the fresh death, the seed death, the green death, to the time before the beginning. A touch of a hand might do it, the merest touch of a hand.

"Unbelievable." Eckels breathed, the light of the Machine on his thin face. "A real Time Machine." He shook his head. "Makes you think. If the election had gone badly yesterday, I might be here now running away from the results. Thank God Keith won. He'll make a fine President of the United States."

"Yes," said the man behind the desk. "We're lucky. If Deutscher had gotten in, we'd have the worst kind of dictatorship. There's an anti-everything man for you, a militarist, anti-Christ, anti-human, anti-intellectual. People called us up, you know, joking but not joking. Said if Deutscher became President they wanted to go live in 1492. Of course it's not our business to conduct Escapes, but to form Safaris. Anyway, Keith's President now. All you got to worry about is—"

"Shooting my dinosaur," Eckels finished it for him.

"A *Tyrannosaurus rex.* The Tyrant Lizard, the most incredible monster in history. Sign this release. Anything happens to you, we're not responsible. Those dinosaurs are hungry."

Eckels flushed angrily. "Trying to scare me!"

"Frankly, yes. We don't want anyone going who'll panic at the first shot. Six Safari leaders were killed last year, and a dozen hunters. We're here to give you the severest thrill a *real* hunter ever asked for. Traveling you back sixty million years to bag the biggest game in all of Time. Your personal check's still there. Tear it up."

Mr. Eckels looked at the check. His fingers twitched.

"Good luck," said the man behind the desk. "Mr. Travis, he's all yours."

They moved silently across the room, taking their guns with them, toward the Machine, toward the silver metal and the roaring light.

First a day and then a night and then a day and then a night, then it was day-night-day-night-day. A week, a month, a year, a decade! A.D. 2055. A.D. 2019. 1999! 1957! Gone! The Machine roared.

They put on their oxygen helmets and tested the inter-coms.

Eckels swayed on the padded seat, his face pale, his jaw stiff. He felt the trembling in his arms and he looked down and found his hands tight on the new rifle. There were four other men in the Machine. Travis, the Safari Leader, his assistant, Lesperance, and two other hunters, Billings and Kramer. They sat looking at each other, and the years blazed around them.

"Can these guns get a dinosaur cold?" Eckels felt his mouth saying.

"If you hit them right," said Travis on the helmet radio. "Some dinosaurs have two brains, one in the head, another far down the spinal column. We stay away from those. That's stretching luck. Put your first two shots into the eyes, if you can, blind them, and go back into the brain."

The Machine howled. Time was a film run backward. Suns fled and ten million moons fled after them. "Think," said Eckels. "Every hunter that ever lived would envy us today. This makes Africa seem like Illinois."

The Machine slowed; its scream fell to a murmur. The Machine stopped.

The sun stopped in the sky.

The fog that had enveloped the Machine blew away and they were in an old time, a very old time indeed, three hunters and two Safari Heads with their blue metal guns across their knees.

"Christ isn't born yet," said Travis. "Moses has not gone to the mountain to talk with God. The Pyramids are still in the earth, waiting to be cut out and put up. Remember that. Alexander, Caesar, Napoleon, Hitler—none of them exists."

The man nodded.

"That"—Mr. Travis pointed—"is the jungle of sixty mil-

lion two thousand and fifty-five years before President
Keith."

He indicated a metal path that struck off into green wilderness, over streaming swamp, among giant ferns and
palms.

"And that," he said, "is the Path, laid by Time Safari for
your use. It floats six inches above the earth. Doesn't touch
so much as one grass blade, flower, or tree. It's an anti-
gravity metal. Its purpose is to keep you from touching this
world of the past in any way. Stay on the Path. Don't go off
it. I repeat. *Don't go off.* For *any* reason! If you fall off,
there's a penalty. And don't shoot any animal we don't
okay."

"Why?" asked Eckels.

They sat in the ancient wilderness. Far birds' cries blew
on a wind, and the smell of tar and an old salt sea, moist
grasses, and flowers the color of blood.

"We don't want to change the Future. We don't belong
here in the Past. The government doesn't *like* us here. We
have to pay big graft to keep our franchise. A Time Machine is finicky business. Not knowing it, we might kill an
important animal, a small bird, a roach, a flower even, thus
destroying an important link in a growing species."

"That's not clear," said Eckels.

"All right," Travis continued, "say we accidentally kill
one mouse here. That means all the future families of this
one particular mouse are destroyed, right?"

"Right."

"And all the families of the families of the families of
that one mouse! With a stamp of your foot, you annihilate
first one, then a dozen, then a thousand, a million, a *billion*
possible mice!"

"So they're dead," said Eckels. "So what?"

"So what?" Travis snorted quietly. "Well, what about

the foxes that'll need those mice to survive? For want of ten mice, a fox dies. For want of ten foxes, a lion starves. For want of a lion, all manner of insects, vultures, infinite billions of life forms are thrown into chaos and destruction. Eventually it all boils down to this: fifty-nine million years later, a caveman, one of a dozen on the *entire world*, goes hunting wild boar or saber-toothed tiger for food. But you, friend, have *stepped* on all the tigers in that region. By stepping on *one* single mouse. So the caveman starves. And the caveman, please note, is not just *any* expendable man, no! He is an *entire future nation*. From his loins would have sprung ten sons. From *their* loins one hundred sons, and thus onward to a civilization. Destroy this one man, and you destroy a race, a people, an entire history of life. It is comparable to slaying some of Adam's grandchildren. The stomp of your foot, on one mouse, could start an earthquake, the effects of which could shake our earth and destinies down through Time, to their very foundations. With the death of that one caveman, a billion others yet unborn are throttled in the womb. Perhaps Rome never rises on its seven hills. Perhaps Europe is forever a dark forest, and only Asia waxes healthy and teeming. Step on a mouse and you crush the Pyramids. Step on a mouse and you leave your print, like a Grand Canyon, across Eternity. Queen Elizabeth might never be born, Washington might not cross the Delaware, there might never be a United States at all. So be careful. Stay on the Path. Never step off!"

"I see," said Eckels. "Then it wouldn't pay for us even to touch the grass?"

"Correct. Crushing certain plants could add up infinitesimally. A little error here would multiply in sixty million years, all out of proportion. Of course maybe our theory is wrong. Maybe Time *can't* be changed by us. Or maybe it can be changed only in little subtle ways. A dead mouse here makes an insect imbalance there, a population disproportion later, a bad harvest further on, a depression, mass starvation, and, finally, a change in *social* temperament in far-flung countries. Something much more subtle, like that. Perhaps only a soft breath, a whisper, a hair, pollen on the air, such a slight, slight change that unless you looked close you wouldn't see it. Who knows? Who really can say he knows? We don't know. We're guessing. But until we do know for certain whether our messing around in Time *can* make a big roar or a little rustle in history, we're being careful. This Machine, this Path, your clothing and bodies, were sterilized, as you know, before the journey. We wear these oxygen helmets so we can't introduce our bacteria into an ancient atmosphere."

"How do we know which animals to shoot?"

"They're marked with red paint," said Travis. "Today, before our journey, we sent Lesperance here back with the Machine. He came to this particular era and followed certain animals."

"Studying them?"

"Right," said Lesperance. "I track them through their entire existence, noting which of them lives longest. Very few. How many times they mate. Not often. Life's short. When I find one that's going to die when a tree falls on him, or one that drowns in a tar pit, I note the exact hour, minute, and second. I shoot a paint bomb. It leaves a red patch on his side. We can't miss it. Then I correlate our arrival in the Past so that we meet the Monster not more than two minutes before he would have died anyway. This way, we kill only animals with no future, that are never going to mate again. You see how *careful* we are?"

"But if you came back this morning in Time," said Eckels eagerly, "you must've bumped into us, our Safari!

How did it turn out? Was it successful? Did all of us get through—alive?"

Travis and Lesperance gave each other a look.

"That'd be a paradox," said the latter. "Time doesn't permit that sort of mess—a man meeting himself. When such occasions threaten, Time steps aside. Like an airplane hitting an air pocket. You felt the Machine jump just before we stopped? That was us passing ourselves on the way back to the Future. We saw nothing. There's no way of telling *if* this expedition was a success, *if* we got our monster, or whether all of us—meaning you, Mr. Eckels—got out alive."

Eckels smiled palely.

"Cut that," said Travis sharply. "Everyone on his feet!"

They were ready to leave the Machine.

The jungle was high and the jungle was broad and the jungle was the entire world forever and forever. Sounds like music and sounds like flying tents filled the sky, and those were pterodactyls soaring with cavernous gray wings, gigantic bats of delirium and night fever. Eckels, balanced on the narrow Path, aimed his rifle playfully.

"Stop that!" said Travis. "Don't even aim for fun, blast you! If your gun should go off—"

Eckels flushed. "Where's our *Tyrannosaurus?*"

Lesperance checked his wristwatch. "Up ahead. We'll bisect his trail in sixty seconds. Look for the red paint! Don't shoot till we give the word. Stay on the Path. *Stay on the Path!*"

They moved forward in the wind of morning.

"Strange," murmured Eckels. "Up ahead, sixty million years, Election Day over. Keith made President. Everyone celebrating. And here we are, a million years lost, and they don't exist. The things we worried about for months, a lifetime, not even born or thought of yet."

"Safety catches off, everyone!" ordered Travis. "You, first shot, Eckels. Second, Billings, Third, Kramer."

"I've hunted tiger, wild boar, buffalo, elephant, but now, this is *it*," said Eckels. "I'm shaking like a kid."

"Ah," said Travis.

Everyone stopped.

Travis raised his hand. "Ahead," he whispered. "In the mist. There he is. There's His Royal Majesty now."

The jungle was wide and full of twitterings, rustlings, murmurs, and sighs.

Suddenly it all ceased, as if someone had shut a door.

Silence.

A sound of thunder.

Out of the mist, one hundred yards away, came *Tyrannosaurus rex*.

"It," whispered Eckels. "It . . ."

"Sh!"

It came on great oiled, resilient, striding legs. It towered thirty feet above half of the trees, a great evil god, folding its delicate watchmaker's claws close to its oily reptilian chest. Each lower leg was a piston, a thousand pounds of white bone, sunk in thick ropes of muscle, sheathed over in a gleam of pebbled skin like the mail of a terrible warrior. Each thigh was a ton of meat, ivory, and steel mesh. And from the great breathing cage of the upper body those two delicate arms dangled out front, arms with hands which might pick up and examine men like toys, while the snake neck coiled. And the head itself, a ton of sculptured stone, lifted easily upon the sky. Its mouth gaped, exposing a fence of teeth like daggers. Its eyes rolled, ostrich eggs, empty of all expression save hunger. It closed its mouth in a death grin. It ran, its pelvic bones crushing aside trees and bushes, its taloned feet clawing damp earth, leaving prints six inches deep wherever it settled its weight. It ran with a gliding ballet step, far too poised and balanced for its ten tons. It moved into a sunlit arena warily, its beautifully reptilian hands feeling the air.

"Why, why," Eckels twitched his mouth. "It could reach up and grab the moon."

"Sh!" Travis jerked angrily. "He hasn't seen us yet."

"It can't be killed." Eckels pronounced this verdict quietly, as if there could be no argument. He had weighed the evidence and this was his considered opinion. The rifle in his hands seemed a cap gun. "We were fools to come. This is impossible."

"Shut up!" hissed Travis.

"Nightmare."

"Turn around," commanded Travis. "Walk quietly to the Machine. We'll remit one half your fee."

"I didn't realize it would be this *big*," said Eckels. "I miscalculated, that's all. And now I want out."

"It *sees* us!"

"There's the red paint on its chest!"

The Tyrant Lizard raised itself. Its armored flesh glittered like a thousand green coins. The coins, crusted with slime, steamed. In the slime, tiny insects wriggled, so that the entire body seemed to twitch and undulate, even while the monster itself did not move. It exhaled. The stink of raw flesh blew down the wilderness.

"Get me out of here," said Eckels. "It was never like this before. I was always sure I'd come through alive. I had good guides, good safaris, and safety. This time, I figured wrong. I've met my match and admit it. This is too much for me to get hold of."

"Don't run," said Lesperance. "Turn around. Hide in the Machine."

"Yes." Eckels seemed to be numb. He looked at his feet

as if trying to make them move. He gave a grunt of helplessness.

"Eckels!"

He took a few steps, blinking, shuffling.

"Not *that* way!"

The Monster, at the first motion, lunged forward with a terrible scream. It covered one hundred yards in six seconds. The rifles jerked up and blazed fire. A windstorm from the beast's mouth engulfed them in the stench of slime and old blood. The Monster roared, teeth glittering with sun.

Eckels, not looking back, walked blindly to the edge of the Path, his gun limp in his arms, stepped off the Path, and walked, not knowing it, in the jungle. His feet sank into green moss. His legs moved him, and he felt alone and remote from the events behind.

The rifles cracked again. Their sound was lost in shriek and lizard thunder. The great lever of the reptile's tail swung up, lashed sideways. Trees exploded in clouds of leaf and branch. The monster twitched its jeweler's hands down to fondle at the men, to twist them in half, to crush them like berries, to cram them into its teeth and its screaming throat. Its boulder-stone eyes leveled with the men. They saw themselves mirrored. They fired at the metallic eyelids and the blazing black iris.

Like a stone idol, like a mountain avalanche, *Tyrannosaurus* fell. Thundering, it clutched trees, pulled them with it. It wrenched and tore the metal Path. The men flung themselves back and away. The body hit, ten tons of cold flesh and stone. The guns fired. The Monster lashed its armored tail, twitched its snake jaws, and lay still. A fount of blood spurted from its throat. Somewhere inside, a sac of fluids burst. Sickening gushes drenched the hunters. They stood, red and glistening.

The thunder faded.

The jungle was silent. After the avalanche, a green peace. After the nightmare, morning.

Billings and Kramer sat on the pathway and threw up. Travis and Lesperance stood with smoking rifles, cursing steadily.

In the Time Machine, on his face, Eckels lay shivering. He had found his way back to the Path, climbed into the Machine.

Travis came walking, glanced at Eckels, took cotton gauze from a metal box, and returned to the others, who were sitting on the Path.

"Clean up."

They wiped the blood from their helmets. They began to curse too. The Monster lay, a hill of solid flesh. Within, you could hear the sighs and murmurs as the furthest chambers of it died, the organs malfunctioning, liquids running a final instant from pocket to sac to spleen, everything shutting off, closing up forever. It was like standing by a wrecked locomotive or a steam shovel at quitting time, all valves being released or levered tight. Bones cracked; the tonnage of its own flesh, off balance, dead weight, snapped the delicate forearms, caught underneath. The meat settled, quivering.

Another cracking sound. Overhead, a gigantic tree branch broke from its heavy mooring, fell. It crashed upon the dead beast with finality.

"There." Lesperance checked his watch. "Right on time. That's the giant tree that was scheduled to fall and kill this animal originally." He glanced at the two hunters. "You want the trophy picture?"

"What?"

"We can't take a trophy back to the Future. The body has to stay right here where it would have died originally,

so the insects, birds, and bacteria can get at it, as they were
intended to. Everything in balance. The body stays. But we
can take a picture of you standing near it."

The two men tried to think, but gave up, shaking their
heads.

They let themselves be led along the metal Path. They
sank wearily into the Machine cushions. They gazed back
at the ruined Monster, the stagnating mound, where already strange reptilian birds and golden insects were busy
at the steaming armor.

A sound on the floor of the Time Machine stiffened
them. Eckels sat there, shivering.

"I'm sorry," he said at last.

"Get up!" cried Travis.

Eckels got up.

"Go out on that Path alone," said Travis. He had his rifle
pointed. "You're not coming back in the Machine. We're
leaving you here!"

Lesperance seized Travis's arm. "Wait—"

"Stay out of this!" Travis shook his hand away. "This
fool nearly killed us. But it isn't that so much, no. It's his
shoes! Look at them! He ran off the Path. That ruins us!
We'll forfeit! Thousands of dollars of insurance! We guarantee no one leaves the Path. He left it. Oh, the fool! I'll
have to report to the government. They might revoke our
license to travel. Who knows what he's done to Time, to
History!"

"Take it easy, all he did was kick up some dirt."

"How do we know?" cried Travis. "We don't know anything! It's all a mystery! Get out there, Eckels!"

Eckels fumbled his shirt. "I'll pay anything. A hundred
thousand dollars!"

Travis glared at Eckels' checkbook and spat. "Go out
there. The Monster's next to the Path. Stick your arms up

to your elbows in his mouth. Then you can come back with us."

"That's unreasonable!"

"The Monster's dead, you idiot. The bullets! The bullets can't be left behind. They don't belong in the Past; they might change something. Here's my knife. Dig them out!"

The jungle was alive again, full of the old tremorings and bird cries. Eckels turned slowly to regard the primeval garbage dump, that hill of nightmares and terror. After a long time, like a sleepwalker he shuffled out along the Path.

He returned, shuddering, five minutes later, his arms soaked and red to the elbows. He held out his hands. Each held a number of steel bullets. Then he fell. He lay where he fell, not moving.

"You didn't have to make him do that," said Lesperance.

"Didn't I? It's too early to tell." Travis nudged the still body. "He'll live. Next time he won't go hunting game like this. Okay." He jerked his thumb wearily at Lesperance. "Switch on. Let's go home."

1492. 1776. 1812.

They cleaned their hands and faces. They changed their caking shirts and pants. Eckels was up and around again, not speaking. Travis glared at him for a full ten minutes.

"Don't look at me," cried Eckels. "I haven't done anything."

"Who can tell?"

"Just ran off the Path, that's all, a little mud on my shoes—what do you want me to do—get down and pray?"

"We might need it. I'm warning you, Eckels, I might kill you yet. I've got my gun ready."

"I'm innocent. I've done nothing!"

1999. 2000. 2055.

The Machine stopped.

"Get out," said Travis.

The room was there as they had left it. But not the same as they had left it. The same man sat behind the same desk. But the same man did not quite sit behind the same desk.

Travis looked around swiftly. "Everything okay here?" he snapped.

"Fine. Welcome home!"

Travis did not relax. He seemed to be looking at the very atoms of the air itself, at the way the sun poured through the one high window.

"Okay, Eckels, get out. Don't ever come back."

Eckels could not move.

"You heard me," said Travis. "What're you staring at?"

Eckels stood smelling the air, and there was a thing to the air, a chemical taint so subtle, so slight, that only a faint cry of his subliminal senses warned him it was there. The colors, white, gray, blue, orange, in the wall, in the furniture, in the sky beyond the window, were . . . were . . . And there was a feel. His flesh twitched. His hands twitched. He stood drinking the oddness with the pores of his body. Somewhere, someone must have been screaming one of those whistles that only a dog can hear. His body screamed silence in return. Beyond this room, beyond this wall, beyond this man who was not quite the same man seated at this desk that was not quite the same desk . . . lay an entire world of streets and people. What sort of world it was now, there was no telling. He could feel them moving there, beyond the walls, almost, like so many chess pieces blown in a dry wind. . . .

But the immediate thing was the sign painted on the office wall, the same sign he had read earlier today on first entering.

Somehow, the sign had changed:

TYME SEFARI INC.

SEFARIS TU ANY YEER EN THE PAST.

YU NAIM THE ANIMALL.

WEE TAEK YU THAIR.

YU SHOOT ITT.

Eckels felt himself fall into a chair. He fumbled crazily at the thick slime on his boots. He held up a clod of dirt, trembling. "No, it *can't* be. Not a *little* thing like that. No!"

Embedded in the mud, glistening green and gold and black, was a butterfly, very beautiful and very dead.

"Not a little thing like *that!* Not a butterfly!" cried Eckels.

It fell to the floor, an exquisite thing, a small thing that could upset balances and knock down a line of small dominoes and then big dominoes and then gigantic dominoes, all down the years across Time. Eckels' mind whirled. It *couldn't* change things. Killing one butterfly couldn't be *that* important! Could it?

His face was cold. His mouth trembled, asking: "Who— who won the presidential election yesterday?"

The man behind the desk laughed. "You joking? You know very well. Deutscher, of course! Who else? Not that fool weakling Keith. We got an iron man now, a man with guts!" The official stopped. "What's wrong?"

Eckels moaned. He dropped to his knees. He scrabbled at the golden butterfly with shaking fingers. "Can't we," he pleaded to the world, to himself, to the officials, to the machine, "can't we take it *back*, can't we *make* it alive again? Can't we start over? Can't we—"

He did not move. Eyes shut, he waited, shivering. He

heard Travis breathe loud in the room; he heard Travis shift his rifle, click the safety catch, and raise the weapon.

There was a sound of thunder.

Ray Bradbury (1920–   )
Ray Bradbury is one of America's most beloved writers, best known for his poetic short stories and his novel Fahrenheit 451 (1953) which was successfully filmed in 1966 by François Truffaut. Among his many story collections, The Martian Chronicles (1950) and The Illustrated Man (1951) are constant favorites, but his definitive collection is the massive The Stories of Ray Bradbury (1980). Mr. Bradbury was born in Waukegan, Illinois, and most of his stories have a strong Midwestern flavor in spite of the fact that he has spent most of his life in Los Angeles.

LIFE CYCLE

INVARIANT
John R. Pierce

You know the general facts concerning Homer Green, so I
don't need to describe him or his surroundings. I knew as
much and more, yet it was an odd sensation, which you
don't get through reading, actually to dress in that primitive fashion, to go among strange surroundings, and to see
him.

The house is no more odd than the pictures. Hemmed
in by other twentieth-century buildings, it must be indis-
tinguishable from the original structure and its surroundings. To enter it, to tread on rugs, to see chairs covered in
cloth with a nap, to see instruments for smoking, to see and
hear a primitive radio, even though operating really from a

variety of authentic transcriptions, and above all to see an open fire; all this gave me a sense of unreality, prepared though I was. Green sat by the fire in a chair, as we almost invariably find him, with a dog at his feet. He is perhaps the most valuable man in the world, I thought. But I could not shake off the sense of unreality concerning the substantial surroundings. He, too, seemed unreal, and I pitied him.

The sense of unreality continued through the form of self-introduction. How many have there been? I could, of course, examine the records.

"I'm Carew, from the Institute," I said. "We haven't met before, but they told me you'd be glad to see me."

Green rose and extended his hand. I took it obediently, making the unfamiliar gesture.

"Glad to see you," he said. "I've been dozing here. It's little of a shock, the treatment, and I thought I'd rest a few days. I hope it's really permanent.

"Won't you sit down?" he added.

We seated ourselves before the fire. The dog, which had risen, lay down, pressed against his master's feet.

"I suppose you want to test my reactions?" Green asked.

"Later," I replied. "There's no hurry. And it's so very comfortable here."

Green was easily distracted. He relaxed, staring at the fire. This was an opportunity, and I spoke in a somewhat purposeful voice.

"It seems more a time for politics, here," I said. "What the Swede intends, and what the French—"

"Drench our thoughts in mirth—" Green replied.

I had thought from the records the quotation would have some effect.

"But one doesn't leave politics to drench his thoughts in mirth," he continued. "One studies them—"

I won't go into the conversation. You've seen it in Appendix A of my thesis, "An Aspect of Twentieth-Century Politics and Speech." It was brief, as you know. I had been very lucky to get to see Green. I was more lucky to hit on the right thread directly. Somehow, it had never occurred to me before that twentieth-century politicians had meant, or had thought that they meant, what they said; that indeed, they had in their own minds attached a sense of meaning or relevancy to what seem to us meaningless or irrelevant phrases. It's hard to explain so foreign an idea; perhaps an example would help.

For instance, would you believe that a man accused of making a certain statement would seriously reply, "I'm not in the habit of making such statements?" Would you believe that this might even mean that he had not made the statement? Or would you further believe that even if he had made the statement, this would seem to him to classify it as some sort of special instance, and his reply as not truly evasive? I think these conjectures plausible, that is, when I struggle to immerse myself in the twentieth century. But I would never have dreamed them before talking with Green. How truly invaluable the man is!

I have said that the conversation recorded in Appendix A is very short. There was no need to continue along political lines after I had grasped the basic idea. Twentieth-century records are much more complete than Green's memory, and that itself has been thoroughly catalogued. It is not the dry bones of information, but the personal contact, the infinite variation in combinations, the stimulation of the warm human touch, that are helpful and suggestive.

So I was with Green, and most of a morning was still before me. You know that he is given meal times free, and only one appointment between meals, so that there will be no overlapping. I was grateful to the man, and sympathetic, and I was somewhat upset in his presence. I wanted to talk to him of the thing nearest his heart. There was no reason I shouldn't. I've recorded the rest of the conversation, but not published it. It's not new. Perhaps it is trivial, but it means a great deal to me. Maybe it's only my very personal memory of it. But I thought you might like to know.

"What led to your discovery?" I asked him.

"Salamanders," he replied without hesitation. "Salamanders."

The account I got of his perfect regeneration experiments was, of course, the published story. How many thousands of times has it been told? Yet, I swear I detected variations from the records. How nearly infinite the possible combinations are! But the chief points came in the usual order. How the regeneration of limbs in salamanders led to the idea of perfect regeneration of human parts. How, say, a cut heals, leaving not a scar, but a perfect replica of the damaged tissue. How in normal metabolism tissue can be replaced not imperfectly, as in an aging organism, but perfectly, indefinitely. You've seen it in animals, in compulsory biology. The chick whose metabolism replaces its tissues, but always in an exact, invariant form, never changing. It's disturbing to think of it in a man. Green looked so young, as young as I. Since the twentieth century—

When Green had concluded his description, including that of his own inoculation in the evening, he ventured to prophesy.

"I feel confident," he said, "that it will work, indefinitely."

"It does work, Dr. Green," I assured him. "Indefinitely."

"We mustn't be premature," he said. "After all, a short time—"

"Do you recall the date, Dr. Green?" I asked.

"September 11th," he said. "1943, if you want that, too."

"Dr. Green, today is August 4, 2170," I told him earnestly.

"Look here," Green said. "If it were, I wouldn't be here dressed this way, and you wouldn't be there dressed that way."

The impasse could have continued indefinitely. I took my communicator from my pocket and showed it to him. He watched with growing wonder and delight as I demonstrated, finally with projection, binaural and stereo. Not simple, but exactly the sort of electronic development which a man of Green's era associated with the future. Green seemed to have lost all thought of the conversation which had led to my production of the communicator.

"Dr. Green," I said, "the year is 2170. This is the twenty-second century."

He looked at me baffled, but this time not with disbelief. A strange sort of terror was spread over his features.

"An accident?" he asked. "My memory?"

"There has been no accident," I said. "Your memory is intact, as far as it goes. Listen to me. Concentrate."

Then I told him, simply and briefly, so that his thought processes would not lag. As I spoke to him he stared at me apprehensively, his mind apparently racing. This is what I said:

"Your experiment succeeded, beyond anything you had reason to hope. Your tissues took on the ability to reform themselves in exactly the same pattern year after year. Their form became invariant.

"Photographs and careful measurements show this, from year to year, yes, from century to century. You are just as you were over two hundred years ago.

"Your life has not been devoid of accident. Minor, even

major, wounds have left no trace in healing. Your tissues
are invariant.

"Your brain is invariant, too; that is, as far as the cell
patterns are concerned. A brain may be likened to an electrical network. Memory is the network, the coils and con-
densers, and their interconnections. Conscious thought is
the pattern of voltages across them and currents flowing
through them. The pattern is complicated, but transitory—
transient. Memory is changing the network of the brain,
affecting all subsequent thoughts, or patterns in the network. The network of your brain never changes. It is invariant.

"Or thought is like the complicated operation of the re-
lays and switches of a telephone exchange of your century,
but memory is the interconnections of elements. The interconnections on other people's brains change in the process
of thought, breaking down, building up, giving them new
memories. The pattern of connections in your brain never
changes. It is invariant.

"Other people can adapt themselves to new surroundings, learning where objects of necessity are, the pattern of
rooms, adapting themselves unconsciously, without friction. You cannot; your brain is invariant. Your habits are
keyed to a house, your house as it was the day before you
treated yourself. It has been preserved, replaced through
two hundred years so that you could live without friction.
In it, you live, day after day, the day after the treatment
which made your brain invariant.

"Do not think you give no return for this care. You are
perhaps the most valuable man in the world. Morning,
afternoon, evening; you have three appointments a day,
when the lucky few who are judged to merit or need your
help are allowed to seek it.

"I am a student of history. I came to see the twentieth

century through the eyes of an intelligent man of that century. You are a very intelligent, a brilliant man. Your mind has been analyzed in a detail greater than that of any other. Few brains are better. I came to learn from this powerful observant brain what politics meant to a man of your period. I learned from a fresh new source, your brain, which is not overlaid, not changed by the intervening years, but is just as it was in 1943.

"But I am not very important. Important workers: psychologists, come to see you. They ask you questions, then repeat them a little differently, and observe your reactions. One experiment is not vitiated by your memory of an earlier experiment. When your train of thought is interrupted, it leaves no memory behind. Your brain remains invariant. And these men, who otherwise could draw only general conclusions from simple experiments on multitudes of different, differently constituted and differently prepared individuals, can observe undisputable differences of response due to the slightest changes in stimulus. Some of these men have driven you to a frenzy. You do not go mad. Your brain cannot change; it is invariant.

"You are so valuable it seems that the world could scarcely progress without your invariant brain. And yet, we have not asked another to do as you did. With animals, yes. Your dog is an example. What you did was willingly, and you did not know the consequences. You did the world this greatest service unknowingly. But we know."

Green's head had sunk to his chest. His face was troubled, and he seemed to seek solace in the warmth of the fire. The dog at his feet stirred, and he looked down, a sudden smile on his face. I knew that his train of thought had been interrupted. The transients had died from his brain. Our whole meeting was gone from his processes of thought.

I rose and stole away before he looked up. Perhaps I wasted the remaining hour of the morning.

John R. Pierce (1910–   )
Dr. John R. Pierce served as the director of the Bell Telephone Laboratories from 1952 to 1971 and later as a professor of Engineering at California Institute of Technology. He is one of the most distinguished scientists ever to write science fiction, although he wrote only a small number of short stories, beginning in 1930. He is best known in science fiction as the author of articles that appeared in Astounding Science Fiction (later Analog) after World War II, some of which were written under the pseudonym J. J. Coupling. Professor Pierce has written fourteen books on science and resides in Pasadena, California.

CELL BIOLOGY

THE EXTERMINATOR

A. Hyatt Verrill

He was a magnificent specimen of his kind. Translucent—
white, swift in movement, possessing an almost uncanny
faculty for discovering his prey, and invariably triumphing
over his natural enemies. But his most outstanding feature
was his insatiable appetite. He was as merciless and as in-
discriminate a killer as a weasel or a ferret; but unlike those
wanton destroyers who kill for the mere lust of killing, the
Exterminator never wasted his kill. Whatever he fell upon
and destroyed was instantly devoured. To have watched
him would have been fascinating. A rush, as he hurled
himself upon his prey, a brief instant of immobility, of
seeming hesitation, a slight tremor of his substance, and all

was over; the unfortunate thing that had been moving, un-
suspicious of danger, on its accustomed way had vanished
completely, and the Exterminator was hurrying off, seeking
avidly for another victim. He moved continually in an
evenly flowing stream of liquid in absolute darkness. Hence
eyes were non-essential, and he was guided entirely by instinct or by nature rather than by faculties such as we know.

He was not alone. Others of his kind were all about and
the current was crowded with countless numbers of other
organisms: slowly moving roundish things of reddish hue,
wiggling tadpole-like creatures, star-shaped bodies; slender,
attenuated things like sticks endowed with life; globular
creatures; shapeless things constantly altering their form as
they moved or rather swam; minute, almost invisible beings;
thread-like, serpentine, or eel-like organisms, and countless
other forms. Among all these, threading his way in the overcrowding warm current, the Exterminator moved aimlessly, yet ever with one all-consuming purpose—to kill
and devour.

By some mysterious, inexplicable means he recognized
friends and could unerringly distinguish foes. The reddish
multitudes he avoided. He knew they were to remain un-
molested and even when, as often happened, he found himself surrounded, hemmed in, almost smothered by hordes
of the harmless red things and was jostled by them, he
remained unperturbed and made no attempt to injure or
devour them. But the others—the writhing, thread-like
creatures; the globular, ovoid, angular, radiate and bar-like
things; the rapidly wiggling tadpole-like organisms—were
different. Among these he wrought rapid and terrible destruction. Yet even here he exhibited a strange discrimina-
tion. Some he passed by without offering to harm them,
while others he attacked, slaughtered, and devoured with
indescribable ferocity. And on every hand others of his
kind were doing the same. They were like a horde of

ravenous sharks in a sea teeming with mackerel. They seemed obsessed with the one all-consuming desire to destroy, and so successful were they in this that often, for long periods, the ever moving stream in which they dwelt would be totally destitute of their prey.

Still, neither the Exterminator nor his fellows appeared to suffer for lack of sustenance. They were capable of going for long periods without food and they cruised, or rather swam slowly about, apparently as contented as when on a veritable orgy of killing. And even when the current bore no legitimate prey within reach of the Exterminator and his companions, never did they attempt to injure or molest the ever present red forms or the innumerable smaller organisms which they seemed to realize were friends. In fact, had it been possible to have interpreted their sensations, it would have been found that they were far more content, far more satisfied when there were no enemies to kill and devour than when the stream swarmed with their natural prey and there was a ceaseless ferocious urge to kill, kill, kill.

At the latter times the stream in which the Exterminator dwelt became uncomfortably warm, which aroused him and his fellows to renewed activity for a space, but which brought death to many of the savage beings. And always, following these casualties, the hordes of enemies rapidly increased until the Exterminator found it almost impossible to decimate them. At times, too, the stream flowed slowly and weakly and a lethargy came over the Exterminator. Often at such times he floated rather than swam, his strength ebbed, and his lust to kill almost vanished. But always there followed a change. The stream took on a peculiar bitter taste, countless numbers of the Exterminator's foes died and vanished, while the Exterminator himself became endowed with unwonted sudden strength and fell ravenously upon the remaining enemies. At such times, also, the number of his fellows always increased in some mysterious manner, as did the red beings. They seemed to appear from nowhere until the stream was thick with them.

Time did not exist for the Exterminator. He knew nothing of distance, nor of night or day. He was susceptible only to changes of temperature in the stream where he always had dwelt, and to the absence or presence of his natural foes and natural allies. Though he was perhaps aware that the current followed an erratic course, that the stream flowed through seemingly endless tunnels that twisted and turned and branched off in innumerable directions and formed a labyrinth of smaller streams, he knew nothing of their routes, or their sources or limits, but swam, or rather drifted, anywhere and everywhere quite aimlessly. No doubt, somewhere within the hundreds of tunnels, there were others of his kind as large, as powerful, and as insatiable a destroyer as himself. But as he was blind, as he did not possess the sense of hearing or other senses which enabled the higher forms of life to judge of their surroundings, he was quite unaware of such companions near him. And, as it happened, he was the only one of his kind who survived the unwanted event that eventually occurred, and by so doing was worthy of being called the Exterminator.

For an unusually long period the current in the tunnel had been most uncomfortably warm. The stream had teemed with countless numbers of his foes and these, attacking the reddish forms, had decimated them. There had been a woeful decrease in the Exterminator's fellows also, and he and the few survivors had been forced to exert themselves to the utmost to avoid being overwhelmed. Even then the hordes of wiggling, gyrating, darting, weaving enemies seemed to increase faster than they were killed and devoured. It

began to look as if their army would be victorious and the
Exterminator and his fellows would be vanquished, utterly
destroyed, when suddenly the slowly flowing hot stream
took on a strange, pungent, acrid taste. Instantly, almost,
the temperature decreased, the current increased, and as if
exposed to a gas attack, the swarming hosts of innumerable
strange forms dwindled. And almost instantly the Exterminator's fellows appeared as if from nowhere and fell ravenously upon their surviving foes. In an amazingly short time
the avenging white creatures had practically exterminated
their multitudinous enemies. Great numbers of the reddish
organisms filled the stream and the Exterminator dashed
hither and thither seeking chance survivors of his enemies.
In eddies and the smaller tunnels he came upon a few.
Almost instantly he dashed at them, destroyed them, swallowed them. Guided by some inexplicable power or force
he swept along a tiny tunnel. Before him he was aware of a
group of three tiny thread-like things, his deadliest foes—
and hurled himself forward in chase. Overtaking one, he
was about to seize it when a terrific cataclysm occurred.
The wall of the tunnel was split assunder, a great rent appeared, and with a rush like water through an opened
sluice-way the enclosed stream poured upward through the
opening.

Helpless in the grip of the current, the Exterminator was
borne whirling, gyrating madly into the aperture. But his
one obsession, an all-consuming desire to kill, overcame all
terror, all other sensations. Even as the fluid hurled him
onward he seized the wriggling foe so near him and swallowed it alive. At the same instant the remaining two were
carried by the rushing current almost within his reach.
With a sudden effort he threw himself upon the nearest,
and as the thing vanished in his maw, he was borne from
eternal darkness into blinding light.

Instantly the current ceased to flow. The liquid became

stagnant and the countless red beings surrounding the Exterminator moved feebly, slowly, and gathered in clusters
where they clung together as if for mutual support. Somewhere near at hand, the Exterminator sensed the presence
of the last surviving member of the trio he had been chas-
ing when the disaster took place. But in the stagnant, thick
liquid, obstructed by the red beings, he could not move
freely. He struggled, fought to reach this one remaining
foe; but in vain. He felt suffocating, becoming weaker and
weaker. And he was alone. Of all his comrades, he was the
only one that had been carried through the rent in the tunnel that for so long had been his home.

Suddenly he felt himself lifted. Together with a few of
the reddish things and a small portion of his native element,
he was drawn up. Then, with the others, he was dropped,
and as he fell, new life coursed through him, for he realized
that his hereditary enemy—that wiggling thread-like thing
—was close beside him, that even yet he might fall upon
and destroy it.

The next instant some heavy object fell upon him. He
was imprisoned there with his archenemy an infinitesimal
distance from him, but hopelessly out of reach. A mad
desire to wreak vengeance swept over him. He was losing
strength rapidly. Already the red beings about him had
become inert, motionless. Only he and that thread-like, tiny
thing still showed signs of life. And the fluid was rapidly
thickening. Suddenly, for a fraction of a second, he felt
free, and with a final spasmodic effort he moved, reached
the enemy, and, triumphant at the last, became a motionless inert thing.

"Strange!" muttered a human voice as its owner peered
through the microscope at the blood drop on the slide
under the objective. "I could have sworn I caught a glimpse

of a bacillus there a moment ago. But there's not a trace of it now."

"That new formula we injected had an almost miraculous effect," observed a second voice.

"Yes," agreed the first. "The crisis is past and the patient is out of danger. Not a single bacillus in this specimen. I would not have believed it possible."

But neither physician was aware of the part the Exterminator had played. To them he was merely a white corpuscle lying dead in the rapidly drying blood drop on the glass-slide.

A. Hyatt Verrill (1871–1954)

A. Hyatt Verrill was in on the beginning of American magazine science fiction, selling stories to Amazing in its first year of publication in 1926. He was also a natural-history illustrator, the inventor of the autochrome process of photography, and an explorer who traveled through the wilds of Central and South America. Latin America and the West Indies provide the setting for most of his science fiction stories.

GENETICS

TOMORROW'S CHILDREN
Poul Anderson

On the world's loom
Weave the Norns doom,
Nor may they guide it nor change.
  —Wagner, Siegfried

Ten miles up, it hardly showed. Earth was a cloudy green
and brown blur, the vast vault of the stratosphere reaching
changelessly out to spatial infinities, and beyond the pulsing engine there was silence and serenity no man could
ever touch. Looking down, Hugh Drummond could see the
Mississippi gleaming like a drawn sword, and its slow curve
matched the contours shown on his map. The hills, the sea,
the sun and wind and rain, they didn't change. Not in less
than a million slow-striding years, and human efforts flickered too briefly in the unending night for that.

Farther down, though, and especially where cities had
been— The lone man in the solitary stratojet swore softly,

bitterly, and his knuckles whitened on the controls. He was a big man, his gaunt rangy form sprawling awkwardly in the tiny pressure cabin, and he wasn't quite forty. But his dark hair was streaked with gray, in the shabby flying suit his shoulders stooped, and his long homely face was drawn into haggard lines. His eyes were black-rimmed and sunken with weariness, dark and dreadful in their intensity. He'd seen too much, survived too much, until he began to look like most other people of the world. *Heir of the ages,* he thought dully.

Mechanically, he went through the motions of following his course. Natural landmarks were still there, and he had powerful binoculars to help him. But he didn't use them much. They showed too many broad shallow craters, their vitreous smoothness throwing back sunlight in the flat blank glitter of a snake's eye, the ground about them a churned and blasted desolation. And there were the worse regions of—deadness. Twisted dead trees, blowing sand, tumbled skeletons, perhaps at night a baleful blue glow of fluorescence. The bombs had been nightmares, riding in on wings of fire and horror to shake the planet with the death blows of cities. But the radioactive dust was worse than any nightmare.

He passed over villages, even small towns. Some of them were deserted, the blowing colloidal dust, or plague, or economic breakdown making them untenable. Others still seemed to be living a feeble half-life. Especially in the Midwest, there was a pathetic struggle to return to an agricultural system, but the insects and blights—

Drummond shrugged. After nearly two years of this, over the scarred and maimed planet, he should be used to it. The United States had been lucky. Europe, now—

Der Untergang des Abendlandes, he thought grayly. *Spengler foresaw the collapse of a topheavy civilization. He* didn't foresee atomic bombs, radioactive-dust bombs, bacteria bombs, blight bombs—the bombs, the senseless inanimate bombs flying like monster insects over the shivering world. So he didn't guess the extent of the collapse.

Deliberately he pushed the thoughts out of his conscious mind. He didn't want to dwell on them. He'd lived with them two years, and that was two eternities too long. And anyway, he was nearly home now.

The capital of the United States was below him, and he sent the stratojet slanting down in a long thunderous dive toward the mountains. Not much of a capital, the little town huddled in a valley of the Cascades, but the waters of the Potomac had filled the grave of Washington. Strictly speaking, there was no capital. The officers of the government were scattered over the country, keeping in precarious touch by plane and radio, but Taylor, Oregon, came as close to being the nerve center as any other place.

He gave the signal again on his transmitter, knowing with a faint spine-crawling sensation of the rocket batteries trained on him from the green of those mountains. When one plane could carry the end of a city, all planes were under suspicion. Not that anyone outside was supposed to know that that innocuous little town was important. But you never could tell. The war wasn't officially over. It might never be, with sheer personal survival overriding the urgency of treaties.

A light-beam transmitter gave him a cautious: "O.K. Can you land in the street?"

It was a narrow, dusty track between two wooden rows of houses, but Drummond was a good pilot and this was a good jet. "Yeah," he said. His voice had grown unused to speech.

He cut speed in a spiral descent until he was gliding with only the faintest whisper of wind across his ship. Touching wheels to the street, he slammed on the brake and bounced to a halt.

Silence struck at him like a physical blow. The engine stilled, the sun beating down from a brassy blue sky on the drabness of rude "temporary" houses, the total-seeming desertion beneath the impassive mountains—home! Hugh Drummond laughed, a short harsh bark with nothing of humor in it, and swung open the cockpit canopy.

There were actually quite a few people, he saw, peering from doorways and side streets. They looked fairly well fed and dressed, many in uniform, they seemed to have purpose and hope. But this, of course, was the capital of the United States of America, the world's most fortunate country.

"Get out—quick!"

The peremptory voice roused Drummond from the introspection into which those lonely months had driven him. He looked down at a gang of men in mechanics' outfits, led by a harassed-looking man in captain's uniform. "Oh—of course," he said slowly. "You want to hide the plane. And, naturally, a regular landing field would give you away."

"Hurry, get out, you infernal idiot! Anyone, anyone might come over and see—"

"They wouldn't get unnoticed by an efficient detection system, and you still have that," said Drummond, sliding his booted legs over the cockpit edge. "And anyway, there won't be any more raids. The war's over."

"Wish I could believe that, but who are you to say? Get a move on!"

The grease monkeys hustled the plane down the street. With an odd feeling of loneliness, Drummond watched it go. After all, it had been his home for—how long?

The machine was stopped before a false house whose whole front was swung aside. A concrete ramp led downward, and Drummond could see a cavernous immensity below. Light within it gleamed off silvery rows of aircraft.

"Pretty neat," he admitted. "Not that it matters any more. Probably it never did. Most of the hell came over on robot rockets. Oh, well." He fished his pipe from his jacket. Colonel's insignia glittered briefly as the garment flipped back.

"Oh . . . sorry, sir!" exclaimed the captain. "I didn't know—"

" 'S O.K. I've gotten out of the habit of wearing a regular uniform. A lot of places I've been, an American wouldn't be very popular." Drummond stuffed tobacco into his briar, scowling. He hated to think how often he'd had to use the Colt at his hip, or even the machine guns in his plane, to save himself. He inhaled smoke gratefully. It seemed to drown out some of the bitter taste.

"General Robinson said to bring you to him when you arrived, sir," said the captain. "This way, please."

They went down the street, their boots scuffing up little acrid clouds of dust. Drummond looked sharply about him. He'd left very shortly after the two-month Ragnarok which had tapered off when the organization of both sides broke down too far to keep on making and sending the bombs, and maintaining order with famine and disease starting their ghastly ride over the homeland. At that time, the United States was a cityless, anarchic chaos, and he'd had only the briefest of radio exchanges since then, whenever he could get at a long-range set still in working order. They'd made remarkable progress meanwhile. How much, he didn't know, but the mere existence of something like a capital was sufficient proof.

Robinson— His lined face twisted into a frown. He didn't know the man. He'd been expecting to be received by the President, who had sent him and some others out. Unless the others had— No, he was the only one who had been in eastern Europe and western Asia. He was sure of that.

Two sentries guarded the entrance to what was obviously a converted general store. But there were no more stores. There was nothing to put in them. Drummond entered the cool dimness of an antechamber. The clatter of a typewriter, the Wac operating it— He gaped and blinked. That was—impossible! Typewriters, secretaries—hadn't they gone out with the whole world, two years ago? If the Dark Ages had returned to Earth, it didn't seem—*right*— that there should still be typewriters. It didn't fit, didn't—

He grew aware that the captain had opened the inner door for him. As he stepped in, he grew aware of how tired he was. His arm weighed a ton as he saluted the man behind the desk.

"At ease, at ease." Robinson's voice was genial. Despite the five stars on his shoulders, he wore no tie or coat, and his round face was smiling. Still, he looked tough and competent underneath. To run things nowadays, he'd have to be.

"Sit down, Colonel Drummond." Robinson gestured to a chair near his and the aviator collapsed into it, shivering. His haunted eyes traversed the office. It was almost well enough outfitted to be a prewar place.

Prewar! A word like a sword, cutting across history with a brutality of murder, hazing everything in the past until it was a vague golden glow through drifting, red-shot black clouds. And—only two years. *Only two years!* Surely sanity was meaningless in a world of such nightmare inversions. Why, he could barely remember Barbara and the kids. Their faces were blotted out in a tide of other visages —starved faces, dead faces, human faces become beast-formed with want and pain and eating throttled hate. His

grief was lost in the agony of the world, and in some ways
he had become a machine himself.

"You look plenty tired," said Robinson.

"Yeah . . . yes, sir—"

"Skip the formality. I don't go for it. We'll be working
pretty close together, can't take time to be diplomatic."

"Uh-huh. I came over the North Pole, you know.
Haven't slept since— Rough time. But, if I may ask,
you—" Drummond hesitated.

"I? I suppose I'm President. Ex officio, pro tem, or something. Here, you need a drink." Robinson got bottle and
glasses from a drawer. The liquor gurgled out in a pungent
stream. "Prewar Scotch. Till it gives out I'm laying off this
modern hooch. *Gambai.*"

The fiery, smoky brew jolted Drummond to wakefulness.
Its glow was pleasant in his empty stomach. He heard Robinson's voice with a surrealistic sharpness:

"Yes, I'm at the head now. My predecessors made the
mistake of sticking together, and of traveling a good deal in
trying to pull the country back into shape. So I think the
sickness got the President, and I know it got several others.
Of course, there was no means of holding an election. The
armed forces had almost the only organization left, so we
had to run things. Berger was in charge, but he shot himself
when he learned he'd breathed radiodust. Then the com-
mand fell to me. I've been lucky."

"I see." It didn't make much difference. A few dozen
more deaths weren't much, when over half the world was
gone. "Do you expect to—continue lucky?" A brutally
blunt question, maybe, but words weren't bombs.

"I do." Robinson was firm about that. "We've learned by
experience, learned a lot. We've scattered the army, broken
it into small outposts at key points throughout the country.
For quite a while, we stopped travel altogether except for
absolute emergencies, and then with elaborate precautions.

That smothered the epidemics. The microorganisms were bred to work in crowded areas, you know. They were almost immune to known medical techniques, but without hosts and carriers they died. I guess natural bacteria ate up most of them. We still take care in traveling, but we're fairly safe now."

"Did any of the others come back? There were a lot like me, sent out to see what really had happened to the world."

"One did, from South America. Their situation is similar to ours, though they lacked our tight organization and have gone further toward anarchy. Nobody else returned but you."

It wasn't surprising. In fact, it was a cause for astonishment that anyone had come back. Drummond had volunteered after the bomb erasing St. Louis had taken his family, not expecting to survive and not caring much whether he did. Maybe that was why he had.

"You can take your time in writing a detailed report," said Robinson, "but in general, how are things over there?"

Drummond shrugged. "The war's over. Burned out. Europe has gone back to savagery. They were caught between America and Asia, and the bombs came both ways. Not many survivors, and they're starving animals. Russia, from what I saw, has managed something like you've done here, though they're worse off than we. Naturally, I couldn't find out much there. I didn't get to India or China, but in Russia I heard rumors— No, the world's gone too far into disintegration to carry on war."

"Then we can come out in the open," said Robinson softly. "We can really start rebuilding. I don't think there'll ever be another war, Drummond. I think the memory of this one will be carved too deeply on the race for us ever to forget."

"Can you shrug it off that easily?"

"No, no, of course not. Our culture hasn't lost its con-

tinuity, but it's had a terrific setback. We'll never wholly get
over it. But—we're on our way up again."

The general rose, glancing at his watch. "Six o'clock.
Come on, Drummond, let's get home."

"Home?"

"Yes, you'll stay with me. Man, you look like the original zombie. You'll need a month or more of sleeping between clean sheets, of home cooking and home atmosphere.
My wife will be glad to have you; we see almost no new
faces. And as long as we'll work together, I'd like to keep
you handy. The shortage of competent men is terrific."

They went down the street, an aide following. Drummond
was again conscious of the weariness aching in every bone
and fiber of him. A home—after two years of ghost towns,
of shattered chimneys above blood-dappled snow, of flimsy
lean-tos housing starvation and death.

"Your plane will be mighty useful, too," said Robinson.
"Those atomic-powered craft are scarcer than hens' teeth
used to be." He chuckled hollowly, as at a rather grim joke.
"Got you through close to two years of flying without need-
ing fuel. Any other trouble?"

"Some, but there were enough spare parts." No need to
tell of those frantic hours and days of slaving, of desperate
improvisation with hunger and plague stalking him who
stayed overlong. He'd had his troubles getting food, too,
despite the plentiful supplies he'd started out with. He'd
fought for scraps in the winters, beaten off howling mani-
acs who would have killed him for a bird he'd shot or a
dead horse he'd scavenged. He hated that plundering, and
would not have cared personally if they'd managed to destroy him. But he had a mission, and the mission was all
he'd had left as a focal point for his life, so he'd clung to it
with fanatic intensity.

And now the job was over, and he realized he couldn't

rest. He didn't dare. Rest would give him time to remember. Maybe he could find surcease in the gigantic work of reconstruction. Maybe.

"Here we are," said Robinson.

Drummond blinked in new amazement. There was a car, camouflaged under brush, with a military chauffeur—a car! And in pretty fair shape, too.

"We've got a few oil wells going again, and a small patched-up refinery," explained the general. "It furnishes enough gas and oil for what traffic we have."

They got in the rear seat. The aide sat in front, a rifle ready. The car started down a mountain road.

"Where to?" usked Drummond a little dazedly.

Robinson smiled. "Personally," he said, "I'm almost the only lucky man on Earth. We had a summer cottage on Lake Taylor, a few miles from here. My wife was there when the war came, and stayed, and nobody came along till I brought the head officers here with me. Now I've got a home all to myself."

"Yeah. Yeah, you're lucky," said Drummond. He looked out the window, not seeing the sun-spattered woods. Presently he asked, his voice a little harsh: "How is the country really doing now?"

"For a while it was rough. Damn rough. When the cities went, our transportation, communication, and distribution systems broke down. In fact, our whole economy disintegrated, though not all at once. Then there was the dust and the plagues. People fled, and there was open fighting when overcrowded safe places refused to take in any more refugees. Police went with the cities, and the army couldn't do much patrolling. We were busy fighting the enemy troops that'd flown over the Pole to invade. We still haven't gotten them all. Bands are roaming the country, hungry and desperate outlaws, and there are plenty of Americans who turned to banditry when everything else failed. That's why we have this guard, though so far none have come this way.

"The insect and blight weapons just about wiped out our crops, and that winter everybody starved. We checked the pests with modern methods, though it was touch and go for a while, and next year got some food. Of course, with no distribution as yet, we failed to save a lot of people. And farming is still a tough proposition. We won't really have the bugs licked for a long time. If we had a research center as well equipped as those which produced the things— But we're gaining. We're gaining."

"Distribution—" Drummond rubbed his chin. "How about railroads? Horse-drawn vehicles?"

"We have some railroads going, but the enemy was as careful to dust most of ours as we were to dust theirs. As for horses, they were nearly all eaten that first winter. I know personally of only a dozen. They're on my place; I'm trying to breed enough to be of use, but"—Robinson smiled wryly—"by the time we've raised that many, the factories should have been going quite a spell."

"And so now—?"

"We're over the worst. Except for outlaws, we have the population fairly well controlled. The civilized people are fairly well fed, with some kind of housing. We have machine shops, small factories, and the like going, enough to keep our transportation and other mechanisms 'level.' Presently we'll be able to expand these, begin actually increasing what we have. In another five years or so, I guess, we'll be integrated enough to drop martial law and hold a general election. A big job ahead, but a good one."

The car halted to let a cow lumber over the road, a calf trotting at her heels. She was gaunt and shaggy, and skittered nervously from the vehicle into the brush.

"Wild," explained Robinson. "Most of the real wild life was killed off for food in the last two years, but a lot of farm animals escaped when their owners died or fled, and have run free ever since. They—" He noticed Drummond's fixed gaze. The pilot was looking at the calf. Its legs were half the normal length.

"Mutant," said the general. "You find a lot of such animals. Radiation from bombed or dusted areas. There are even a lot of human abnormal births." He scowled, worry clouding his eyes. "In fact, that's just about our worst problem. It—"

The car came out of the woods onto the shore of a small lake. It was a peaceful scene, the quiet waters like molten gold in the slanting sunlight, trees ringing the circumference and all about them the mountains. Under one huge pine stood a cottage, a woman on the porch.

It was like one summer with Barbara—Drummond cursed under his breath and followed Robinson toward the little building. It wasn't, it wasn't, it could never be. Not ever again. There were soldiers guarding this place from chance marauders, and— There was an odd-looking flower at his foot. A daisy, but huge and red and irregularly formed.

A squirrel chittered from a tree. Drummond saw that its face was so blunt as to be almost human.

Then he was on the porch, and Robinson was introducing him to "my wife Elaine." She was a nice-looking young woman with eyes that were sympathetic on Drummond's exhausted face. The aviator tried not to notice that she was pregnant.

He was led inside, and reveled in a hot bath. Afterward there was supper, but he was numb with sleep by then, and hardly noticed it when Robinson put him to bed.

Reaction set in, and for a week or so Drummond went about in a haze, not much good to himself or anyone else. But it was surprising what plenty of food and sleep could do, and one evening Robinson came home to find him scribbling on sheets of paper.

"Arranging my notes and so on," he explained. "I'll write out the complete report in a month, I guess."

"Good. But no hurry." Robinson settled tiredly into an armchair. "The rest of the world will keep. I'd rather you'd just work at this off and on, and join my staff for your main job."

"O.K. Only what'll I do?"

"Everything. Specialization is gone; too few surviving specialists and equipment. I think your chief task will be to head the census bureau."

"Eh?"

Robinson grinned lopsidedly. "You'll be the census bureau, except for what few assistants I can spare you." He leaned forward, said earnestly: "And it's one of the most important jobs there is. You'll do for this country what you did for central Eurasia, only in much greater detail. Drummond, we have to *know*."

He took a map from a desk drawer and spread it out. "Look, here's the United States. I've marked regions known to be uninhabitable in red." His fingers traced out the ugly splotches. "Too many of 'em, and doubtless there are others we haven't found yet. Now, the blue X's are army posts." They were sparsely scattered over the land, near the centers of population groupings. "Not enough of those. It's all we can do to control the more or less well-off, orderly people. Bandits, enemy troops, homeless refugees—they're still running wild, skulking in the backwoods and barrens, and raiding whenever they can. And they spread the plague. We won't really have it licked till everybody's settled down, and that'd be hard to enforce. Drummond, we don't even have enough soldiers to start a feudal system for protection. The plague spread like a prairie fire in those concentrations of men.

"We have to know. We have to know how many people survived—half the population, a third, a quarter, whatever it is. We have to know where they are, and how they're fixed for supplies, so we can start up an equitable distribution system. We have to find all the small-town shops and labs and libraries still standing, and rescue their priceless contents before looters or the weather beat us to it. We have to locate doctors and engineers and other professional men, and put them to work rebuilding. We have to find the outlaws and round them up. We— I could go on forever. Once we have all that information, we can set up a master plan for redistributing population, agriculture, industry, and the rest most efficiently, for getting the country back under civil authority and police, for opening regular transportation and communication channels—for getting the nation back on its feet."

"I see," nodded Drummond. "Hitherto, just surviving and hanging on to what was left has taken precedence. Now you're in a position to start expanding, if you know where and how much to expand."

"Exactly," Robinson rolled a cigarette, grimacing. "Not much tobacco left. What I have is perfectly foul. Lord, that war was crazy!"

"All wars are," said Drummond dispassionately, "but technology advanced to the point of giving us a knife to cut our throats with. Before that, we were just beating our heads against the wall. Robinson, we can't go back to the old ways. We've got to start on a new track—a track of sanity."

"Yes. And that brings up—" The other man looked

toward the kitchen door. They could hear the cheerful rattle of dishes there, and smell mouth-watering cooking odors. He lowered his voice. "I might as well tell you this now, but don't let Elaine know. She . . . she shouldn't be worried. Drummond, did you see our horses?"

"The other day, yes. The colts—"

"Uh-huh. There've been five colts born of eleven mares in the last year. Two of them were so deformed they died in a week, another in a few months. One of the two left has cloven hoofs and almost no teeth. The last one looks normal—so far. One out of eleven, Drummond."

"Were those horses near a radioactive area?"

"They must have been. They were rounded up wherever found and brought here. The stallion was caught near the site of Portland, I know. But if he were the only one with mutated genes, it would hardly show in the first generation, would it? I understand nearly all mutations are Mendelian recessives. Even if there were one dominant, it would show in all the colts, but none of these looked alike."

"Hm-m-m—I don't know much about genetics, but I do know hard radiation, or rather the secondary charged particles it produces, will cause mutation. Only mutants are rare, and tend to fall into certain patterns—"

"Were rare!" Suddenly Robinson was grim, something coldly frightened in his eyes. "Haven't you noticed the animals and plants? They're fewer than formerly, and . . . well, I've not kept count, but at least half those seen or killed have something wrong, internally or externally."

Drummond drew heavily on his pipe. He needed something to hang onto, in a new storm of insanity. Very quietly, he said: "In my college biology course, they told me the vast majority of mutations are unfavorable. More ways of not doing something than of doing it. Radiation might sterilize an animal, or might produce several degrees of genetic change. You could have a mutation so violently lethal the possessor never gets born, or soon dies. You could have all kinds of more or less handicapping factors, or just random changes not making much difference one way or the other. Or in a few cases you might get something actually favorable, but you couldn't really say the possessor is a true member of the species. And favorable mutations themselves usually involve a price in the partial or total loss of some other function."

"Right." Robinson nodded heavily. "One of your jobs on the census will be to try and locate any and all who know genetics, and send them here. But your real task, which only you and I and a couple of others must know about, the job overriding all other considerations, will be to find the human mutants."

Drummond's throat was dry. "There've been a lot of them?" he whispered.

"Yes. But we don't know how many or where. We only know about those people who live near an army post, or have some other fairly regular intercourse with us, and they're only a few thousand all told. Among them, the birth rate has gone down to about half the prewar ratio. And over half the births they do have are abnormal."

"Over half—"

"Yeah. Of course, the violently different ones soon die, or are put in an institution we've set up in the Alleghenies. But what can we do with viable forms, if their parents still love them? A kid with deformed or missing or abortive organs, twisted internal structure, a tail, or something even worse . . . well, it'll have a tough time in life, but it can generally survive. And perpetuate itself—"

"And a normal-looking one might have some unnoticeable quirk, or a characteristic that won't show up for years.

Or even a normal one might be carrying recessives, and pass them on— God!" The exclamation was half blasphemy, half prayer. "But how'd it happen? People weren't all near atom-hit areas."

"Maybe not, though a lot of survivors escaped from the outskirts. But there was that first year, with everybody on the move. One could pass near enough to a blasted region to be affected, without knowing it. And that damnable radiodust, blowing on the wind. It's got a long half-life. It'll be active for decades. Then, as in any collapsing culture, promiscuity was common. Still is. Oh, it'd spread itself, all right."

"I still don't see why it spread itself so much. Even here—"

"Well, I don't know why it shows up here. I suppose a lot of the local flora and fauna came in from elsewhere. This place is safe. The nearest dusted region is three hundred miles off, with mountains between. There must be many such islands of comparatively normal conditions. We have to find them too. But elsewhere—"

"Soup's on," announced Elaine, and went from the kitchen to the dining room with a loaded tray.

The men rose. Grayly, Drummond looked at Robinson and said tonelessly: "O.K. I'll get your information for you. We'll map mutation areas and safe areas, we'll check on our population and resources, we'll eventually get all the facts you want. But—what are you going to do then?"

"I wish I knew," said Robinson haggardly. "I wish I knew."

Winter lay heavily on the north, a vast gray sky seeming frozen solid over the rolling white plains. The last three winters had come early and stayed long. Dust, colloidal dust of the bombs, suspended in the atmosphere and cutting down the solar constant by a deadly percent or two. There had even been a few earthquakes, set off in geologically unstable parts of the world by bombs planted right. Half California had been ruined when a sabotage bomb started the San Andreas Fault on a major slip. And that kicked up still more dust.

Fimbulwinter, thought Drummond bleakly. *The doom of the prophecy. But no, we're surviving. Though maybe not as men—*

Most people had gone south, and there overcrowding had made starvation and disease and internecine struggle the normal aspects of life. Those who'd stuck it out up here, and had luck with their pest-ridden crops, were better off.

Drummond's jet slid above the cratered black ruin of the Twin Cities. There was still enough radioactivity to melt the snow, and the pit was like a skull's empty eye socket. The man sighed, but he was becoming calloused to the sight of death. There was so much of it. Only the struggling agony of life mattered any more.

He strained through the sinister twilight, swooping low over the unending fields. Burned-out hulks of farmhouses, bones of ghost towns, sere deadness of dusted land—but he'd heard travelers speak of a fairly powerful community up near the Canadian border, and it was up to him to find it.

A lot of things had been up to him in the last six months. He'd had to work out a means of search, and organize his few, overworked assistants into an efficient staff, and go out on the long hunt.

They hadn't covered the country. That was impossible. Their few planes had gone to areas chosen more or less at random, trying to get a cross section of conditions. They'd penetrated wildernesses of hill and plain and forest, establishing contact with scattered, still demoralized out-dwellers. On the whole, it was more laborious than anything else. Most were pathetically glad to see any symbol of law and order and the paradisical-seeming "old days." Now and then there was danger and trouble, when they encountered wary or sullen or outright hostile groups suspicious of a government they associated with disaster, and once there had even been a pitched battle with roving outlaws. But the work had gone ahead, and now the preliminaries were about over.

Preliminaries— It was a bigger job to find out exactly how matters stood than the entire country was capable of undertaking right now. But Drummond had enough facts for reliable extrapolation. He and his staff had collected most of the essential data and begun correlating it. By questioning, by observation, by seeking and finding, by any means that came to hand they'd filled their notebooks. And in the sketchy outlines of a Chinese drawing, and with the same stark realism, the truth was there.

Just this one more place, and I'll go home, thought Drummond for the—thousandth?—time. His brain was getting into a rut, treading the same terrible circle and finding no way out. *Robinson won't like what I tell him, but there it is.* And darkly, slowly: *Barbara, maybe it was best you and the kids went as you did. Quickly, cleanly, not even knowing it. This isn't much of a world. It'll never be our world again.*

He saw the place he sought, a huddle of buildings near the frozen shores of the Lake of the Woods, and his jet murmured toward the white ground. The stories he'd heard of this town weren't overly encouraging, but he supposed he'd get out all right. The others had his data anyway, so it didn't matter.

By the time he'd landed in the clearing just outside the

village, using the jet's skis, most of the inhabitants were there waiting. In the gathering dusk they were a ragged and wild-looking bunch, clumsily dressed in whatever scraps of cloth and leather they had. The bearded, hard-eyed men were armed with clubs and knives and a few guns. As Drummond got out, he was careful to keep his hands away from his own automatics.

"Hello," he said. "I'm friendly."

"Y' better be," growled the big leader. "Who are you, where from, an' why?"

"First," lied Drummond smoothly, "I want to tell you I have another man with a plane who knows where I am. If I'm not back in a certain time, he'll come with bombs. But we don't intend any harm or interference. This is just a sort of social call. I'm Hugh Drummond of the United States Army."

They digested that slowly. Clearly, they weren't friendly to the government, but they stood in too much awe of aircraft and armament to be openly hostile. The leader spat. "How long you staying?"

"Just overnight, if you'll put me up. I'll pay for it." He held up a small pouch. "Tobacco."

Their eyes gleamed, and the leader said, "You'll stay with me. Come on."

Drummond gave him the bribe and went with the group. He didn't like to spend such priceless luxuries thus freely, but the job was more important. And the boss seemed thawed a little by the fragrant brown flakes. He was sniffing them greedily.

"Been smoking bark an' grass," he confided. "Terrible."

"Worse than that," agreed Drummond. He turned up his jacket collar and shivered. The wind starting to blow was bitterly cold.

"Just what y' here for?" demanded someone else.

"Well, just to see how things stand. We've got the government started again, and are patching things up. But we have to know where folks are, what they need, and so on."

"Don't want nothing t' do with the gov'ment," muttered a woman. "They brung all this on us."

"Oh, come now. We didn't ask to be attacked." Mentally, Drummond crossed his fingers. He neither knew nor cared who was to blame. Both sides, letting mutual fear and friction mount to hysteria— In fact, he wasn't sure the United States hadn't sent out the first rockets, on orders of some panicky or aggressive officials. Nobody was alive who admitted knowing.

"It's the jedgment o' God, for the sins o' our leaders," persisted the woman. "The plague, the fire-death, all that, ain't it foretold in the Bible? Ain't we living in the last days o' the world?"

"Maybe." Drummond was glad to stop before a long low cabin. Religious argument was touchy at best, and with a lot of people nowadays it was dynamite.

They entered the rudely furnished but fairly comfortable structure. A good many crowded in with them. For all their suspicion, they were curious, and an outsider in an aircraft was a blue-moon event these days.

Drummond's eyes flickered unobtrusively about the room, noticing details. Three women—that meant a return to concubinage. Only to be expected in a day of few men and strong-arm rule. Ornaments and utensils, tools and weapons of good quality—yes, that confirmed the stories. This wasn't exactly a bandit town, but it had waylaid travelers and raided other places when times were hard, and built up a sort of dominance of the surrounding country. That, too, was common.

There was a dog on the floor nursing a litter. Only three

pups, and one of those was bald, one lacked ears, and one had more toes than it should. Among the wide-eyed children present, there were several two years old or less, and with almost no obvious exceptions, they were also different.

Drummond sighed heavily and sat down. In a way, this clinched it. He'd known for a long time, and finding mutation here, as far as any place from atomic destruction, was about the last evidence he needed.

He had to get on friendly terms, or he wouldn't find out much about things like population, food production, and whatever else there was to know. Forcing a smile to stiff lips, he took a flask from his jacket. "Prewar rye," he said. "Who wants a nip?"

"Do we!" The answer barked out in a dozen voices and words. The flask circulated, men pawing and cursing and grabbing to get at it. *Their homebrew must be pretty bad,* thought Drummond wryly.

The chief shouted an order, and one of his women got busy at the primitive stove. "Rustle you a mess o' chow," he said heartily. "An' my name's Sam Buckman."

"Pleased to meet you, Sam." Drummond squeezed the hairy paw hard. He had to show he wasn't a weakling, a conniving city slicker.

"What's it like, outside?" asked someone presently. "We ain't heard for so long—"

"You haven't missed much," said Drummond between bites. The food was pretty good. Briefly, he sketched conditions. "You're better off than most," he finished.

"Yeah. Mebbe so." Sam Buckman scratched his tangled beard. "What I'd give f'r a razor blade—! It ain't easy, though. The first year we weren't no better off 'n anyone else. Me, I'm a farmer, I kept some ears o' corn an' a little wheat an' barley in my pockets all that winter, even though I was starving. A bunch o' hungry refugees plundered my

place, but I got away an' drifted up here. Next year I took
an empty farm here an' started over."

Drummond doubted that it had been abandoned, but
said nothing. Sheer survival outweighed a lot of considerations.

"Others came an' settled here," said the leader reminis-
cently. "We farm together. We have to; one man couldn't
live by hisself, not with the bugs an' blight, an' the crops
sproutin' into all new kinds, an' the outlaws aroun'. Not
many up here, though we did beat off some enemy troops
last winter." He glowed with pride at that, but Drummond
wasn't particularly impressed. A handful of freezing starve-
ling conscripts, lost and bewildered in a foreign enemy's
land, with no hope of ever getting home, weren't for-
midable.

"Things getting better, though," said Buckman. "We're
heading up." He scowled blackly, and a palpable chill crept
into the room. "If 'twern't for the births—"

"Yes—the births. The new babies. Even the stock an'
plants." It was an old man speaking, his eyes glazed with
near-madness. "It's the mark o' the beast. Satan is loose in
the world—"

"Shut up!" Huge and bristling with wrath, Buckman
launched himself out of his seat and grabbed the oldster by
his scrawny throat. "Shut up 'r I'll bash y'r lying head in.
Ain't no son o' mine being marked by the devil."

"Or mine—" "Or mine—" The rumble of voices ran
about the cabin, sullen and afraid.

"It's God's jedgment, I tell you!" The woman was shrill-
ing again. "The end o' the world is near. Prepare f'r the
second coming—"

"An' you shut up too, Mag Schmidt," snarled Buckman.
He stood bent over, gnarled arms swinging loose, hands
flexing, little eyes darting red and wild about the room.

"Shut y'r trap an' keep it shut. I'm still boss here, an' if you don't like it you can get out. I still don't think that gunny-looking brat o' y'rs fell in the lake by accident."

The woman shrank back, lips tight. The room filled with a crackling silence. One of the babies began to cry. It had two heads.

Slowly and heavily, Buckman turned to Drummond, who sat immobile against the wall. "You see?" he asked dully. "You see how it is? Maybe it is the curse o' God. Maybe the world is ending. I dunno. I just know there's few enough babies, an' most o' them deformed. Will it go on? Will all our kids be monsters? Should we . . . kill these an' hope we get some human babies? What is it? What to do?"

Drummond rose. He felt a weight as of centuries on his shoulders, the weariness, blank and absolute, of having seen that smoldering panic and heard that desperate appeal too often, too often.

"Don't kill them," he said. "That's the worst kind of murder, and anyway it'd do no good at all. It comes from the bombs, and you can't stop it. You'll go right on having such children, so you might as well get used to it."

By atomic-powered stratojet it wasn't far from Minnesota to Oregon, and Drummond landed in Taylor about noon the next day. This time there was no hurry to get his machine under cover, and up on the mountain was a raw scar of earth where a new airfield was slowly being built. Men were getting over their terror of the sky. They had another fear to face now, and it was one from which there was no hiding.

Drummond walked slowly down the icy main street to the central office. It was numbingly cold, a still, relentless intensity of frost eating through clothes and flesh and bone. It wasn't much better inside. Heating systems were still poor improvisations.

"You're back!" Robinson met him in the antechamber, suddenly galvanized with eagerness. He had grown thin and nervous, looking ten years older, but impatience blazed from him. "How is it? How is it?"

Drummond held up a bulky notebook. "All here," he said grimly. "All the facts we'll need. Not formally correlated yet, but the picture is simple enough."

Robinson laid an arm on his shoulder and steered him into the office. He felt the general's hand shaking, but he'd sat down and had a drink before business came up again.

"You've done a good job," said the leader warmly. "When the country's organized again, I'll see you get a medal for this. Your men in the other planes aren't in yet."

"No, they'll be gathering data for a long time. The job won't be finished for years. I've only got a general outline here, but it's enough. It's enough." Drummond's eyes were haunted again.

Robinson felt cold at meeting that too-steady gaze. He whispered shakily: "Is it—bad?"

"The worst. Physically, the country's recovering. But biologically, we've reached a crossroads and taken the wrong fork."

"What do you mean? What do you mean?"

Drummond let him have it then, straight and hard as a bayonet thrust. "The birth rate's a little over half the prewar," he said, "and about seventy-five percent of all births are mutant, of which possibly two-thirds are viable and presumably fertile. Of course, that doesn't include late-maturing characteristics, or those undetectable by naked-eye observation, or the mutated recessive genes that must be carried by a lot of otherwise normal zygotes. And it's everywhere. There are no safe places."

"I see," said Robinson after a long time. He nodded, like a man struck a stunning blow and not yet fully aware of it. "I see. The reason—"

"Is obvious."

"Yes. People going through radioactive areas—"

"Why, no. That would only account for a few. But—"

"No matter. The fact's there, and that's enough. We have to decide what to do about it."

"And soon." Drummond's jaw set. "It's wrecking our culture. We at least preserved our historical continuity, but even that's going now. People are going crazy as birth after birth is monstrous. Fear of the unknown, striking at minds still stunned by the war and its immediate aftermath. Frustration of parenthood, perhaps the most basic instinct there is. It's leading to infanticide, desertion, despair, a cancer at the root of society. We've got to act."

"How? How?" Robinson stared numbly at his hands.

"I don't know. You're the leader. Maybe an educational campaign, though that hardly seems practicable. Maybe an acceleration of your program for re-integrating the country. Maybe— I don't know."

Drummond stuffed tobacco into his pipe. He was near the end of what he had, but would rather take a few good smokes than a lot of niggling puffs. "Of course," he said thoughtfully, "it's probably not the end of things. We won't know for a generation or more, but I rather imagine the mutants can grow into society. They'd better, for they'll outnumber the humans. The thing is, if we just let matters drift there's no telling where they'll go. The situation is unprecedented. We may end up in a culture of specialized variations, which would be very bad from an evolutionary standpoint. There may be fighting between mutant types, or with humans. Interbreeding may produce worse freaks, particularly when accumulated recessives start showing up. Robinson, if we want any say at all in what's going to happen in the next few centuries, we have to act quickly. Otherwise it'll snowball out of all control."

"Yes. Yes, we'll have to act fast. And hard." Robinson straightened in his chair. Decision firmed his countenance, but his eyes were staring. "We're mobilized," he said. "We have the men and the weapons and the organization. They won't be able to resist."

The ashy cold of Drummond's emotions stirred, but it was with a horrible wrenching of fear. "What are you getting at?" he snapped.

"Racial death. All mutants and their parents to be sterilized whenever and wherever detected."

"You're crazy!" Drummond sprang from his chair, grabbed Robinson's shoulders across the desk, and shook him. "You . . . why, it's impossible! You'll bring revolt, civil war, final collapse!"

"Not if we go about it right." There were little beads of sweat studding the general's forehead. "I don't like it any better than you, but it's got to be done or the human race is finished. Normal births a minority—" He surged to his feet, gasping. "I've thought a long time about this. Your facts only confirmed my suspicions. This tears it. Can't you see? Evolution has to proceed slowly. Life wasn't meant for such a storm of change. Unless we can save the true human stock, it'll be absorbed and differentiation will continue till humanity is a collection of freaks, probably intersterile. Or . . . there must be a lot of lethal recessives. In a large population, they can accumulate unnoticed till nearly everybody has them and then start emerging all at once. That'd wipe us out. It's happened before, in rats and other species. If we eliminate mutant stock now, we can still save the race. It won't be cruel. We have sterilization techniques which are quick and painless, not upsetting the endocrine balance. But it's got to be done." His voice rose to a raw scream, broke. "It's got to be done!"

Drummond slapped him, hard. He drew a shuddering breath, sat down, and began to cry, and somehow that was the most horrible sight of all. "You're crazy," said the aviator. "You've gone nuts with brooding alone on this the last six months, without knowing or being able to act. You've lost all perspective.

"We can't use violence. In the first place, it would break our tottering, cracked culture irreparably, into a mad-dog finish fight. We'd not even win it. We're outnumbered, and we couldn't hold down a continent, eventually a planet. And remember what we said once, about abandoning the old savage way of settling things, that never brings a real settlement at all? We'd throw away a lesson our noses were rubbed in not three years ago. We'd return to the beast—to ultimate extinction.

"And anyway," he went on very quietly, "it wouldn't do a bit of good. Mutants would still be born. The poison is everywhere. Normal parents will give birth to mutants, somewhere along the line. We just have to accept that fact, and live with it. The new human race will have to."

"I'm sorry." Robinson raised his face from his hands. It was a ghastly visage, gone white and old, but there was calm on it. "I—blew my top. You're right. I've been thinking of this, worrying and wondering, living and breathing it, lying awake nights, and when I finally sleep I dream of it. I . . . yes, I see your point. And you're right."

"It's O.K. You've been under a terrific strain. Three years with never a rest, and the responsibility for a nation, and now this— Sure, everybody's entitled to be a little crazy. We'll work out a solution, somehow."

"Yes, of course." Robinson poured out two stiff drinks

and gulped his. He paced restlessly, and his tremendous ability came back in waves of strength and confidence. "Let me see— Eugenics, of course. If we work hard, we'll have the nation tightly organized inside of ten years. Then . . . well, I don't suppose we can keep the mutants from interbreeding, but certainly we can pass laws to protect humans and encourage their propagation. Since radical mutations would probably be intersterile anyway, and most mutants handicapped one way or another, a few generations should see humans completely dominant again."

Drummond scowled. He was worried. It wasn't like Robinson to be unreasonable. Somehow, the man had acquired a mental blind spot where this most ultimate of human problems was concerned. He said slowly, "That won't work either. First, it'd be hard to impose and enforce. Second, we'd be repeating the old *Herrenvolk* notion. Mutants are inferior, mutants must be kept in their place—to enforce that, especially on a majority, you'd need a full-fledged totalitarian state. Third, that wouldn't work either, for the rest of the world, with almost no exceptions, is under no such control and we'll be in no position to take over that control for a long time—generations. Before then, mutants will dominate everywhere over there, and if they resent the way we treat their kind here, we'd better run for cover."

"You assume a lot. How do you know those hundreds or thousands of diverse types will work together? They're less like each other than like humans, even. They could be played off against each other."

"Maybe. But *that* would be going back onto the old road of treachery and violence, the road to Hell. Conversely, if every not-quite-human is called a 'mutant,' like a separate class, he'll think he is, and act accordingly against the lumped-together 'humans.' No, the only way to sanity—to *survival*—is to abandon class prejudice and race hate alto-

gether, and work as individuals. We're all . . . well, Earth-
lings, and subclassification is deadly. We all have to live
together, and might as well make the best of it."

"Yeah . . . yeah, that's right too."

"Anyway, I repeat that all such attempts would be useless. All Earth is infected with mutation. It will be for a
long time. The purest human stock will still produce mutants."

"Y-yes, that's true. Our best bet seems to be to find all
such stock and withdraw it into the few safe areas left. It'll
mean a small human population, but a *human* one."

"I tell you, that's impossible," clipped Drummond.
"There is no safe place. Not one."

Robinson stopped pacing and looked at him as at a physical antagonist. "That so?" he almost growled. "Why?"

Drummond told him, adding incredulously, "Surely you
knew that. Your physicists must have measured the amount
of it. Your doctors, your engineers, that geneticist I dug up
for you. You obviously got a lot of this biological information you've been slinging at me from him. They must all
have told you the same thing."

Robinson shook his head stubbornly. "It can't be. It's not
reasonable. The concentration wouldn't be great enough."

"Why, you poor fool, you need only look around you.
The plants, the animals— Haven't there been any births in
Taylor?"

"No. This is still a man's town, though women are trick-
ling in and several babies are on the way—" Robinson's
face was suddenly twisted with desperation. "Elaine's is due
any time now. She's in the hospital here. Don't you see, our
other kid died of the plague. This one's all we have. We
want him to grow up in a world free of want and fear, a
world of peace and sanity where he can play and laugh and
become a man, not a beast starving in a cave. You and I

are on our way out. We're the old generation, the one that wrecked the world. It's up to us to build it again, and then retire from it to let our children have it. The future's theirs. We've got to make it ready for them."

Sudden insight held Drummond motionless for long seconds. Understanding came, and pity, and an odd gentleness that changed his sunken bony face. "Yes," he murmured, "yes, I see. That's why you're working with all that's in you to build a normal, healthy world. That's why you nearly went crazy when this threat appeared. That . . . that's why you can't, just can't comprehend—"

He took the other man's arm and guided him toward the door. "Come on," he said. "Let's go see how your wife's making out. Maybe we can get her some flowers on the way."

The silent cold bit at them as they went down the street. Snow crackled underfoot. It was already grimy with town smoke and dust, but overhead the sky was incredibly clean and blue. Breath smoked whitely from their mouths and nostrils. The sound of men at work rebuilding drifted faintly between the bulking mountains.

"We couldn't emigrate to another planet, could we?" asked Robinson, and answered himself: "No, we lack the organization and resources to settle them right now. We'll have to make out on Earth. A few safe spots—there must be others besides this one—to house the true humans till the mutation period is over. Yes, we can do it."

"There are no safe places," insisted Drummond. "Even if there were, the mutants would still outnumber us. Does your geneticist have any idea how this'll come out, biologically speaking?"

"He doesn't know. His specialty is still largely unknown. He can make an intelligent guess, and that's all."

"Yeah. Anyway, our problem is to learn to live with the mutants, to accept anyone as—Earthling—no matter how he looks, to quit thinking anything was ever settled by violence or connivance, to build a culture of individual sanity. Funny," mused Drummond, "how the impractical virtues, tolerance and sympathy and generosity, have become the fundamental necessities of simple survival. I guess it was always true, but it took the death of half the world and the end of a biological era to make us see that simple little fact. The job's terrific. We've got half a million years of brutality and greed, superstition and prejudice, to lick in a few generations. If we fail, mankind is done. But we've got to try."

They found some flowers, potted in a house, and Robinson bought them with the last of his tobacco. By the time he reached the hospital, he was sweating. The sweat froze on his face as he walked.

The hospital was the town's biggest building, and fairly well equipped. A nurse met them as they entered.

"I was just going to send for you, General Robinson," she said. "The baby's on the way."

"How . . . is she?"

"Fine, so far. Just wait here, please."

Drummond sank into a chair and with haggard eyes watched Robinson's jerky pacing. *The poor guy. Why is it expectant fathers are supposed to be so funny? It's like laughing at a man on the rack. I know, Barbara, I know.*

"They have some anesthetics," muttered the general. "They . . . Elaine never was very strong."

"She'll be all right." *It's afterward that worries me.*

"Yeah— Yeah— How long, though, how long?"

"Depends. Take it easy." With a wrench, Drummond made a sacrifice to a man he liked. He filled his pipe and handed it over. "Here, you need a smoke."

"Thanks." Robinson puffed raggedly.

The slow minutes passed, and Drummond wondered vaguely what he'd do when—it—happened. It didn't have to happen. But the chances were all against such an easy solution. He was no psychologist. Best just to let things happen as they would.

The waiting broke at last. A doctor came out, seeming an inscrutable high priest in his white garments. Robinson stood before him, motionless.

"You're a brave man," said the doctor. His face, as he removed the mask, was stern and set. "You'll need your courage."

"She—" It was hardly a human sound, that croak.

"Your wife is doing well. But the baby—"

A nurse brought out the little wailing form. It was a boy. But his limbs were rubbery tentacles terminating in boneless digits.

Robinson looked, and something went out of him as he stood there. When he turned, his face was dead.

"You're lucky," said Drummond, and meant it. He'd seen too many other mutants. "After all, if he can use those hands he'll get along all right. He'll even have an advantage in certain types of work. It isn't a deformity, really. If there's nothing else, you've got a good kid."

"*If!* You can't tell with mutants."

"I know. But you've got guts, you and Elaine. You'll see this through, together." Briefly, Drummond felt an utter personal desolation. He went on, perhaps to cover that emptiness:

"I see why you didn't understand the problem. You *wouldn't.* It was a psychological bloc, suppressing a fact you didn't dare face. That boy is really the center of your life. You couldn't think the truth about him, so your subconscious just refused to let you think rationally on that subject at all.

"Now you know. Now you realize there's no safe place,

not on all the planet. The tremendous incidence of mutant births in the first generation could have told you that alone. Most such new characteristics are recessive, which means both parents have to have it for it to show in the zygote. But genetic changes are random, except for a tendency to fall into roughly similar patterns. Four-leaved clovers, for instance. Think how vast the total number of such changes must be, to produce so many corresponding changes in a couple of years. Think how many, many recessives there must be, existing only in gene patterns till their mates show up. We'll just have to take our chances of something really deadly accumulating. We'd never know till too late."

"The dust—"

"Yeah. The radiodust. It's colloidal, and uncountable other radiocolloids were formed when the bombs went off, and ordinary dirt gets into unstable isotopic forms near the craters. And there are radiogases too, probably. The poison is all over the world by now, spread by wind and air currents. Colloids can be suspended indefinitely in the atmosphere.

"The concentration isn't too high for life, though a physicist told me he'd measured it as being very near the safe limit and there'll probably be a lot of cancer. But it's everywhere. Every breath we draw, every crumb we eat and drop we drink, every clod we walk on, the dust is there. It's in the stratosphere, clear on down to the surface, probably a good distance below. We could only escape by sealing ourselves in air-conditioned vaults and wearing spacesuits whenever we got out, and under present conditions that's impossible.

"Mutations were rare before, because a charged particle has to get pretty close to a gene and be moving fast before its electromagnetic effect causes physico-chemical changes, and then that particular chromosome has to enter into reproduction. Now the charged particles, and the gamma rays producing still more, are everywhere. Even at the comparatively low concentration, the odds favor a given organism having so many cells changed that at least one will give rise to a mutant. There's even a good chance of like recessives meeting in the first generation, as we've seen. Nobody's safe, no place is free."

"The geneticist thinks some true humans will continue."

"A few, probably. After all, the radioactivity isn't too concentrated, and it's burning itself out. But it'll take fifty or a hundred years for the process to drop to insignificance, and by then the pure stock will be way in the minority. And there'll still be all those unmatched recessives, waiting to show up."

"You were right. We should never have created science. It brought the twilight of the race."

"I never said that. The race brought its own destruction, through misuse of science. Our culture was scientific anyway, in all except its psychological basis. It's up to us to take that last and hardest step. If we do, the race may yet survive."

Drummond gave Robinson a push toward the inner door. "You're exhausted, beat up, ready to quit. Go on in and see Elaine. Give her my regards. Then take a long rest before going back to work. I still think you've got a good kid."

Mechanically, the de facto President of the United States left the room. Hugh Drummond stared after him a moment, then went out into the street.

Poul Anderson (1926–   )
Since his first appearance as a science fiction writer in 1947, Poul Anderson has produced well over seventy novels and story

collections. He is one of those rare writers who are equally at home with high fantasy and "hard" science fiction, and he is particularly popular for his two best-known series, the stories and books about intergalactic agent Dominic Flandry and the tales featuring the merchant trader Van Rijn. Mr. Anderson has won the highly coveted Hugo Award six times, and the Nebula Award of the Science Fiction Writers of America twice.

GENETICS

MARY AND JOE
Naomi Mitchison

Her husband looked up from his newspaper. "Jaycie seems to be getting into trouble again," he said.

She nodded. "Yes. I had a short letter from her. I wish— oh, Joe, I do wish she could take things a bit more lightly!"

"Get herself married," said Joe.

Mary didn't exactly answer that, but went on: "I know so well what she feels about politics. After all, we both had liberal sympathies in our time—hadn't we, Joe? But—it's more than politics to her. Much more. And when she's feeling like that she seems to forget all about human relationships."

Her husband grinned a bit. "Not like Simon. Nor yet my

107

little Martha! What time did that kid get back from her date? Oh, well . . ." He finished his coffee. "I must be off, Mary. I'll take the car—right? How's your stuff going?"

"Not bad," she said. "We've got all the routine tests for the new skin grafts to check before we can get on. These internal ones are a bit tricky."

"Poor old rabbits!" said Joe lightly and shrugged himself into his coat. He respected Mary's work, knew about it, but somehow didn't care much for it.

Mary, however, was thinking about the next series of experiments and checks while she cleared up the breakfast dishes. Dear Joe, couldn't he ever learn to put his stubs into the ashtray! She left a tidy place for Martha, who was running the bath upstairs and singing to herself, saw that there was plenty of cereal left in the packet, and all the time the shape of the work was clear in her mind.

The basic genetics were reasonably simple, though not as simple as they had seemed ten years earlier. But then, nothing was! At its simplest, blood from two different blood groups, with all that this implies, cannot live together in the same body. Equally, cells of one genetic constitution will not accept cells of another—and are all genetically different, except for identical twins and (if we happen to be laboratory mice) pure-line strains. If living tissue is grafted onto a host animal, the grafted cells produce antigens and the host cells in reply produce antibodies which destroy the grafter cells. As long as the cells come from genetically different individuals, this natural process goes on. But it can be checked; this had to be done for surgical transplants. The host cells producing the antibodies could be killed by radiation, or checked by a series of drugs which most hospitals of that period called XQ, or else could be, in a sense, paralyzed by certain methods of presentation.

All this meant a long series of experiments, often involv-

ing the death of the host animal; yet they had to go on
before the essential knowledge was complete and could be
used on humans without dangerous reactions. Grafts from
a genetically different individual can take in certain fa-
vored situations, such as the cornea of the eye and in bone
structure; some organs transplanted better than others. The
choice of donor mattered a lot; Mary was working on this,
especially on the possibility of using an anti-lymphatic
serum. In practical terms, to delay rejection by the antibodies was important; but this involved a series of experiments, mostly during the last year or two on rabbits *in
utero*, with typed donors. Naturally, the parent-to-child
transfer was not likely to be successful, even at a very immature stage, since there was necessarily a great difference between the genes of one parent and the genes of the
child which were mixed with another quite different set.

Sometimes, too, she worked with individual graft hosts,
not only *in utero*, but at a still earlier stage, in the egg. One
experiment, with all the apparatus which it involved, and
which Mary rather enjoyed devising, led to another. This
was the field in which she had worked for a couple of
decades, exchanging views with other workers in the same
field and occasionally going to conferences when the family
could spare her. It was an absorbing and in many ways a
happy life.

On her way to the big teaching hospital where she
worked she bought another newspaper. It looked as if these
strikes were going to develop the way Jaycie had said they
would in her letter. It is odd, she thought to herself, how
often things do work out the way Jaycie says. But if they
bring in troops . . . She couldn't really think about it sensibly. She hadn't got the data. Jaycie hadn't been home for
six months; it wasn't that she didn't get on with the others,
and dear Joe always going out of his way to be nice and

welcoming, but—well, sometimes it seemed as if nothing they did at home was worth her attention. She would try, especially with Martha, yes, she would try, but it was like a clumsy grown-up talking to kids! Jaycie could be annoying. Yes. And yet—people followed her. A great many people really. And whatever happened her mother loved her.

The newspapers were beginning to get on to Jaycie now. They had ignored her at first. Put things down to anyone and everything else. After all, it was a bit awkward for them having to do with a woman who was beautiful but apparently had no sex life; they didn't know what to try and smear her with. But now—Mary wished she knew, wished she could read between the lines. Were they frightened? She had been too busy these last ten years or so to think much about politics. When Jaycie turned up: yes. But when she left, Mary went back to her work thankfully as though to something simple and relatively clean—though some people wouldn't think so! Back to thinking about problems of genetics and immunology. And an undertow in her mind always busy on the other children and dear Joe and something especially nice for supper and perhaps a show at the weekend and the new hyacinth bulbs to plant. But now it looked as if all Jaycie had said last time was going to develop into something she would need to think about, something real. And dangerous.

But this was the hospital stop. She had come by bus, for it was an easy journey and she didn't care for driving herself. She was apt to get abstracted and slow down, so that people hooted at her, but here in the bus she could work. She knew the conductor would call to her, amused if she was deep in calculations when it came to her stop: "This is you, Doctor!"

She got out, nodded to a colleague, and walked a bit abstractedly along the corridor with the marble bust of the

Founder, on which young Bowles had, as usual, hung his hat. There was a lot of routine work and checking. She could do it with half her mind. But instead of concentrating on the next phase she kept on thinking about Jaycie. Had she done the right thing to tell her? Had she? Had she? Or would it have been better to let her believe the same thing dear Joe believed, the story about a sudden overwhelming fascination—women's magazine stuff really. But easy to make up and equally easy to believe. Much easier than— whatever the truth was. You couldn't expect anyone to believe that and still remain normal. And she had so wanted that: the lovely solid, warm normalness of dear Joe. If she hadn't told Joe the lie to which he never afterward referred they mightn't have had their life together, they mightn't have had Simon and darling naughty Martha. No. No. Any other way didn't bear thinking about.

Yet perhaps she should have told Jaycie the same—lie. If she had done that, Jaycie too might have grown up to be a normal girl. She might have fallen in love and married, and then there would have been grandchildren, lovely normal babies and the happiness that goes with them. Or if Jaycie hadn't felt like that she could have done some absorbing professional job. She could have been a scientist like her mother perhaps or an architect like Simon, one of the thousand satisfying things which are open to modern men and women alike.

Why had she told Jaycie? Mary thought back, frowning. It was that time when Jaycie was so depressed about being a woman, about the undoubted fact that there were rather fewer females than males of undoubted genius. That it is so much harder for a woman to take the clear, unswerving line toward—whatever it might be—because women are ordinarily more pliable, more likely to be interrupted, more aware of other people's feelings and apt to be deflected by them: especially if they are loved people. She remembered Jaycie sitting curled up on the sofa, her chin dropped on her hand; and she herself had been standing beside the fire, so much wanting to help, but knowing that Jaycie needed more than the comfort of a mother's arm around her.

Jaycie had said: "I suppose, Mother, that's what it means to be a Son of God, as they used to say. You go straight to the light. You know." And Mary had said yes and had felt something gripping at her, a rush of adrenaline no doubt! Jaycie had said: "No daughters of God, of course!" and had laughed a little. And then she had stood up and looked straight toward her mother and said: "But I too, I know. Directly."

And then Mary had to speak, had to tell her. It was, after all, true. And since then Jaycie had never curled up again on the sofa. Never seemed to want the comforting arms. And Mary had hardly liked to touch her. Only on the rare nights when Jaycie slept at home Mary used to go up to her room when she was asleep, so deeply and peacefully it seemed, and stand there and want to take the one who had been her baby into her arms and share and share and comfort. But luckily she had managed the self-control never to do anything of the kind. Because if she had tried it Jaycie wouldn't ever have come home again. She was fairly sure of that.

Mary had forgotten to make her own sandwiches, so she went down to the canteen for lunch. There were rather more newspapers than usual being read. Young Bowles was having an argument with another of the lecturers; they frowned at her, but perhaps not deliberately. The Professor made some sympathetic remark to her about Jaycie. Nice old bird, the Prof. But who did *he* think Jaycie's father was? Simple enough: that wasn't the kind of thing he thought about.

Things looked worse in the headlines of the evening editions. Mary seldom bought an evening paper, but this time she felt she had to. "Look, old girl, don't worry," said Joe. "They—they always write this sort of bilge. Makes people buy their rotten old papers. Nobody takes it seriously."

"It's so childish of them—calling names!" she said, and stupidly found herself crying.

"Jaycie wouldn't give a damn for that, would she now?" said Joe cheerfully. But all the same, he thought, if only she and her crowd knew when to stop!

"I bet Jaycie likes it!" Martha chipped in and, of course, in a way that hit the nail on the head.

Three days. And suddenly the headlines got bigger, blotting out any other news. Now she was stuffing things into a small bag and Joe beside her was talking. "I won't try and stop you, Mary, if you feel you must." And she wasn't listening to him, wasn't thinking about him. She was only thinking about Jaycie.

They hadn't done anything really out of the ordinary to Jaycie. And the police as a matter of fact hadn't been the worst. But nobody who wants things to go on as they are—and that goes for most of us—cares for someone who is intent on changing them and looks likely to succeed. An agitator is bad enough; a successful agitator is not to be borne. There was something about Jaycie that made her audiences believe her; she never lied to them, not even at a big meeting with the lights on and the voices clamoring, the time when lies come easy to most people. But Jaycie stayed steady and unmoved by that temptation. You couldn't catch her out.

But it was not during the actual arrest that most of the damage had been done, nor even when she was questioned. At first the police had been rather inhibited at doing their worst on a woman. But—she got them annoyed. Not reacting the way they wanted. Then they let go a bit. But the really nasty thing was the accident—at least they said afterward that it was an accident—with the petrol. Apart from everything else, Jaycie had lost considerable areas of superficial tissue and skin, including some on the face. Too much for safety. Very much too much.

It had perhaps not been intended that she should get to an ordinary hospital. But Jaycie had more friends than was usually supposed, and in some curious places. Someone took fright and reversed an order. The body of Jaycie was bundled into an ambulance; she might well die before getting to the hospital. That was to be hoped. But she didn't.

At the hospital they knew Mary by reputation; most of them had read one or two of her papers at least. But someone who has been a printed name at the end of a scientific paper looks different when she is the mother of a young woman who is probably dying of shock and what have you and who has been considerably disfigured. Who will be up for trial if she recovers. But she won't. Even in the hospital some of them felt that this would be just as well. Doctors and surgeons no less than other citizens have a considerable interest in the preservation of the existing order of things. They were, of course, extremely busy in Casualties. That was to be expected after the last few days. But it did account for the fact that the house surgeon paid little attention to what was happening at this particular screened bed. Mary got the ward sister to agree. Then she took the skin grafts off her own thighs under a local anesthetic. It was not really at all difficult. She had often worked with this type of scalpel like an old-fashioned cutthroat razor. It took the strips off neatly, though it is always a rather peculiar feeling to do such things to oneself. The slight reluctance of the skin to the blade and then the curious ease of the shaving off of the strips can be felt by the operating

hand but not by the anesthetized tissue. The sister brings
the necessary dressings. The new, still living skin is in place
over the cleaned burns on the young woman's thin, partly
broken body.

The ward sister couldn't help noticing the extreme care
with which the mother was laying on the skin grafts over
burned cheek and neck and forehead, above all the corner
of the mouth.

"I couldn't have done it," she said afterward over a nice
cup of tea. "Not on my own child. My own daughter. Nice-
looking she must have been, you could tell that. And there
was the mother going straight ahead, not batting an eye.
And bound to be in pain herself. And all for nothing!
Those grafts'll never take, and that poor thing will look a
proper mess if she lives. And that's not likely. In a proper
surgical transplant, we'd either do radiation or at least we'd
type the patient up and give her a shot of XQ. Well, you
know how things are this week. Couldn't be done. And the
mother must have known." She shook her head.

"Well, I for one wouldn't have bothered to do it!" said
another nurse who had been reading the papers.

"And what wouldn't you have done, may I ask?" said
the ward sister, standing up with the finished cup in her
hand.

"I wouldn't have bothered myself to take any trouble to
type up an agitator like her! Anyway, even if she lives,
this'll stop her speaking at those meetings!"

"We'll keep her, all the same. I'm not having deaths in
my ward. That mother of hers, well, there was something
about her, there sure was, the way she went about it. Kind
of cool. But the scar tissue's going to twist that girl's face."
The ward sister put down her cup and prepared to go back
on duty. "Remember that woman we had in after the big
Palladium fire? Shocking, wasn't it? This'll be worse. But

mind, agitator or no agitator, she gets proper nursing!"

The morphia was wearing off. Jaycie was whispering in half-sleep, arguing and refusing. Even like this, her voice kept much of its strange persuasive beauty. The ward sister was whispering to the house surgeon: "I know these skin grafts can't take; you don't have to tell me! They'll slough off. If she doesn't die first. Do more harm than good. Too late now for radiation or for XQ. But the mother—well, she's kind of distinguished; I couldn't very well say no, could I now? Besides she had some theory—oh, I can't remember now—yes, yes, it'll be worse for her when she sees her daughter's face the way it's bound to be. I know. But don't you fuss now! Haven't we all got our hands full these days!"

After that there was rather less scope for fussing about any individual patient. The wards were jammed with temporary beds. Mary waited beside Jaycie as she gradually awoke into pain and mastered it. They were getting short of analgesics by now, and besides Jaycie had said quite firmly that she needed none. Mary did not ask for much herself; the pain, though at times severe, was bearable. On her own thighs the skinned strips were healing by first intention; all had been aseptic from the start, competently done. She helped the ward sister when she could. It kept her mind off what might be happening at home. For the usual channels of communication were no longer functioning. The military had taken over successfully. Or had they . . . ? Perhaps not.

Days and nights went by. In the third week the ward sister, still surprised that Jaycie went on living when so many had died, said to herself that now those skin grafts were lifting, would slough off like a dead scab, leaving everything worse. "They can't do anything else," she said. Then you'd begin to see the mess the scarring was bound to make of her face. And that wouldn't be nice for the mother.

But the new skin didn't lift off, didn't die. The edge of it visibly and redly lived and grew on to the damaged flesh in healthy granulations. The thin scar lines would be there, but not the hideous twisting and lumping of raw flesh. You took off the dressings and there was the undeniable fact: the skin grafts had taken. The area of damage, the hideous wounds were covered in. No wonder Jaycie lived.

The ward sister shook her head. It shouldn't have happened. But it had. In a way, however, Sister was rather pleased; the doctors were wrong again. Them and their theories that they were always having to change! And it just showed how, in spite of all the troubles and difficulties of overcrowding and medical shortages, good nursing—her pride, the thing she insisted on in her ward—had somehow done the trick.

The house surgeon looked too. He wouldn't commit himself and he hadn't time just then to look it all up in the textbooks. Later on he'd mention the matter to his chief. But after a while, with Jaycie getting stronger every day, he and Sister decided on a few tactful questions. The odd thing was that Mary found it comparatively easy telling them. She didn't mind what the effect on them might be of what she was telling. Indeed, she hardly noticed. She had plenty of other things to worry about. It was much less easy telling Joe.

For he came at last, bless him, bringing all sorts of delicious things to eat. Yes, they were all rather hungry at the hospital; supplies had been cut off. There hadn't been much news either. "Oh, Joe," she said, "dear, dear Joe, is everything all right?"

"Yes," he said, "and my little Martha turned up trumps. We never guessed what a head that kid had! And I got Simon on long distance. Naturally he couldn't say much, but he's okay. Now, Mary, what's all this story about skin grafts?"

Mary said: "Jaycie had a very large area of skin torn and burned off. On purpose. Joe, they—they were so horrible to her. Some of her friends told me. They didn't mean her to live. I didn't realize people could be like that about politics in this country. Though I suppose they really are everywhere when it gets serious. You know, she was very nearly dead when I got here."

She stopped for a moment and dabbed her eyes. It came fleetingly through Joe's mind that this might have been the best thing. For the world, for things as they are. For himself and Simon and Martha. Maybe for Mary herself in the long run. But he wasn't going to let himself think that just now, not with his wife sobbing on to the edge of his waistcoat. He stroked her hair, a bit sticky and unwashed and the white collar of her dress all mucked up, poor sweet.

She looked up a little and said: "So it seemed to me that the best chance was a skin graft."

"But, Mary," he said, "a skin graft's no good from someone else. Even I know that!"

"It's all right from someone identical: genetically the same."

"But Mary, you aren't, you can't be . . ." Joe had an uncomfortable feeling, though he didn't quite know why.

"Because of the father. His genes make the child different from the mother. I know. Joe, I told you a long time ago that Jaycie had a father. Joe, dear, dear Joe, I only told you that because I thought it would upset you more to think she hadn't a father. There now, you are upset—"

"Mary darling, don't worry about me, I just don't understand."

"She didn't have a father, Joe. I—I never had a lover. I

was—well, I suppose there is nothing else for it, I was a virgin, Joe."

"But you had a baby. Sweet, you can't have been."

"I was. You see, something started one of my ova developing. That's all. Oh, that's all! It doesn't sound too odd that way, does it?"

"But what could start it? What's the stimulus?"

"It might be anything I expect. Some—metabolic change."

"What was it with you?"

She did not answer. Even now she could not think quite calmly. It might have been imagination. It must have been. Lower than far thunder, higher than the bat's squeak, the whispering of a million leaves. Sometimes the murmur of wind-shifted leaves in summer reminded her. It couldn't possibly have been what she was certain it was. She took a breath: "Whatever the stimulus was, the ovum developed normally. The child had to be a female, an identical female. Without the Y chromosome that comes from the male and goes to a male. I don't know what happened in the process of chromosome division. Of course, there was the possibility—perhaps the probability—of a haploid. Of the chromosomes splitting unevenly. You see what I mean, Joe? But they didn't."

"That—that was odd," said Joe, looking away from his wife's face. "There must have been—some kind of pattern-making machinery behind it—"

"You could call it that," said Mary; "yes, of course, Joe, you could call it that. But the way things worked out, Jaycie and I are genetically identical."

Joe swallowed: "Did you—did you know this from the start, Mary?"

"Not for sure," she said. "But—when she was a baby I started by taking the tiniest pinch-graft from her to me.

That took. But it wasn't certain. I mean, it was almost sure that my antibodies wouldn't affect her graft. But it wasn't sure the other way round. So, when she was a little older, I tried it that way too."

"But if you were genetically identical, Mary, you—you'd have been as alike as—identical twins."

"We are, physically. But there's a big difference in nurture, Joe, as well as age. I'm going gray and wrinkled."

Gallantly he said "No!" but she only smiled a little.

"You see, my dearest, there's a different best treatment for babies every generation. And then—we started thinking about different kinds of things. Using the same brain perhaps, but—"

"I'd have thought I'd have noticed," Joe muttered, "seeing you both all the time."

"You were used to me, Joe. And besides, by the time she was adult, you thought of her as herself. Though you've always thought she was like me. You were pleased she was like me and not—like someone else. Weren't you? And I always had a different hairdo from hers. On purpose, Joe."

"And all that time, you never told me, Mary."

"I—I couldn't. Not by then. The other thing—we'd got used to it, you and I—as a story. Oh, Joe, you wouldn't have liked it!"

"No," said Joe, "no, I suppose I wouldn't." He looked across the crowded ward at the bed; one of Jaycie's friends was sitting there with a notebook, questioning and taking down the answers. Jaycie's friends were going about openly now. Beginning to take over here and there, to put Jaycie's ideas into practice. Bad, bad. At least, that was what one had to suppose. The alternative—the military alternative—had not succeeded. There would be no trial for Jaycie. Instead, there were going to be changes. Changes he knew he was going to hate. Even if they were supposed to be

going to be good in the end. A lot of people were sold on
that, but not Joe. Changes—everything changed before it
was done! His own whole life: set another way, not the way
he wanted! But all the same, he thought, this was the baby
he had accepted when he got Mary to say she would marry
him all that long while back. She was a sweet baby right
enough. Pretty. Those great eyes. There was always something about babies that got you. Maybe, he thought, I shall
have to accept Jaycie's changes and not say a word. Because of Mary.

Mary went on: "Perhaps that's why she's always been a
bit different. Why she's been—single-hearted." She wasn't
going to let Joe know—not ever—that she had told Jaycie
before she told him. That would hurt him, and she couldn't
bear to hurt him any more. She was Joe's Mary as much as
she was Jaycie's. Almost as much.

"So you don't know what the stimulus was," Joe said
half aloud. "You don't know. It's—yes, it's a bit scaring,
Mary."

"I know. That's why I told you the other thing. The easy
thing. And you were so sweet. Forgive me, Joe."

"That's all right, Mary. Funny, I sometimes wondered
what the other chap was like. Whether Jaycie took after
him. Whether you ever thought about him. And now there
isn't another chap."

"No," said Mary. "No."

"And you got the doctor here to take this skin graft—"

"I took it myself," said Mary. "There's nothing to it if it's
done in good conditions."

"Didn't it hurt?"

"Just a bit afterward. But not nearly as much as thinking
she was going to die. Goodness, Joe, any mother would do
it for her child; jump at the chance of doing it if it was to be
any use. But of course it wouldn't be any use—normally."

"Yes," said Joe. "Yes. But you've always liked normal things, haven't you, Mary?"

"For everything but this, Joe," she said, and held on tight to his hand. Deliberately and with a slow effort he made the hand respond, warmly, gently, normally. For the hand left to itself had wanted to pull away, not to touch her. Not to touch.

Naomi Mitchison (1897–   )

Naomi Mitchison is the author of scores of books for adults and children, but only two of them are science fiction: Memoirs of a Spacewoman *(1962) and* Solution Three *(1975). The sister of the famous scientist J. B. S. Haldane and a friend of Aldous Huxley, Ms. Mitchison started writing science fiction in her sixties, and in addition to the above mentioned novels has about seven so far uncollected science fiction short stories. Ms. Mitchison had a home in Botswana for many years and was an adopted member of the Bakgatla tribe. A native of Scotland, she now resides in that part of the United Kingdom.*

PHYSIOLOGY

SEA CHANGE
Thomas N. Scortia

Gleaming . . . like a needle of fire . . .

Whose voice? He didn't know.

The interstellar . . . two of them . . .

They were talking all at once then, their voices blending chaotically.

They're moving one out beyond Pluto for the test, someone said.

Beautiful . . . We're waiting . . . waiting.

That was her voice. He felt coldness within his chest.

That was the terrible part of his isolation, he thought. He could still hear everything. Not just in the Superintendent's office in Marsopolis where he sat.

123

Everywhere.

All the whispers of sound, spanning the system on pulses of c-cube radio. All the half-words, half-thoughts from the inner planets to the space stations far beyond Pluto.

And the loneliness was a sudden agonizing thing. The loneliness and the loss of two worlds.

Not that he couldn't shut out the voices if he wished, the distant voices that webbed space with the cubed speed of light. But . . . might as well shut out all thought of living and seek the mindless fetal state of merely being.

There was the voice droning cargo numbers. He made the small mental change and the tight mass of transistors, buried deep in his metal and plastic body, brought the voice in clear and sharp. It was a Triplanet ship in the twilight belt of Mercury.

He had a fleeting image of flame-shriveled plains under a blinding monster sun.

Then there was the voice, saying, *Okay . . . bearing three-ought-six and count down ten to free fall . . .*

That one was beyond Saturn . . . Remembered vision of bright ribbons of light, lacing a startling blue sky.

He thought, *I'll never see that again.*

And: *Space Beacon Three to MRX two two . . . Space Beacon Three . . . Bishop to queen's rook four . . .*

And there was the soft voice, the different voice: *Matt . . . Matt . . . Where are you? . . . Matt, come in . . . Oh, Matt . . .*

But he ignored that one.

Instead he looked at the receptionist and watched her fingers dance intricate patterns over the keyboard of her electric typewriter.

Matt . . . Matt . . .

No, no more, he thought. There was nothing there for him but bitterness. The isolation of being apart from hu-

manity. The loneliness. Love? Affection? The words had
no meaning in that existence.

It had become a ritual with him, he realized, this trip the
first Tuesday of every month down through the silent Martian town to the Triplanet Port. A formalized tribute to
something that was quite dead. An empty ritual, a weak
ineffectual gesture.

He had known that morning that there would be nothing.

"No, nothing," the girl in the Super's office had said.
"Nothing at all."

Nothing for him in his gray robot world of no-touch, no-
taste.

She looked at him the way they all did, the ones who saw
past the clever human disguise of plastic face and muted
eyes.

He waited . . . listening.

When the Super came in, he smiled and said, "Hello,
Matt," and then, with a gesture of his head, "Come on
in."

The girl frowned silent disapproval.

After they found seats, the Super said, "Why don't you
go home?"

"Home?"

"Back to Earth."

"Is that home?"

The voices whispered in his ear while the Super frowned
and puffed a black cigar alight.

And: . . . *Matt* . . . *Matt* . . . *Knight four to* . . . *three
down* . . . *two down* . . . *Out past Deimos, the sun blazing
on its sides* . . . *Matt* . . .

"What are you trying to do?" the Super demanded. "Cut
yourself off from the world completely?"

"That's been done already," he said. "Very effectively."

"Look, let's be brutal about it. We don't owe you any-thing."

"No," he said.

"It was a business arrangement purely," the Super said. "And if this hadn't been done"—he gestured at the body Freck wore—"Matthew Freck would have been little more than a page in some dusty official records.

"Or worse," he added.

"I suppose so," Freck said.

"You could go back tomorrow. To Earth. To a new life. No one has to know who you are or what you are unless you tell them."

Freck looked down at his hands, the carefully veined, very human hands and the hard muscled thighs where the cellotherm trousers hugged his legs.

"The technicians did a fine job," he said. "Actually, it's better than my old body. Younger and stronger. And it'll last longer. But . . . ."

He flexed his hands sensuously, watching the way the smooth bands of contractile plastic articulated his fingers.

"But the masquerade won't work. We were made for one thing."

"I can't change Company policy," the Super said. "Oh, I know the experiment didn't work. Actually technology is moving too fast. It was a bad compromise anyway. We needed something a little faster, more than human to pilot the new ships. Human reactions, the speed of a nerve im-pulse wasn't sufficient, electronic equipment was too bulky, and the organic memory units we built for our first cyber-netic pilots didn't have enough initiative. That's why we jumped at the chance to use you people when Marshal Jenks first came to us. But we weren't willing to face facts. We tried to compromise . . . keep the human form."

"Well, we gave you what you needed then. You do owe us something in return," he said.

"We lived up to our contract," the Super said. "With you and a hundred like you whom we could save. All in exchange for the ability only you had. It was a fair trade."

"All right, give me a ship then. That's all I want."

"I told you before. Direct hook-up."

"No. If you knew what you were asking . . ."

"Look, one of the interstellars is being tested right this minute. And there are the stations beyond Pluto."

"The stations? That's like the Director all over again. Completely immobile. What kind of a life would that be, existing as a self-contained unit for years on end without the least contact with humanity?"

"The stations are not useless," the Super said. He leaned forward and slapped his palm on the surface of his desk.

"You of all people should know the Bechtoldt Drive can't be installed within the system's heavy gravitational fields. That's why we need the stations. They're set up to install the drive after the ship leaves the system proper on its atomic motors."

"You still haven't answered my question."

"Stargazer I is outbound for one of the trans-Plutonian stations now. Stargazer II will follow in a few days."

"So?"

"You can have one of them if you want it. Oh, don't get the idea that this is a handout. We don't play that way. The last two ships blew up because the pilots weren't skilled enough to handle the hook-up. We need the best and that's you."

He paused for a long second.

"You may as well know," the Super said. "We've put all our eggs in those two baskets. We've been losing political strength in the past three years, and if either one fails, Triplanet and the other combines stand to lose their subsidies from the government. Then it'll be a century before anyone tries again, if they ever do. We're tired of being tied to a petty nine planets. We're doing the thing you worked for all your life. We're going to the stars now . . . and you can still be a part of that."

"That used to mean something to me," he said, "but after a time, you start losing your identification with humanity and its drives."

When he started to rise, the Super said, "You know you can't operate a modern ship or station, tied down to a humanoid body. It's too inefficient. You've got to become a part of the setup."

"I've told you before. I can't do that."

"What are you afraid of? The loneliness?"

"I've been lonely before," he said.

"What then?"

"What am I afraid of?" He smiled his mechanical smile. "Something you could never understand. I'm afraid of what's happened to me already."

The Super was silent.

"When you start losing the basic emotions, the basic ways of thinking that make you human, well . . . What am I afraid of?

"I'm afraid of becoming more of a machine," he said.

And before the Super could say more, he left.

Outside he zipped up the cellotherm jacket and adjusted his respirator. Then he advanced the setting of the rheostat on the chest of his jacket until the small jewel light above the mechanism glowed in the morning's half-dusk. He had no need for the heat that the clothing furnished, of course, but the masquerade, the pretending to be wholly human would have been incomplete without this vital touch.

All the way back through the pearl-gray light, he listened to the many voices flashing back and forth across the ship lanes. He heard the snatches of commerce from a hundred separate ports and he followed in his mind's eye the swift progress of *Stargazer I* out past the orbit of Uranus to her rendezvous with the station that would fit her with the Bechtoldt Drive.

And he thought, *Lord, if I could make the jump with her,* and then, *But not at that price, not for what it's cost the others, Jim and Martha and Art and . . . Beth. (Forget the name . . . forget the name . . . lost from you like all the others . . .)*

The city had turned to full life in the interval he had spent in the Super's office and he passed numerous hurrying figures, bearlike in cellotherm clothing and transparent respirators. They ignored him completely and for a moment he had an insane impulse to tear the respirator from his face and stand waiting . . .

Waiting savagely, defiantly for someone to notice him.

The tortured writhings of neon signs glowed along the wide streets and occasionally an electric run-about, balanced lightly on two wheels, passed him with a soft whirr, its headlights cutting a bright swath across his path. He had never become fully accustomed to the twilight of the Martian day. But that was the fault of the technicians who had built his body. In their pathetic desire to ape the human body, they had often built in human limitations as well as human strengths.

He stopped a moment before a shop, idly inspecting the window display of small things, fragile and alien, from the dead Martian towns to the north. The shop window, he realized, was as much out of place here as the street and the individual pressurized buildings that lined it. It would have been better, as someone had suggested, to house the entire city under one pressurized unit. But this was how the Martian settlements had started and men still held to habits more suited to another world.

Well, that was a common trait that he shared with his

race. The Super was right, of course. He was as much of a compromise as the town was. The old habits of thought prevailed, molding the new forms.

He thought that he should get something to eat. He hadn't had breakfast before setting out for the port. They'd managed to give him a sense of hunger, though taste had been too elusive for them to capture.

But the thought of food was somehow unpleasant.

And then he thought perhaps he should get drunk.

But even that didn't seem too satisfying.

He walked on for a distance and found a bar that was open and he walked in. He shed his respirator in the airlock and, under the half-watchful eyes of a small fat man, fumbling with his wallet, he pretended to turn off the rheostat of his suit.

Then he went inside, nodded vaguely at the bored bartender and sat at a corner table. After the bartender had brought him a whiskey and water, he sat and listened.

Six and seven . . . and twenty-ought-three . . .

. . . read you . . .

. . . and out there you see nothing, absolutely nothing. It's like . . . Matt . . . Matt . . .

. . . to king's knight four . . . check in three . . .

Matt . . .

And for the first time in weeks, he made the change. He could talk without making an audible sound, which was fortunate. A matter of subverbalizing.

He said silently, *Come on in.*

Matt, where are you?

In a bar.

I'm far out . . . very far out. The sun's like a pinhole in a black sheet.

I think I'm going to get very drunk.

Why?

Because I want to. Isn't that reason enough? Because it's the one wholly, completely human thing that I can do well.

I've missed you.

Missed me? My voice perhaps. There's little else.

You should be out here with us . . . with me and Art . . . , she said breathlessly. *They're bringing the new ones out. The big ships. They're beautiful. Bigger and faster than anything you and I ever rode.*

They're bringing Stargazer I out for her tests, he told her.

I know. My station has one of the drives. Station three is handling Stargazer I now.

He swallowed savagely, thinking of what the Super had said.

Oh, I wish I were one of them, Beth said.

His hand tensed on the glass and for a moment he thought it would shatter in his fingers. She hadn't said "on."

Were . . . were . . . I wish I were one of them.

Do you, he said. *That's fine.*

Oh, that's fine, starry eyes, he thought, *I love you and the ship and the stars and the sense of being . . . I am the ship . . . I am the station . . . I am anything but human . . .*

What's wrong, Matt?

I'm going to get drunk.

There's a ship coming in. Signaling.

The bartender, he saw, was looking at him oddly. He realized that he had been nursing the same drink for fifteen minutes. He raised the glass and very deliberately drank and swallowed.

I've got to leave for a minute, she said.

Do that, he said.

Then: *I'm sorry, Beth. I didn't mean to take it out on you.*

I'll be back, she said.

And he was alone, wrapped in the isolation he had come to know so well. He wondered if such loneliness would eventually drive him to the change that . . . No, that would never be . . . The memory of what that had been like still haunted him.

He would rather have died in that distant cold Plutonian valley, he told himself, than to have ever come to this day. He thought of Jenks and Catherine and David and he envied them the final unthinking blackness that they shared. Even death was better than again facing that frightening loss of humanity he had once suffered.

He sat, looking out over the room, for the first time really noticing his surroundings. There were two tourists at the bar—a fat, weak-chinned man in a plaid, one-piece business suit and a woman, probably his wife, thin, thyroid-looking. They were talking animatedly, the man gesturing heatedly. He wondered what had brought them out so early in the morning.

It was funny, he thought, the image of the fat man, chattering like a nervous magpie, his pudgy hands making weaving motions in the air before him.

He saw that his glass was empty and he rose and went over to the bar. He found a stool and ordered another whiskey.

"I'll break him," the little man was saying in a high, thin voice. "Consolidation or no consolidation . . ."

"George," the woman said gratingly, "you shouldn't drink in the morning."

"You know very well that . . ."

"George, I want to go to the ruins today."

Matt . . . Matt . . .

"They've got the cutest pottery down in the shop on the corner. From the ruins. Those little dwarf figures . . . You know, the Martians."

Only she pronounced it "Mar-chans" with a spitting *ch* sound.

It's the big one, Matt. The Stargazer. It's coming in. Maybe I'll see it warp. Beautiful . . . You should see the way the sides catch the light from the station's beacon. Like a big needle of pure silver.

"Pardon me," the woman said, turning on the stool to him. "Do you know what time the tours to the ruins start?"

He tried to smile. He told her and she said, "Thank you."

"I suppose you people get tired of tourists," she said, large eyes questioning.

"Don't be silly," George said. "Got to be practical. Lots of money from tourists."

"That's true," he said.

Matt . . .

"Well," the woman said, "when you don't get away from Earth too often, you've got to crowd everything in."

Matt . . . Uneasy.

"That's true," he told the woman aloud and tried to sip his drink and say silently, *What's wrong?*

Matt, there's something wrong with the ship. The way Art described it that time . . . The field . . . flickering . . .

She started to fade.

Come back, he shouted silently.

Silence.

"I'm in the Manta business back home," George said.

"Manta?" He raised a mechanical eyebrow carefully.

"You know, the jet airfoil planes. That's our model name. Manta. 'Cause they look like a ray, the fish. The jets squirt a stream of air directly over the airfoil. They hover just like a 'copter. But speed? You've never seen that kind of speed from a 'copter."

"I've never seen one," he said.

Beth . . . Beth . . . , his silent voice shouted. For a moment he felt like shouting aloud, but an iron control stopped his voice.

"Oh, I tell you," George said, "we'll really be crowding the market in another five years. The air's getting too crowded for 'copters. They're not safe any longer. Why, the turbulence over Rochester is something . . ."

"We're from Rochester," the thyroid woman explained.

Matt, listen. It's the field generator, I think . . . The radiation must have jammed the pilot's synapses. I can't raise him. And there's no one else aboard. Only instruments.

How far from the station?

Half a mile.

My God, if the thing goes . . .

I go with it! He could feel the fear in her words.

"So we decided now was the time, before the new merger. George would never find the time after . . ."

Try to raise the pilot.

Matt . . . I'm afraid.

Try!

"Is something wrong?" The thyroid woman asked.

He shook his head.

"You need a drink," George said as he signaled the bartender.

Beth, what's the count?

Oh, Matt, I'm scared.

The count . . .

"Good whiskey," George said.

Getting higher . . . I can't raise the pilot.

"Lousiest whiskey on the ship coming in. Those things give me the creeps."

"George, shut up."

Beth, where are you?

What do you mean?

Where are you positioned? Central or to one side?

I'm five hundred yards off station center.

"I told you not to drink in the morning," the woman said.

Any secondary movers? Robot handlers?

Yes, I have to handle the drive units.

All right, tear your auxiliary power pile down.

But . . .

Take the bricks and stack them against the far wall of the station. You're shielded enough against their radiation. Then you'll have to rotate the bulk of the station between you and the ship.

But how . . . ?

Uranium's dense. It'll shield you from the radiation when the ship goes. And break orbit. Get as far away as possible.

I can't. The station's not powered.

If you don't . . .

I can't . . .

Then silence.

The woman and George looked at him expectantly. He raised his drink to his lips, marveling at the steadiness of his hands.

"I'm sorry," he said aloud. "I didn't catch what you said."

Beth, the drive units . . .

Yes?

Can you activate them?

They'll have to be jury-rigged in place. Quick welded.

How long?

Five, maybe ten minutes. But the field. It'll collapse the way the one on the ship's doing.

If you, of all people, can't handle it . . . Anyway, you'll have to chance it. Otherwise . . .

"I said," George said thickly, "have you ever ridden one of those robot ships?"

"Robot ships?"

"Oh, I know, they're not robots exactly."

"I've ridden one," he said. "After all, I wouldn't be on Mars if I hadn't."

George looked confused.

"George is a little dull sometimes," the woman said.

Beth . . .

Almost finished. The count's mounting.

Hurry . . .

If the field collapses . . .

Don't think about it.

"They give me the creeps," George said. "Like riding a ship that's haunted."

"The pilot is very much alive," he said. "And very human."

Matt, the pile bricks are in place. A few more minutes . . .

Hurry . . . hurry . . . hurry . . .

"George talks too much," the woman said.

"Oh, hell," George said, "it's just that . . . well, those things aren't actually human any more."

Matt, I'm ready . . . Scared . . .

Can you control your thrust?

With the remote control units. Just as if I were the Stargazer.

Her voice was chill . . . frightened.

All right, then . . .

Count's climbing fast . . . I'll . . . Matt! It's blinding . . . a ball of fire . . . it's . . .

Beth . . .

Silence.

"I don't give a damn," George told the woman petulantly. "A man's got a right to say what he feels."

Beth . . .

"George, will you shut up and let's go."

Beth . . .

He looked out at the bar and thought of flame blossoming in utter blackness and . . .

"They aren't men any more," he told George. "And perhaps not even quite human. But they're not machines."

Beth . . .

"George didn't mean . . ."

"I know," he said. "George is right in a way. But they've got something normal men will never have. They've found a part in the biggest dream that man has ever dared dream. And that takes courage . . . courage to be what they are. Not men and yet a part of the greatest thing that men have ever reached for."

Beth . . .

Silence.

George rose from his stool.

"Maybe," he said. "But . . . well . . ." He thrust out his hand. "We'll see you around," he said.

He winced when Freck's hand closed on his, and for a moment sudden awareness shone in his eyes. He mumbled something in a confused voice and headed for the door.

Matt . . .

Beth, are you all right?

The woman stayed behind for a moment.

Yes, I'm all right, but the ship . . . *the* Stargazer . . .

Forget it.

But will there be another? Will they dare try again?

You're safe. That's all that counts.

The woman was saying, "George hardly ever sees past his own nose." She smiled, her thin lips embarrassed. "Maybe that's why he married me."

Matt . . .

Just hang on. They'll get to you.

No, I don't need help. The acceleration just knocked me out for a minute. But don't you see?

See?

I have the drive installed. I'm a self-contained system.

No, you can't do that. Get it out of your mind.

Someone has to prove it can be done. Otherwise they'll never build another.

It'll take you years. You can't make it back.

"I knew right away," the woman was saying. "About you, I mean."

"I didn't mean to embarrass you," he said.

Beth, come back . . . Beth.

Going out . . . faster each minute. Matt, I'll be there before anyone else. The first. But you'll have to come after me. I won't have enough power in the station to come back.

"You didn't embarrass me," the thyroid woman said.

Her eyes were large and filmed.

"It's something new," she said, "to meet someone with an object in living."

Beth, come back.

Far out now . . . accelerating all the while . . . Come for me, Matt. I'll wait for you out there . . . circling Centaurus.

He stared at the woman by the bar, his eyes scarcely seeing her.

"You know," the woman said, "I think I could be very much in love with you."

"No," he told her. "No, you wouldn't like that."

"Perhaps," she said, "but you were right. In what you told George, I mean. It does take a lot of courage to be what you are."

Then she turned and followed her husband through the door. Before the door closed, she looked back longingly.

Don't worry, Beth. I'll come. As fast as I can.

And then he sensed the sounds of the others, the worried sounds that filtered through the space blackness from the burned plains of Mercury to the nitrogen oceans of dark Pluto.

And he told them what she was doing.

For moments his inner hearing rustled with their wonder of it.

There was a oneness then. He knew what he must do, the next step he must take.

We're all with you, he told her, wondering if she could still hear his voice. *From now on, we always will be.*

And he reached out, feeling himself unite in a silent wish with all those other hundreds of minds, stretching in a brotherhood of metal across the endless spaces.

Stretching in a tight band of metal, a single organism reaching . . .

Reaching for the stars.

Thomas N. Scortia (1926–   )
Readers not familiar with science fiction may know Thomas N. Scortia as the author (with Frank M. Robinson) of the best-selling novel The Glass Inferno *(1974), which partly inspired the popular film* The Towering Inferno. *However, Mr. Scortia is well known to science fiction readers for his many excellent short stories, the best of which can be found in two collections,* Caution! Inflammable! *(1975) and* The Best of Thomas N. Scortia *(1981). Other notable novels (both in collaboration with Frank M. Robinson) are* The Nightmare Factor *(1978) and* The Gold Crew *(1980).*

ANATOMY

CAUGHT IN THE ORGAN DRAFT
Robert Silverberg

Look there, Kate, down by the promenade. Two splendid
seniors, walking side by side near the water's edge. They
radiate power, authority, wealth, assurance. He's a judge, a
senator, a corporation president, no doubt, and she's—
what?—a professor emeritus of international law, let's say.
There they go toward the plaza, moving serenely, smiling,
nodding graciously to passersby. How the sunlight gleams
in their white hair! I can barely stand the brilliance of that
reflected aura: it blinds me, it stings my eyes. What are
they—eighty, ninety, a hundred years old? At this distance
they seem much younger—they hold themselves upright,
their backs are straight, they might pass for being only fifty

or sixty. But I can tell. Their confidence, their poise, mark
them for what they are. And when they were nearer I could
see their withered cheeks, their sunken eyes. No cosmetics
can hide that. These two are old enough to be our great-
grandparents. They were well past sixty before we were
even born, Kate. How superbly their bodies function! But
why not? We can guess at their medical histories. She's had
at least three hearts, he's working on his fourth set of lungs,
they apply for new kidneys every five years, their brittle
bones are reinforced with hundreds of skeletal snips from
the arms and legs of hapless younger folk, their dimming
sensory apparatus is aided by countless nerve grafts obtained the same way, their ancient arteries are freshly
sheathed with sleek Teflon. Ambulatory assemblages of
second-hand human parts, spiced here and there with synthetic or mechanical organ substitutes, that's all they are.
And what am I, then, or you? Nineteen years old and vulnerable. In their eyes I'm nothing but a ready stockpile of
healthy organs, waiting to serve their needs. Come here,
son. What a fine strapping young man you are! Can you
spare a kidney for me? A lung? A choice little segment of
intestine? Ten centimeters of your ulnar nerve? I need a
few pieces of you, lad. You won't deny a distinguished
elder leader like me what I ask, will you? *Will you?*

Today my draft notice, a small crisp document, very official looking, came shooting out of the data slot when I
punched for my morning mail. I've been expecting it all
spring: no surprise, no shock, actually rather an anticlimax
now that it's finally here. In six weeks I am to report to
Transplant House for my final physical exam—only a formality, they wouldn't have drafted me if I didn't already
rate top marks as organ reservoir potential—and then I go
on call. The average call time is about two months. By

autumn they'll be carving me up. Eat, drink, and be merry, for soon comes the surgeon to my door.

A straggly band of senior citizens is picketing the central headquarters of the League for Bodily Sanctity. It's a counterdemonstration, an anti-anti-transplant protest, the worst kind of political statement, feeding on the ugliest of negative opinions. The demonstrators carry glowing signs that say:

> BODILY SANCTITY—OR BODILY SELFISHNESS?

And:

> YOU OWE YOUR LEADERS YOUR VERY LIVES

And:

> LISTEN TO THE VOICE OF EXPERIENCE

The picketers are low-echelon seniors, barely across the qualifying line, the ones who can't really be sure of getting transplants. No wonder they're edgy about the league. Some of them are in wheelchairs and some are encased right up to the eyebrows in portable life support systems. They croak and shout bitter invective and shake their fists. Watching the show from an upper window of the league building, I shiver with fear and dismay. These people don't just want my kidneys or my lungs. They'd take my eyes, my liver, my pancreas, my heart, anything they might happen to need.

I talked it over with my father. He's forty-five years old— too old to have been personally affected by the organ draft, too young to have needed any transplants yet. That puts him in a neutral position, so to speak, except for one minor factor: his transplant status is 5-G. That's quite high on the eligibility list, not the top-priority class but close enough. If he fell ill tomorrow and the Transplant Board ruled that his life would be endangered if he didn't get a new heart or lung or kidney, he'd be given one practically immediately. Status like that simply has to influence his objectivity on the whole organ issue. Anyway, I told him I was planning to appeal and maybe even to resist. "Be reasonable," he said, "be rational, don't let your emotions run away with you. Is it worth jeopardizing your whole future over a thing like this? After all, not everybody who's drafted loses vital organs."

"Show me the statistics," I said. "Show me."

He didn't know the statistics. It was his impression that only about a quarter or a fifth of the draftees actually got an organ call. That tells you how closely the older generation keeps in touch with the situation—and my father's an educated man, articulate, well informed. Nobody over the age of thirty-five that I talked to could show me any statistics. So I showed them. Out of a league brochure, it's true, but based on certified National Institute of Health reports. Nobody escapes. They always clip you, once you qualify. The need for young organs inexorably expands to match the pool of available organpower. In the long run they'll get us all and chop us to bits. That's probably what they want, anyway. To rid themselves of the younger members of the species, always so troublesome, by cannibalizing us for spare parts, and recycling us, lung by lung, pancreas by pancreas, through their own deteriorating bodies.

Fig. 4. On March 23, 1964, this dog's own liver was removed and replaced with the liver of a non-related mongrel donor. The animal was treated with azathioprine for four months and all therapy then stopped. He remains in perfect health 6 ⅔ years after transplantation.

The war goes on. This is, I think, its fourteenth year. Of course they're beyond the business of killing now. They

haven't had any field engagements since '93 or so, certainly
—none since the organ draft legislation went into effect.
The old ones can't afford to waste precious young bodies
on the battlefield. So robots wage our territorial struggles
for us, butting heads with a great metallic clank, laying
land mines and twitching their sensors at the enemy's
mines, digging tunnels beneath his screens, et cetera, et
cetera. Plus, of course, the quasi-military activity—
economic sanctions, third-power blockades, propaganda
telecasts beamed as overrides from merciless orbital satel-
lites, and stuff like that. It's a subtler war than the kind they
used to wage: nobody dies. Still, it drains national resources. Taxes are going up again this year, the fifth or
sixth year in a row, and they've just slapped a special Peace
Surcharge on all metal-containing goods, on account of the
copper shortage. There once was a time when we could
hope that our crazy old leaders would die off or at least
retire for reasons of health, stumbling away to their country villas with ulcers or shingles or scabies or scruples and
allowing new young peacemakers to take office. But now
they just go on and on, immortal and insane, our senators,
our cabinet members, our generals, our planners. And their
war goes on and on too, their absurd, incomprehensible,
diabolical, self-gratifying war.

I know people my age or a little older who have taken
asylum in Belgium or Sweden or Paraguay or one of the
other countries where Bodily Sanctity laws have been
passed. There are about twenty such countries, half of them
the most progressive nations in the world and half of them
the most reactionary. But what's the sense of running
away? I don't want to live in exile. I'll stay here and fight.

Naturally they don't ask a draftee to give up his heart or his
liver or some other organ essential to life, say his medulla

oblongata. We haven't yet reached that stage of political enlightenment at which the government feels capable of legislating fatal conscription. Kidneys and lungs, the paired organs, the dispensable organs, are the chief targets so far. But if you study the history of conscription over the years you see that it can always be projected on a curve rising from rational necessity to absolute lunacy. Give them a fingertip, they'll take an arm. Give them an inch of bowel, they'll take your guts. In another fifty years they'll be drafting hearts and stomachs and maybe even brains, mark my words; let them get the technology of brain transplants together and nobody's skull will be safe. It'll be human sacrifice all over again. The only difference between us and the Aztecs is one of method: we have anesthesia, we have antisepsis and asepsis, we use scalpels instead of obsidian blades to cut out the hearts of our victims.

MEANS OF OVERCOMING THE HOMOGRAFT REACTION

The pathway that has led from the demonstration of the immunological nature of the homograft reaction and its universality to the development of relatively effective but by no means completely satisfactory means of overcoming it for therapeutic purposes is an interesting one that can only be touched upon very briefly. The year 1950 ushered in a new era in transplantation immunobiology in which the discovery of various means of weakening or abrogating a host's response to a homograft—such as sublethal whole body x-irradiation, or treatment with certain adrenal corticosteroid hormones, notably cortisone—began to influence the direction of the mainstream of research and engender confidence that a workable clinical solution might not be too far off. By the end of the decade powerful immunosuppressive drugs, such as 6-mercaptopurine, had been shown to be capable of holding in abeyance the reactivity

of dogs to renal homografts, and soon afterward this principle was successfully extended to man.

Is my resistance to the draft based on an ingrained abstract distaste for tyranny in all forms or rather on the mere
desire to keep my body intact? Could it be both, maybe?
Do I need an idealistic rationalization at all? Don't I have
an inalienable right to go through my life wearing my own
native-born kidneys?

The law was put through by an administration of old men.
You can be sure that all laws affecting the welfare of the
young are the work of doddering moribund ancients
afflicted with angina pectoris, atherosclerosis, prolapses of
the infundibulum, fulminating ventricles, and dilated via-
ducts. The problem was this: not enough healthy young
people were dying of highway accidents, successful suicide
attempts, diving board miscalculations, electrocutions, and
football injuries; therefore there was a shortage of transplantable organs. An effort to restore the death penalty for
the sake of creating a steady supply of state-controlled
cadavers lost out in the courts. Volunteer programs of
organ donation weren't working out too well, since most of
the volunteers were criminals who signed up in order to
gain early release from prison: a lung reduced your sentence by five years, a kidney got you three years off, and so
on. The exodus of convicts from the jails under this clause
wasn't so popular among suburban voters. Meanwhile there
was an urgent and mounting need for organs; a lot of important seniors might in fact die if something didn't get
done fast. So a coalition of senators from all four parties
rammed the organ draft measure through the upper chamber in the face of a filibuster threat from a few youth-
oriented members. It had a much easier time in the House

of Representatives, since nobody in the House ever pays much attention to the text of a bill up for a vote, and word had been circulated on this one that if it passed, everybody over sixty-five who had any political pull at all could count on living twenty or thirty extra years, which to a representative means a crack at ten to fifteen extra terms of office. Naturally there have been court challenges, but what's the use? The average age of the eleven justices of the Supreme Court is seventy-eight. They're human and mortal. They need our flesh. If they throw out the organ draft now, they're signing their own death warrants.

For a year and a half I was the chairman of the antidraft campaign on our campus. We were the sixth or seventh local chapter of the League for Bodily Sanctity to be organized in this country, and we were real activists. Mainly we would march up and down in front of the draft board offices carrying signs proclaiming things like:

KIDNEY POWER

And:

A MAN'S BODY IS HIS CASTLE

And:

THE POWER TO CONSCRIPT ORGANS IS
THE POWER TO DESTROY LIVES

We never went in for the rough stuff, though, like bombing organ transplant centers or hijacking refrigerator trucks. Peaceful agitation, that was our motto. When a couple of our members tried to swing us to a more violent policy, I delivered an extemporaneous two-hour speech arguing for moderation. Naturally I was drafted the moment I became eligible.

"I can understand your hostility to the draft," my college advisor said. "It's certainly normal to feel queasy about surrendering important organs of your body. But you ought to consider the countervailing advantages. Once you've given an organ you get a 6-A classification, Preferred Recipient, and you remain forever on the 6-A roster. Surely you realize that this means that if you ever need a transplant yourself, you'll automatically be eligible for one, even if your other personal and professional qualifications don't lift you to the optimum level. Suppose your career plans don't work out and you become a manual laborer, for instance. Ordinarily you wouldn't rate even a first look if you developed heart disease, but your Preferred Recipient status would save you. You'd get a new lease on life, my boy."

I pointed out the fallacy inherent in this. Which is that as the number of draftees increases, it will come to encompass a majority or even a totality of the population, and eventually everybody will have a 6-A Preferred Recipient status by virtue of having donated, and the term Preferred Recipient will cease to have any meaning. A shortage of transplantable organs would eventually develop as each past donor stakes his claim to a transplant when his health fails, and in time they'd have to arrange the Preferred Recipients by order of personal and professional achievement anyway, for the sake of arriving at some kind of priorities within the 6-A class, and we'd be right back where we are now.

Fig. 7. The course of a patient who received antilymphocyte globulin (ALG) before and for the first four months after renal homotransplantation. The donor was an older brother. There was no early rejection. Prednisone therapy was started forty days postoperatively. Note the insidious onset of late rejection after cessation of globulin therapy. This was treated by a moderate increase in the maintenance doses of steroids. This delayed complication occurred in only two of

*the first twenty recipients of intrafamilial homografts who
were treated with ALG. It has been seen with about the
same low frequency in subsequent cases. (By permission of
Surg. Gynec. Obstet. 126 [1968]: p. 1023.)*

So I went down to Transplant House today, right on
schedule, to take my physical. A couple of my friends
thought I was making a tactical mistake by reporting at all;
if you're going to resist, they said, resist at every point
along the line. Make them drag you in for the physical. In
purely idealistic (and ideological) terms I suppose they're
right. But there's no need yet for me to start kicking up a
fuss. Wait till they actually say, "We need your kidney,
young man." Then I can resist, if resistance is the course I
ultimately choose. (Why am I wavering? Am I afraid of
the damage to my career plans that resisting might do? Am
I not entirely convinced of the injustice of the entire organ
draft system? I don't know. I'm not even sure that I *am*
wavering. Reporting for your physical isn't really a sellout
to the system.) I went, anyway. They tapped this and x-
rayed that and peered into the other thing. Yawn, please.
Bend over, please. Cough, please. Hold out your left arm,
please. They marched me in front of a battery of diagnostat
machines and I stood there hoping for the red light to flash
—*tilt,* get out of here!—but I was, as expected, in perfect
physical shape, and I qualified for call. Afterward I met
Kate and we walked in the park and held hands and
watched the glories of the sunset and discussed what I'll do,
when and if the call comes. *If?* Wishful thinking, boy!

If your number is called you become exempt from military
service, and they credit you with a special $750 tax deduc-
tion every year. Big deal.

Another thing they're very proud of is the program of voluntary donation of unpaired organs. This has nothing to do with the draft, which—thus far, at least—requisitions only paired organs, organs that can be spared without loss of life. For the last twelve years it's been possible to walk into any hospital in the United States and sign a simple release form allowing the surgeons to slice you up. Eyes, lungs, heart, intestines, pancreas, liver, anything, you give it all to them. This process used to be known as suicide in a simpler era and it was socially disapproved, especially in times of labor shortages. Now we have a labor surplus, because even though our population growth has been fairly slow since the middle of the century, the growth of labor-eliminating mechanical devices and processes has been quite rapid, even exponential. Therefore to volunteer for this kind of total donation is considered a deed of the highest social utility, removing as it does a healthy young body from the overcrowded labor force and at the same time providing some elder statesman with the assurance that the supply of vital organs will not unduly diminish. Of course, you have to be crazy to volunteer, but there's never been any shortages of lunatics in our society.

If you're not drafted by the age of twenty-one, through some lucky fluke, you're safe. And a few of us do slip through the net, I'm told. So far there are more of us in the total draft pool than there are patients in need of transplants. But the ratios are changing rapidly. The draft legislation is still relatively new. Before long they'll have drained the pool of eligible draftees, and then what? Birth rates nowadays are low; the supply of potential draftees is finite. But death rates are even lower; the demand for organs is essentially infinite. I can give you only one of my kidneys, if I am to survive; but you, as you live on and on, may require more than one kidney transplant. Some recipients may need five or six sets of kidneys or lungs before they finally get beyond hope of repair at age seventy-one or so. As those who've given organs come to requisition organs later on in life, the pressure on the under-twenty-one group will get even greater. Those in need of transplants will come to outnumber those who can donate organs, and everybody in the pool will get clipped. And then? Well, they could lower the draft age to seventeen or sixteen or even fourteen. But even that's only a short-term solution. Sooner or later, there won't be enough spare organs to go around.

Will I stay? Will I flee? Will I go to court? Time's running out. My call is sure to come up in another few weeks. I feel a tickling sensation in my back, now and then, as though somebody's quietly sawing at my kidneys.

Cannibalism. At Chou-kou-tien, Dragon Bone Hill, twenty-five miles southwest of Peking, paleontologists excavating a cave early in the twentieth century discovered the fossil skulls of Peking Man, *Pithecanthropus pekinensis.* The skulls had been broken away at the base, which led Franz   .
Weidenreich, the director of the Dragon Bone Hill digs, to speculate that Peking Man was a cannibal who had killed his own kind, extracted the brains of his victims through openings in the base of their skulls, cooked and feasted on the cerebral meat—there were hearths and fragments of charcoal at the site—and left the skulls behind in the cave as trophies. To eat your enemy's flesh: to absorb his skills, his strengths, his knowledge, his achievements, his virtues. It took mankind five hundred thousand years to struggle upward from cannibalism. But we never lost the old craving, did we? There's still easy comfort to gain by devouring

those who are younger, stronger, more agile than you. We've improved the techniques, is all. And so now they eat us raw, the old ones, they gobble us up, organ by throbbing organ. Is that really an improvement? At least Peking Man cooked his meat.

Our brave new society, where all share equally in the triumphs of medicine, and the deserving senior citizens need not feel that their merits and prestige will be rewarded only by a cold grave—we sing its praises all the time. How pleased everyone is about the organ draft! Except, of course, a few disgruntled draftees.

The ticklish question of priorities. Who gets the stockpiled organs? They have an elaborate system by which hierarchies are defined. Supposedly a big computer drew it up, thus assuring absolute godlike impartiality. You earn salvation through good works: accomplishments in career and benevolence in daily life win you points that nudge you up the ladder until you reach one of the high-priority classifications, 4-G or better. No doubt the classification system is impartial and is administered justly. But is it rational? Whose needs does it serve? In 1943, during World War II, there was a shortage of the newly discovered drug penicillin among the American military forces in North Africa. Two groups of soldiers were most in need of its benefits: those who were suffering from infected battle wounds and those who had contracted venereal disease. A junior medical officer, working from self-evident moral principles, ruled that the wounded heroes were more deserving of treatment than the self-indulgent syphilitics. He was overruled by the medical officer in charge, who observed that the VD cases could be restored to active duty more quickly, if treated; besides, if they remained untreated they served as vectors of further infection. Therefore he gave them the penicillin and left the wounded groaning on their beds of pain. The logic of the battlefield, incontrovertible, unassailable.

The great chain of life. Little creatures in the plankton are eaten by larger ones, and the greater plankton falls prey to little fishes, and little fishes to bigger fishes, and so on up to the tuna and the dolphin and the shark. I eat the flesh of the tuna and I thrive and flourish and grow fat, and store up energy in my vital organs. And am eaten in turn by the shriveled wizened senior. All life is linked. I see my destiny.

In the early days rejection of the transplanted organ was the big problem. Such a waste! The body failed to distinguish between a beneficial though alien organ and an intrusive, hostile microorganism. The mechanism known as the immune response was mobilized to drive out the invader. At the point of invasion enzymes came into play, a brush fire war designed to rip down and dissolve the foreign substances. White corpuscles poured in via the circulatory system, vigilant phagocytes on the march. Through the lymphatic network came antibodies, high-powered protein missiles. Before any technology of organ grafts could be developed, methods had to be devised to suppress the immune response. Drugs, radiation treatment, metabolic shock —one way and another, the organ rejection problem was long ago conquered. I can't conquer my draft rejection problem. Aged and rapacious legislators, I reject you and your legislation.

My call notice came today. They'll need one of my kidneys. The usual request. "You're lucky," somebody said at lunchtime. "They might have wanted a lung."

Kate and I walk into the green glistening hills and stand among the blossoming oleanders and corianders and frangipani and whatever. How good it is to be alive, to breathe this fragrance, to show our bodies to the bright sun! Her skin is tawny and glowing. Her beauty makes me weep. She will not be spared. None of us will be spared. I go first, then she, or is it she ahead of me? Where will they make the incision? Here, on her smooth rounded back? Here, on the flat taut belly? I can see the high priest standing over the altar. At the first blaze of dawn his shadow falls across her. The obsidian knife that is clutched in his upraised hand has a terrible fiery sparkle. The choir offers up a discordant hymn to the god of blood. The knife descends.

My last chance to escape across the border. I've been up all night, weighing the options. There's no hope of appeal. Running away leaves a bad taste in my mouth. Father, friends, even Kate, all say stay, stay, stay, face the music. The hour of decision. Do I really have a choice? I have no choice. When the time comes, I'll surrender peacefully.

I report to Transplant House for conscriptive donative surgery in three hours.

After all, he said coolly, what's a kidney? I'll still have another one, you know. And if that one malfunctions, I can always get a replacement. I'll have Preferred Recipient status, 6-A, for what that's worth. But I won't settle for my automatic 6-A. I know what's going to happen to the priority system; I'd better protect myself. I'll go into politics. I'll climb. I'll attain upward mobility out of enlightened self-interest, right? Right. I'll become so important that society will owe me a thousand transplants. And one of these years I'll get that kidney back. Three or four kidneys, fifty kidneys, as many as I need. A heart or two. A few lungs. A pancreas, a spleen, a liver. They won't be able to refuse me anything. I'll show them. I'll show them. I'll out-senior the seniors. There's your Bodily Sanctity for you, eh? I suppose I'll have to resign from the league. Goodbye, idealism. Goodbye, moral superiority. Goodbye, kidney. Goodbye, goodbye, goodbye.

It's done. I've paid my debt to society. I've given up unto the powers that be my humble pound of flesh. When I leave the hospital in a couple of days, I'll carry a card testifying to my new 6-A status.

Top priority for the rest of my life.

Why, I might live for a thousand years.

Robert Silverberg (1935–   )
Robert Silverberg is a remarkable writer in terms both of quality and quantity. He is the author of well over one hundred books, on subjects ranging from lost cities to the history of Israel to novels like Lord Valentine's Castle (1980). He has won two Hugo Awards and four Nebula Awards (and been nominated for several others) within the science fiction field. Mr. Silverberg served as president of the Science Fiction Writers of America from 1967 to 1968.

REPRODUCTION

NINE LIVES
Ursula K. Le Guin

She was alive inside but dead outside, her face a black and dun net of wrinkles, tumors, cracks. She was bald and blind. The tremors that crossed Libra's face were mere quiverings of corruption. Underneath, in the black corridors, the halls beneath the skin, there were crepitations in darkness, ferments, chemical nightmares that went on for centuries. "O the damned flatulent planet," Pugh murmured as the dome shook and a boil burst a kilometer to the southwest, spraying silver pus across the sunset. The sun had been setting for the last two days. "I'll be glad to see a human face."

"Thanks," said Martin.

"Yours is human to be sure," said Pugh, "but I've seen it so long I can't see it."

Radvid signals cluttered the communicator which Martin was operating, faded, returned as face and voice. The face filled the screen, the nose of an Assyrian king, the eyes of a samurai, skin bronze, eyes the color of iron: young, magnificent. "Is that what human beings look like?" said Pugh with awe. "I'd forgotten."

"Shut up, Owen, we're on."

"Libra Exploratory Mission Base, come in please, this is *Passerine* launch."

"Libra here. Beam fixed. Come on down, launch."

"Expulsion in seven E-seconds. Hold on." The screen blanked and sparkled.

"Do they all look like that? Martin, you and I are uglier men than I thought."

"Shut up, Owen. . . ."

For twenty-two minutes Martin followed the landing craft down by signal and then through the cleared dome they saw it, small star in the blood-colored east, sinking. It came down neat and quiet, Libra's thin atmosphere carrying little sound. Pugh and Martin closed the headpieces of their imsuits, zipped out of the dome airlocks, and ran with soaring strides, Nijinsky and Nureyev, toward the boat. Three equipment modules came floating down at four-minute intervals from each other and hundred-meter intervals east of the boat. "Come on out," Martin said on his suit radio, "we're waiting at the door."

"Come on in, the methane's fine," said Pugh.

The hatch opened. The young man they had seen on the screen came out with one athletic twist and leaped down onto the shaky dust and clinkers of Libra. Martin shook his hand, but Pugh was staring at the hatch, from which another young man emerged with the same neat

twist and jump, followed by a young woman who emerged
with the same neat twist, ornamented by a wriggle, and the
jump. They were all tall, with bronze skin, black hair, high-
bridged noses, epicanthic fold, the same face. They all had
the same face. The fourth was emerging from the hatch
with a neat twist and jump. "Martin bach," said Pugh,
"we've got a clone."

"Right," said one of them, "we're a tenclone. John
Chow's the name. You're Lieutenant Martin?"

"I'm Owen Pugh."

"Alvaro Guillen Martin," said Martin, formal, bowing
slightly. Another girl was out, the same beautiful face;
Martin stared at her and his eyes rolled like a nervous
pony's. Evidently he had never given any thought to cloning and was suffering technological shock. "Steady," Pugh
said in the Argentine dialect, "it's only excess twins." He
stood close by Martin's elbow. He was glad himself of the
contact.

It is hard to meet a stranger. Even the greatest extrovert
meeting even the meekest stranger knows a certain dread,
though he may not know he knows it. Will he make a fool
of me wreck my image of myself invade me destroy me
change me? Will he be different from me? Yes, that he will.
There's the terrible thing: the strangeness of the stranger.

After two years on a dead planet, and the last half year
isolated as a team of two, oneself and one other, after that
it's even harder to meet a stranger, however welcome he
may be. You're out of the habit of difference, you've lost
the touch; and so the fear revives, the primitive anxiety, the
old dread.

The clone, five males and five females, had got done in a
couple of minutes what a man might have got done in
twenty: greeted Pugh and Martin, had a glance at Libra,
unloaded the boat, made ready to go. They went, and the

dome filled with them, a hive of golden bees. They hummed and buzzed quietly, filled up all silences, all spaces with a honey-brown swarm of human presence. Martin looked bewildered at the long-limbed girls, and they smiled at him, three at once. Their smile was gentler than that of the boys, but no less radiantly self-possessed.

"Self-possessed," Owen Pugh murmured to his friend, "that's it. Think of it, to be oneself ten times over. Nine seconds for every motion, nine ayes on every vote. It would be glorious." But Martin was asleep. And the John Chows had all gone to sleep at once. The dome was filled with their quiet breathing. They were young, they didn't snore. Martin sighed and snored, his Hershey-bar-colored face relaxed in the dim afterglow of Libra's primary, set at last. Pugh had cleared the dome and stars looked in, Sol among them, a great company of lights, a clone of splendors. Pugh slept and dreamed of a one-eyed giant who chased him through the shaking halls of Hell.

From his sleeping bag Pugh watched the clone's awakening. They all got up within one minute except for one pair, a boy and a girl, who lay snugly tangled and still sleeping in one bag. As Pugh saw this there was a shock like one of Libra's earthquakes inside him, a very deep tremor. He was not aware of this and in fact thought he was pleased at the sight; there was no other such comfort on this dead hollow world. More power to them, who made love. One of the others stepped on the pair. They woke and the girl sat up flushed and sleepy, with bare golden breasts. One of her sisters murmured something to her; she shot a glance at Pugh and disappeared in the sleeping bag; from another direction came a fierce stare, from still another direction a voice: "Christ, we're used to having a room to ourselves. Hope you don't mind, Captain Pugh."

"It's a pleasure," Pugh said half truthfully. He had to stand up then wearing only the shorts he slept in, and he felt like a plucked rooster, all white scrawn and pimples. He had seldom envied Martin's compact brownness so much. The United Kingdom had come through the Great Famines well, losing less than half its population: a record achieved by rigorous food control. Black marketeers and hoarders had been executed. Crumbs had been shared. Where in richer lands most had died and a few had thriven, in Britain fewer died and none throve. They all got lean. Their sons were lean, their grandsons lean, small, brittle-boned, easily infected. When civilization became a matter of standing in lines, the British had kept queue, and so had replaced the survival of the fittest with the survival of the fair-minded. Owen Pugh was a scrawny little man. All the same, he was there.

At the moment he wished he wasn't.

At breakfast a John said, "Now if you'll brief us, Captain Pugh—"

"Owen, then."

"Owen, we can work out our schedule. Anything new on the mine since your last report to your Mission? We saw your reports when *Passerine* was orbiting Planet V, where they are now."

Martin did not answer, though the mine was his discovery and project, and Pugh had to do his best. It was hard to talk to them. The same faces, each with the same expression of intelligent interest, all leaned toward him across the table at almost the same angle. They all nodded together.

Over the Exploitation Corps insigne on their tunics each had a nameband, first name John and last name Chow of course, but the middle names different. The men were Aleph, Kaph, Yod, Gimel, and Samekh; the women

Sadhe, Daleth, Zayin, Beth, and Resh. Pugh tried to use the
names but gave it up at once; he could not even tell sometimes which one had spoken, for all the voices were alike.

Martin buttered and chewed his toast, and finally interrupted: "You're a team. Is that it?"

"Right," said two Johns.

"God, what a team! I hadn't seen the point. How much
do you each know what the others are thinking?"

"Not at all, properly speaking," replied one of the girls,
Zayin. The others watched her with the proprietary, ap-
proving look they had. "No ESP, nothing fancy. But we
think alike. We have exactly the same equipment. Given
the same stimulus, the same problem, we're likely to be
coming up with the same reactions and solutions at the
same time. Explanations are easy—don't even have to
make them, usually. We seldom misunderstand each other.
It does facilitate our working as a team."

"Christ yes," said Martin. "Pugh and I have spent seven
hours out of ten for six months misunderstanding each
other. Like most people. What about emergencies, are you
as good at meeting the unexpected problem as a nor . . .
an unrelated team?"

"Statistics so far indicate that we are," Zayin answered
readily. Clones must be trained, Pugh thought, to meet
questions, to reassure and reason. All they said had the
slightly bland and stilted quality of answers furnished to the
Public. "We can't brainstorm as singletons can, we as a
team don't profit from the interplay of varied minds; but we
have a compensatory advantage. Clones are drawn from
the best human material, individuals of IIQ ninety-ninth
percentile, Genetic Constitution alpha double A, and so
on. We have more to draw on than most individuals do."

"And it's multiplied by a factor of ten. Who is—who was
John Chow?"

"A genius surely," Pugh said politely. His interest in cloning was not so new and avid as Martin's.

"Leonardo Complex type," said Yod. "Biomath, also a cellist and an undersea hunter, and interested in structural engineering problems and so on. Died before he'd worked out his major theories."

"Then you each represent a different facet of his mind, his talents?"

"No," said Zayin, shaking her head in time with several others. "We share the basic equipment and tendencies, of course, but we're all engineers in Planetary Exploitation. A later clone can be trained to develop other aspects of the basic equipment. It's all training; the genetic substance is identical. We are John Chow. But we are differently trained."

Martin looked shell-shocked. "How old are you?"

"Twenty-three."

"You say he died young—had they taken germ cells from him beforehand or something?"

Gimel took over: "He died at twenty-four in an air car crash. They couldn't save the brain, so they took some intestinal cells and cultured them for cloning. Reproductive cells aren't used for cloning, since they have only half the chromosomes. Intestinal cells happen to be easy to despecialize and reprogram for total growth."

"All chips off the old block," Martin said valiantly. "But how can . . . some of you be women . . . ?"

Beth took over: "It's easy to program half the clonal mass back to the female. Just delete the male gene from half the cells and they revert to the basic, that is, the female. It's trickier to go the other way, have to hook in artificial Y chromosomes. So they mostly clone from males, since clones function best bisexually."

Gimel again: "They've worked these matters of technique and function out carefully. The taxpayers wants the best for his money, and of course clones are expensive. With the cell manipulations, and the incubation in Ngama Placentae, and the maintenance and training of the foster-parent groups, we end up costing about three million apiece."

"For your next generation," Martin said, still struggling, "I suppose you . . . you breed?"

"We females are sterile," said Beth with perfect equanimity. "You remember that the Y chromosome was deleted from our original cell. The males can interbreed with approved singletons, if they want to. But to get John Chow again as often as they want, they just reclone a cell from this clone."

Martin gave up the struggle. He nodded and chewed cold toast. "Well," said one of the Johns, and all changed mood, like a flock of starlings that change course in one wingflick, following a leader so fast that no eye can see which leads. They were ready to go. "How about a look at the mine? Then we'll unload the equipment. Some nice new models in the roboats; you'll want to see them. Right?" Had Pugh or Martin not agreed they might have found it hard to say so. The Johns were polite but unanimous; their decisions carried. Pugh, Commander of Libra Base 2, felt a qualm. Could he boss around this superman/woman-entity-of-ten? and a genius at that? He stuck close to Martin as they suited for outside. Neither said anything.

Four apiece in the three large airjets, they slipped off north from the dome, over Libra's dun rugose skin, in starlight.

"Desolate," one said.

It was a boy and girl with Pugh and Martin. Pugh wondered if these were the two that had shared a sleeping bag last night. No doubt they wouldn't mind if he asked them.

Sex must be as handy as breathing to them. Did you two
breathe last night?

"Yes," he said, "it is desolate."

"This is our first time off, except training on Luna." The
girl's voice was definitely a bit higher and softer.

"How did you take the big hop?"

"They doped us. I wanted to experience it." That was
the boy; he sounded wistful. They seemed to have more
personality, only two at a time. Did repetition of the individual negate individuality?

"Don't worry," said Martin, steering the sled, "you can't
experience no-time because it isn't there."

"I'd just like to once," one of them said. "So we'd know."

The Mountains of Merioneth showed leprotic in starlight to the east, a plume of freezing gas trailed silvery from
a vent-hole to the west, and the sled tilted groundward. The
twins braced for the stop at one moment, each with a slight
protective gesture to the other. Your skin is my skin, Pugh
thought, but literally, no metaphor. What would it be like,
then, to have someone as close to you as that? Always to
be answered when you spoke; never to be in pain alone.
Love your neighbor as you love yourself. . . . That hard old
problem was solved. The neighbor was the self: the love
was perfect.

And here was Hellmouth, the mine.

Pugh was the Exploratory Mission's E.T. geologist, and
Martin his technician and cartographer; but when in the
course of a local survey Martin had discovered the U-mine,
Pugh had given him full credit, as well as the onus of pros-
pecting the lode and planning the Exploitation Team's job.
These kids had been sent out from Earth years before Martin's reports got there and had not known what their job
would be until they got here. The Exploitation Corps simply sent out teams regularly and blindly as a dandelion

sends out its seed, knowing there would be a job for them
on Libra or the next planet out or one they hadn't even
heard about yet. The government wanted uranium too
urgently to wait while reports drifted home across the light-
years. The stuff was like gold, old-fashioned but essential,
worth mining extraterrestrially and shipping interstellar.
Worth its weight in people, Pugh thought sourly, watching
the tall young men and women go one by one, glimmering
in starlight, into the black hole Martin had named Hellmouth.

As they went in their homeostatic forehead-lamps
brightened. Twelve nodding gleams ran along the moist,
wrinkled walls. Pugh heard Martin's radiation counter
peeping twenty to the dozen up ahead. "Here's the drop-
off," said Martin's voice in the suit intercom, drowning out
the peeping and the dead silence that was around them.
"We're in a side-fissure, this is the main vertical vent in
front of us." The black void gaped, its far side not visible in
the headlamp beams. "Last vulcanism seems to have been a
couple of thousand years ago. Nearest fault is twenty-eight
kilos east, in the Trench. This area seems to be as safe
seismically as anything in the area. The big basalt-flow
overhead stabilizes all these substructures, so long as it remains stable itself. Your central lode is thirty-six meters
down and runs in a series of five bubble caverns northeast.
It is a lode, a pipe of very high-grade ore. You saw the
percentage figures, right? Extraction's going to be no problem. All you've got to do is get the bubbles topside."

"Take off the lid and let 'em float up." A chuckle. Voices
began to talk, but they were all the same voice and the suit
radio gave them no location in space. "Open the thing right
up. —Safer that way. —But it's a solid basalt roof, how
thick, ten meters here? —Three to twenty, the report said.
—Blow good ore all over the lot. —Use this access we're in,

straighten it a bit and run slider rails for the robos. —Import burros. —Have we got enough propping material? —What's your estimate of total payload mass, Martin?"

"Say over five million kilos and under eight."

"Transport will be here in ten E-months. —It'll have to go pure. —No, they'll have the mass problem in NAFAL shipping licked by now, remember it's been sixteen years since we left Earth last Tuesday. —Right, they'll send the whole lot back and purify it in Earth orbit. —Shall we go down, Martin?"

"Go on. I've been down."

The first one—Aleph? (Heb., the ox, the leader)— swung onto the ladder and down; the rest followed. Pugh and Martin stood at the chasm's edge. Pugh set his intercom to exchange only with Martin's suit, and noticed Martin doing the same. It was a bit wearing, this listening to one person think aloud in ten voices, or was it one voice speaking the thoughts of ten minds?

"A great gut," Pugh said, looking down into the black pit, its veined and warted walls catching stray gleams of headlamps far below. "A cow's bowel. A bloody great constipated intestine."

Martin's counter peeped like a lost chicken. They stood inside the dead but epileptic planet, breathing oxygen from tanks, wearing suits impermeable to corrosives and harmful radiations, resistant to a 200-degree range of temperatures, tear-proof, and as shock-resistant as possible given the soft vulnerable stuff inside.

"Next hop," Martin said, "I'd like to find a planet that has nothing whatever to exploit."

"You found this."

"Keep me home next time."

Pugh was pleased. He had hoped Martin would want to go on working with him, but neither of them was used to talking much about their feelings, and he had hesitated to ask. "I'll try that," he said.

"I hate this place. I like caves, you know. It's why I came in here. Just spelunking. But this one's a bitch. Mean. You can't ever let down in here. I guess this lot can handle it, though. They know their stuff."

"Wave of the future, whatever," said Pugh.

The wave of the future came swarming up the ladder, swept Martin to the entrance, gabbled at and around him: "Have we got enough material for supports? —If we convert one of the extractor servos to anneal, yes. —Sufficient if we miniblast? —Kaph can calculate stress." Pugh had switched his intercom back to receive them; he looked at them, so many thoughts jabbering in an eager mind, and at Martin standing silent among them, and at Hellmouth and the wrinkled plain. "Settled! How does that strike you as a preliminary schedule, Martin?"

"It's your baby," Martin said.

Within five E-days the Johns had all their material and equipment unloaded and operating and were starting to open up the mine. They worked with total efficiency. Pugh was fascinated and frightened by their effectiveness, their confidence, their independence. He was no use to them at all. A clone, he thought, might indeed be the first truly stable, self-reliant human being. Once adult it would need nobody's help. It would be sufficient to itself physically, sexually, emotionally, intellectually. Whatever he did, any member of it would always receive the support and approval of his peers, his other selves. Nobody else was needed.

Two of the clone stayed in the dome doing calculations and paperwork, with frequent sled trips to the mine for measurements and tests. They were the mathematicians of the clone, Zayin and Kaph. That is, as Zayin explained, all ten had had thorough mathematical training from age three to twenty-one, but from twenty-one to twenty-three she and Kaph had gone on with math while the others intensified study in other specialties, geology, mining, engineering, electronic engineering, equipment robotics, applied atomics, and so on. "Kaph and I feel," she said, "that we're the element of the clone closest to what John Chow was in his singleton lifetime. But of course he was principally in biomath, and they didn't take us far in that."

"They needed us most in this field," Kaph said, with the patriotic priggishness they sometimes evinced.

Pugh and Martin soon could distinguish this pair from the others, Zayin by gestalt, Kaph only by a discolored left fourth fingernail, got from an ill-aimed hammer at the age of six. No doubt there were many such differences, physical and psychological, among them; nature might be identical, nurture could not be. But the differences were hard to find. And part of the difficulty was that they never really talked to Pugh and Martin. They joked with them, were polite, got along fine. They gave nothing. It was nothing one could complain about; they were very pleasant, they had the standardized American friendliness. "Do you come from Ireland, Owen?"

"Nobody comes from Ireland, Zayin."

"There are lots of Irish-Americans."

"To be sure, but no more Irish. A couple of thousand in all the island, the last I knew. They didn't go in for birth control, you know, so the food ran out. By the Third Famine there were no Irish left at all but the priesthood, and they're all celibate, or nearly all."

Zayin and Kaph smiled stiffly. They had no experience of either bigotry or irony. "What are you then, ethnically?" Kaph asked, and Pugh replied, "A Welshman."

"Is it Welsh that you and Martin speak together?"

None of your business, Pugh thought, but said, "No, it's his dialect, not mine: Argentinean. A descendant of Spanish."

"You learned it for private communication?"

"Whom had we here to be private from? It's just that sometimes a man likes to speak his native language."

"Ours is English," Kaph said unsympathetically. Why should they have sympathy? That's one of the things you give because you need it back.

"Is Wells quaint?" asked Zayin.

"Wells? Oh, Wales, it's called. Yes, Wales is quaint." Pugh switched on his rock-cutter, which prevented further conversation by a synapse-destroying whine, and while it whined he turned his back and said a profane word in Welsh.

That night he used the Argentine dialect for private communication. "Do they pair off in the same couples or change every night?"

Martin looked surprised. A prudish expression, unsuited to his features, appeared for a moment. It faded. He too was curious. "I think it's random."

"Don't whisper, man, it sounds dirty. I think they rotate."

"On a schedule?"

"So nobody gets omitted."

Martin gave a vulgar laugh and smothered it. "What about us? Aren't we omitted?"

"That doesn't occur to them."

"What if I proposition one of the girls?"

"She'd tell the others and they'd decide as a group."

"I am not a bull," Martin said, his dark, heavy face heating up. "I will not be judged—"

"Down, down, machismo," said Pugh. "Do you mean to proposition one?"

Martin shrugged, sullen. "Let 'em have their incest."

"Incest is it, or masturbation?"

"I don't care, if they'd do it out of earshot!"

The clone's early attempts at modesty had soon worn off, unmotivated by any deep defensiveness of self or awareness of others. Pugh and Martin were daily deeper swamped under the intimacies of its constant emotional-sexual-mental interchange: swamped yet excluded.

"Two months to go," Martin said one evening.

"To what?" snapped Pugh. He was edgy lately, and Martin's sullenness got on his nerves.

"To relief."

In sixty days the full crew of their Exploratory Mission were due back from their survey of the other planets of the system. Pugh was aware of this.

"Crossing off the days on your calendar?" he jeered.

"Pull yourself together, Owen."

"What do you mean?"

"What I say."

They parted in contempt and resentment.

Pugh came in after a day alone on the Pampas, a vast lava plain the nearest edge of which was two hours south by jet. He was tired but refreshed by solitude. They were not supposed to take long trips alone but lately had often done so. Martin stooped under bright lights, drawing one of his elegant masterly charts. This one was of the whole face of Libra, the cancerous face. The dome was otherwise empty, seeming dim and large as it had before the clone came. "Where's the golden horde?"

Martin grunted ignorance, cross-hatching. He straightened his back to glance round at the sun, which squatted feebly like a great red toad on the eastern plain, and at the clock, which said 18:45. "Some big quakes today," he said, returning to his map. "Feel them down there? Lots of crates were falling around. Take a look at the seismo."

The needle jigged and wavered on the roll. It never stopped dancing here. The roll had recorded five quakes of major intensity back in midafternoon; twice the needle had hopped off the roll. The attached computer had been activated to emit a slip reading, "Epicenter 61' N by 42'4" E."

"Not in the Trench this time."

"I thought it felt a bit different from usual. Sharper."

"In Base One I used to lie awake all night feeling the ground jump. Queer how you get used to things."

"Go spla if you didn't. What's for dinner?"

"I thought you'd have cooked it."

"Waiting for the clone."

Feeling put upon, Pugh got out a dozen dinnerboxes, stuck two in the Instobake, pulled them out. "All right, here's dinner."

"Been thinking," Martin said, coming to table. "What if some clone cloned itself? Illegally. Made a thousand duplicates—ten thousand. Whole army. They could make a tidy power grab, couldn't they?"

"But how many millions did this lot cost to rear? Artificial placentae and all that. It would be hard to keep secret, unless they had a planet to themselves. . . . Back before the Famines when Earth had national governments, they talked about that: clone your best soldiers, have whole regiments of them. But the food ran out before they could play that game."

They talked amicably, as they used to do.

"Funny," Martin said, chewing. "They left early this morning, didn't they?"

"All but Kaph and Zayin. They thought they'd get the first payload above ground today. What's up?"

"They weren't back for lunch."

"They won't starve, to be sure."

"They left at seven."

"So they did." Then Pugh saw it. The air tanks held eight hours' supply.

"Kaph and Zayin carried out spare cans when they left. Or they've got a heap out there."

"They did, but they brought the whole lot in to recharge." Martin stood up, pointing to one of the stacks of stuff that cut the dome into rooms and alleys.

"There's an alarm signal on every imsuit."

"It's not automatic."

Pugh was tired and still hungry. "Sit down and eat, man. That lot can look after themselves."

Martin sat down but did not eat. "There was a big quake, Owen. The first one. Big enough it scared me."

After a pause Pugh sighed and said, "All right."

Unenthusiastically, they got out the two-man sled that was always left for them and headed it north. The long sunrise covered everything in poisonous red jello. The horizontal light and shadow made it hard to see, raised walls of fake iron ahead of them which they slid through, turned the convex plain beyond Hellmouth into a great dimple full of bloody water. Around the tunnel entrance a wilderness of machinery stood, cranes and cables and servos and wheels and diggers and robocarts and sliders and control huts, all slanting and bulking incoherently in the red light. Martin jumped from the sled, ran into the mine. He came out again, to Pugh. "Oh, God, Owen, it's down," he said. Pugh went in and saw, five meters from the entrance, the shiny moist, black wall that ended the tunnel. Newly exposed to air, it looked organic, like visceral tissue. The tunnel entrance, enlarged by blasting and double-tracked for robocarts, seemed unchanged until he noticed thousands of tiny spiderweb cracks in the walls. The floor was wet with some sluggish fluid.

"They were inside," Martin said.

"They may be still. They surely had extra air cans—"

"Look, Owen, look at the basalt flow, at the roof, don't you see what the quake did, look at it."

The low hump of land that roofed the caves still had the unreal look of an optical illusion. It had reversed itself, sunk down, leaving a vast dimple or pit. When Pugh walked on it he saw that it too was cracked with many tiny fissures. From some a whitish gas was seeping, so that the sunlight on the surface of the gas pool was shafted as if by the waters of a dim red lake.

"The mine's not on the fault. There's no fault here!"

Pugh came back to him quickly. "No, there's no fault, Martin— Look, they surely weren't all inside together."

Martin followed him and searched among the wrecked machines dully, then actively. He spotted the airsled. It had come down heading south, and stuck at an angle in a pot-hole of colloidal dust. It had carried two riders. One was half sunk in the dust, but his suit meters registered normal functioning; the other hung strapped onto the tilted sled. Her imsuit had burst open on the broken legs, and the body was frozen hard as any rock. That was all they found. As both regulation and custom demanded, they cremated the dead at once with the laser guns they carried by regulation and had never used before. Pugh, knowing he was going to be sick, wrestled the survivor onto the two-man sled and sent Martin off to the dome with him. Then he vomited and flushed the waste out of his suit, and finding one four-man sled undamaged, followed after Martin, shaking as if the cold of Libra had got through to him.

The survivor was Kaph. He was in deep shock. They found a swelling on the occiput that might mean concussion, but no fracture was visible.

Pugh brought two glasses of food concentrate and two chasers of aquavit. "Come on," he said. Martin obeyed, drinking off the tonic. They sat down on crates near the cot and sipped the aquavit.

Kaph lay immobile, face like beeswax, hair bright black to the shoulders, lips stiffly parted for faintly gasping breaths.

"It must have been the first shock, the big one," Martin said. "It must have slid the whole structure sideways. Till it fell in on itself. There must be gas layers in the lateral rocks, like those formations in the Thirty-first Quadrant. But there wasn't any sign—" As he spoke the world slid out from under them. Things leaped and clattered, hopped and jigged, shouted Ha! Ha! Ha! "It was like this at four-teen hours," said Reason shakily in Martin's voice, amidst the unfastening and ruin of the world. But Unreason sat up, as the tumult lessened and things ceased dancing, and screamed aloud.

Pugh leaped across his spilt aquavit and held Kaph down. The muscular body flailed him off. Martin pinned the shoulders down. Kaph screamed, struggled, choked; his face blackened. "Oxy," Pugh said, and his hand found the right needle in the medical kit as if by homing instinct; while Martin held the mask he struck the needle home to the vagus nerve, restoring Kaph to life.

"Didn't know you knew that stunt," Martin said, breath-ing hard.

"The Lazarus Jab, my father was a doctor. It doesn't often work," Pugh said. "I want that drink I spilled. Is the quake over? I can't tell."

"Aftershocks. It's not just you shivering."

"Why did he suffocate?"

"I don't know, Owen. Look in the book."

Kaph was breathing normally and his color was restored; only the lips were still darkened. They poured a new shot of courage and sat down by him again with their medical guide. "Nothing about cyanosis or asphyxiation under 'Shock' or 'Concussion.' He can't have breathed in anything with his suit on. I don't know. We'd get as much good out of *Mother Mog's Home Herbalist.* . . . 'Anal Hemorrhoids,' fy!" Pugh pitched the book to a crate table. It fell short, because either Pugh or the table was still unsteady.

"Why didn't he signal?"

"Sorry?"

"The eight inside the mine never had time. But he and the girl must have been outside. Maybe she was in the entrance and got hit by the first slide. He must have been outside, in the control hut maybe. He ran in, pulled her out, strapped her onto the sled, started for the dome. And all that time never pushed the panic button in his imsuit. Why not?"

"Well, he'd had that whack on his head. I doubt he ever realized the girl was dead. He wasn't in his senses. But if he had been I don't know if he'd have thought to signal us. They looked to one another for help."

Martin's face was like an Indian mask, grooves at the mouth corners, eyes of dull coal. "That's so. What must he have felt, then, when the quake came and he was outside, alone—"

In answer Kaph screamed.

He came off the cot in the heaving convulsions of one suffocating, knocked Pugh right down with his flailing arm, staggered into a stack of crates and fell to the floor, lips blue, eyes white. Martin dragged him back onto the cot and gave him a whiff of oxygen, then knelt by Pugh, who was sitting up, and wiped at his cut cheekbone. "Owen, are you all right, are you going to be all right, Owen?"

"I think I am," Pugh said. "Why are you rubbing that on my face?"

It was a short length of computer tape, now spotted with

Pugh's blood. Martin dropped it. "Thought it was a towel. You clipped your cheek on that box there."

"Is he out of it?"

"Seems to be."

They stared down at Kaph lying stiff, his teeth a white line inside dark parted lips.

"Like epilepsy. Brain damage maybe?"

"What about shooting him full of meprobamate?"

Pugh shook his head. "I don't know what's in that shot I already gave him for shock. Don't want to overdose him."

"Maybe he'll sleep it off now."

"I'd like to myself. Between him and the earthquake I can't seem to keep on my feet."

"You got a nasty crack there. Go on, I'll sit up awhile."

Pugh cleaned his cut cheek and pulled off his shirt, then paused.

"Is there anything we ought to have done—have tried to do—"

"They're all dead," Martin said heavily, gently.

Pugh lay down on top of his sleeping bag and one instant later was wakened by a hideous, sucking, struggling noise. He staggered up, found the needle, tried three times to jab it in correctly and failed, began to massage over Kaph's heart. "Mouth-to-mouth," he said, and Martin obeyed. Presently Kaph drew a harsh breath, his heartbeat steadied, his rigid muscles began to relax.

"How long did I sleep?"

"Half an hour."

They stood up sweating. The ground shuddered, the fabric of the dome sagged and swayed. Libra was dancing her awful polka again, her *Totentanz*. The sun, though rising, seemed to have grown larger and redder; gas and dust must have been stirred up in the feeble atmosphere.

"What's wrong with him, Owen?"

"I think he's dying with them."

"Them— But they're all dead, I tell you."

"Nine of them. They're all dead, they were crushed or suffocated. They were all him, he is all of them. They died, and now he's dying their deaths one by one."

"Oh, pity of God," said Martin.

The next time was much the same. The fifth time was worse, for Kaph fought and raved, trying to speak but getting no words out, as if his mouth were stopped with rocks or clay. After that the attacks grew weaker, but so did he. The eighth seizure came at about four-thirty; Pugh and Martin worked till five-thirty doing all they could to keep life in the body that slid without protest into death. They kept him, but Martin said, "The next will finish him." And it did; but Pugh breathed his own breath into the inert lungs, until he himself passed out.

He woke. The dome was opaqued and no light on. He listened and heard the breathing of two sleeping men. He slept, and nothing woke him till hunger did.

The sun was well up over the dark plains, and the planet had stopped dancing. Kaph lay asleep. Pugh and Martin drank tea and looked at him with proprietary triumph.

When he woke Martin went to him: "How do you feel, old man?" There was no answer. Pugh took Martin's place and looked into the brown, dull eyes that gazed toward but not into his own. Like Martin he quickly turned away. He heated food concentrate and brought it to Kaph. "Come on, drink."

He could see the muscles in Kaph's throat tighten. "Let me die," the young man said.

"You're not dying."

Kaph spoke with clarity and precision: "I am nine-tenths dead. There is not enough of me left alive."

That precision convinced Pugh, and he fought the conviction. "No," he said, peremptory. "They are dead. The others. Your brothers and sisters. You're not them, you're alive. You are John Chow. Your life is in your own hands."

The young man lay still, looking into a darkness that was not there.

Martin and Pugh took turns taking the Exploitation hauler and a spare set of robos over to Hellmouth to salvage equipment and protect it from Libra's sinister atmosphere, for the value of the stuff was, literally, astronomical. It was slow work for one man at a time, but they were unwilling to leave Kaph by himself. The one left in the dome did paperwork, while Kaph sat or lay and stared into his darkness and never spoke. The days went by, silent.

The radio spat and spoke: the Mission calling from the ship. "We'll be down on Libra in five weeks, Owen. Thirty-four E-days nine hours I make it as of now. How's tricks in the old dome?"

"Not good, chief. The Exploit team were killed, all but one of them, in the mine. Earthquake. Six days ago."

The radio crackled and sang starsong. Sixteen seconds' lag each way; the ship was out around Planet II now. "Killed, all but one? You and Martin were unhurt?"

"We're all right, chief."

Thirty-two seconds.

"*Passerine* left an Exploit team out here with us. I may put them on the Hellmouth project then, instead of the Quadrant Seven project. We'll settle that when we come down. In any case you and Martin will be relieved at Dome Two. Hold tight. Anything else?"

"Nothing else."

Thirty-two seconds.

"Right then. So long, Owen."

Kaph had heard all this, and later on Pugh said to him, "The chief may ask you to stay here with the other Exploit team. You know the ropes here." Knowing the exigencies of Far Out life, he wanted to warn the young man. Kaph made no answer. Since he had said, "There is not enough of me left alive," he had not spoken a word.

"Owen," Martin said on suit intercom, "he's spla. Insane. Psycho."

"He's doing very well for a man who's died nine times."

"Well? Like a turned-off android is well? The only emotion he has left is hate. Look at his eyes."

"That's not hate, Martin. Listen, it's true that he has, in a sense, been dead. I cannot imagine what he feels. But it's not hatred. He can't even see us. It's too dark."

"Throats have been cut in the dark. He hates us because we're not Aleph and Yod and Zayin."

"Maybe. But I think he's alone. He doesn't see us or hear us, that's the truth. He never had to see anyone else before. He never was alone before. He had himself to see, talk with, live with, nine other selves all his life. He doesn't know how you go it alone. He must learn. Give him time."

Martin shook his heavy head. "Spla," he said. "Just remember when you're alone with him that he could break your neck one-handed."

"He could do that," said Pugh, a short, soft-voiced man with a scarred cheekbone; he smiled. They were just outside the dome airlock, programming one of the servos to repair a damaged hauler. They could see Kaph sitting inside the great half-egg of the dome like a fly in amber.

"Hand me the insert pack there. What makes you think he'll get any better?"

"He has a strong personality, to be sure."

"Strong? Crippled. Nine-tenths dead, as he put it."

"But he's not dead. He's a live man: John Kaph Chow. He had a jolly queer upbringing, but after all every boy has got to break free of his family. He will do it."

"I can't see it."

"Think a bit, Martin bach. What's this cloning for? To repair the human race. We're in a bad way. Look at me. My IIQ and GC are half this John Chow's. Yet they wanted me so badly for the Far Out Service that when I volunteered they took me and fitted me out with an artificial lung and corrected my myopia. Now if there were enough good sound lads about would they be taking one-lunged short-sighted Welshmen?"

"Didn't know you had an artificial lung."

"I do then. Not tin, you know. Human, grown in a tank from a bit of somebody; cloned, if you like. That's how they make replacement organs, the same general idea as cloning, but bits and pieces instead of whole people. It's my own lung now, whatever. But what I am saying is this, there are too many like me these days and not enough like John Chow. They're trying to raise the level of the human genetic pool, which is a mucky little puddle since the population crash. So then if a man is cloned, he's a strong and clever man. It's only logic, to be sure."

Martin grunted; the servo began to hum.

Kaph had been eating little; he had trouble swallowing his food, choking on it, so that he would give up trying after a few bites. He had lost eight or ten kilos. After three weeks or so, however, his appetite began to pick up, and one day he began to look through the clone's possessions, the sleeping bags, kits, papers which Pugh had stacked neatly in a far angle of a packing-crate alley. He sorted, destroyed a heap of papers and oddments, made a small packet of what remained, then relapsed into his walking coma.

Two days later he spoke. Pugh was trying to correct a flutter in the tape-player and failing; Martin had the jet out, checking their maps of the Pampas. "Hell and damnation!"

Pugh said, and Kaph said in a toneless voice, "Do you want me to do that?"

Pugh jumped, controlled himself, and gave the machine to Kaph. The young man took it apart, put it back together, and left it on the table.

"Put on a tape," Pugh said with careful casualness, busy at another table.

Kaph put on the topmost tape, a chorale. He lay down on his cot. The sound of a hundred human voices singing together filled the dome. He lay still, his face blank.

In the next days he took over several routine jobs, unasked. He undertook nothing that wanted initiative, and if asked to do anything he made no response at all.

"He's doing well," Pugh said in the dialect of Argentina.

"He's not. He's turning himself into a machine. Does what he's programmed to do, no reaction to anything else. He's worse off than when he didn't function at all. He's not human any more."

Pugh sighed. "Well, good night," he said in English. "Good night, Kaph."

"Good night," Martin said; Kaph did not.

Next morning at breakfast Kaph reached across Martin's plate for the toast. "Why don't you ask for it?" Martin said with the geniality of repressed exasperation. "I can pass it."

"I can reach it," Kaph said in his flat voice.

"Yes, but look. Asking to pass things, saying good night or hello, they're not important, but all the same when somebody says something a person ought to answer. . . ."

The young man looked indifferently in Martin's direction; his eyes still did not seem to see clear through to the person he looked toward. "Why should I answer?"

"Because somebody has said something to you."

"Why?"

Martin shrugged and laughed. Pugh jumped up and turned on the rock-cutter.

Later on he said, "Lay off that, please, Martin."

"Manners are essential in small isolated crews, some kind of manners, whatever you work out together. He's been taught that, everybody in Far Out knows it. Why does he deliberately flout it?"

"Do you tell yourself good night?"

"So?"

"Don't you see Kaph's never known anyone but himself?"

Martin brooded and then broke out. "Then by God this cloning business is all wrong. It won't do. What are a lot of duplicate geniuses going to do for us when they don't even know we exist?"

Pugh nodded. "It might be wiser to separate the clones and bring them up with others. But they make such a grand team this way."

"Do they? I don't know. If this lot had been ten average inefficient E.T. engineers, would they all have got killed? What if, when the quake came and things started caving in, what if all those kids ran the same way, farther into the mine, maybe, to save the one who was farthest in? Even Kaph was outside and went in. . . . It's hypothetical. But I keep thinking, out of ten ordinary confused guys, more might have got out."

"I don't know. It's true that identical twins tend to die at about the same time, even when they have never seen each other. Identity and death, it is very strange. . . ."

The days went on, the red sun crawled across the dark sky, Kaph did not speak when spoken to, Pugh and Martin snapped at each other more frequently each day. Pugh complained of Martin's snoring. Offended, Martin moved his cot clear across the dome and also ceased speaking to

Pugh for some while. Pugh whistled Welsh dirges until Martin complained, and then Pugh stopped speaking for a while.

The day before the Mission ship was due, Martin announced he was going over to Merioneth.

"I thought at least you'd be giving me a hand with the computer to finish the rock analyses," Pugh said, aggrieved.

"Kaph can do that. I want one more look at the Trench. Have fun," Martin added in dialect, and laughed, and left.

"What is that language?"

"Argentinean. I told you that once, didn't I?"

"I don't know." After a while the young man added, "I have forgotten a lot of things, I think."

"It wasn't important, to be sure," Pugh said gently, realizing all at once how important this conversation was. "Will you give me a hand running the computer, Kaph?"

He nodded.

Pugh had left a lot of loose ends, and the job took them all day. Kaph was a good co-worker, quick and systematic, much more so than Pugh himself. His flat voice, now that he was talking again, got on the nerves; but it didn't matter, there was only this one day left to get through and then the ship would come, the old crew, comrades and friends.

During tea break Kaph said, "What will happen if the Explore ship crashes?"

"They'd be killed."

"To you, I mean."

"To us? We'd radio SOS signals and live on half rations till the rescue cruiser from Area Three Base came. Four and a half E-years away it is. We have life support here for three men for, let's see, maybe between four and five years. A bit tight, it would be."

"Would they send a cruiser for three men?"

"They would."

Kaph said no more.

"Enough cheerful speculations," Pugh said cheerfully, rising to get back to work. He slipped sideways and the chair avoided his hand; he did a sort of half-pirouette and fetched up hard against the dome hide. "My goodness," he said, reverting to his native idiom, "what is it?"

"Quake," said Kaph.

The teacups bounced on the table with a plastic cackle, a litter of papers slid off a box, the skin of the dome swelled and sagged. Underfoot there was a huge noise, half sound, half shaking, a subsonic boom.

Kaph sat unmoved. An earthquake does not frighten a man who died in an earthquake.

Pugh, white-faced, wiry black hair sticking out, a frightened man, said, "Martin is in the Trench."

"What trench?"

"The big fault line. The epicenter for the local quakes. Look at the seismograph." Pugh struggled with the stuck door of a still-jittering locker.

"Where are you going?"

"After him."

"Martin took the jet. Sleds aren't safe to use during quakes. They go out of control."

"For God's sake man, shut up."

Kaph stood up, speaking in a flat voice as usual. "It's unnecessary to go out after him now. It's taking an unnecessary risk."

"If his alarm goes off, radio me," Pugh said, shut the head-piece of his suit, and ran to the lock. As he went out Libra picked up her ragged skirts and danced a belly dance from under his feet clear to the red horizon.

Inside the dome, Kaph saw the sled go up, tremble like a meteor in the dull red daylight, and vanish to the northeast.

The hide of the dome quivered, the earth coughed. A vent south of the dome belched up a slow-flowing bile of black gas.

A bell shrilled and a red light flashed on the central control board. The sign under the light read Suit 2 and scribbled under that, A. G. M. Kaph did not turn the signal off. He tried to radio Martin, then Pugh, but got no reply from either.

When the aftershocks decreased he went back to work and finished up Pugh's job. It took him about two hours. Every half hour he tried to contact Suit 1 and got no reply, then Suit 2 and got no reply. The red light had stopped flashing after an hour.

It was dinnertime. Kaph cooked dinner for one and ate it. He lay down on his cot.

The aftershocks had ceased except for faint rolling tremors at long intervals. The sun hung in the west, oblate, pale red, immense. It did not sink visibly. There was no sound at all.

Kaph got up and began to walk about the messy, half-packed-up, overcrowded, empty dome. The silence continued. He went to the player and put on the first tape that came to hand. It was pure music, electronic, without harmonies, without voices. It ended. The silence continued.

Pugh's uniform tunic, one button missing, hung over a stack of rock samples. Kaph stared at it awhile.

The silence continued.

The child's dream: There is no one else alive in the world but me. In all the world.

Low, north of the dome, a meteor flickered.

Kaph's mouth opened as if he were trying to say something, but no sound came. He went hastily to the north wall and peered out into the gelatinous red light.

The little star came in and sank. Two figures blurred the

airlock. Kaph stood close beside the lock as they came in. Martin's imsuit was covered with some kind of dust so that he looked raddled and warty like the surface of Libra. Pugh had him by the arm.

"Is he hurt?"

Pugh shucked his suit, helped Martin peel off his. "Shaken up," he said, curt.

"A piece of cliff fell onto the jet," Martin said, sitting down at the table and waving his arms. "Not while I was in it though. I was parked, see, and poking about that carbon-dust area when I felt things humping. So I went out onto a nice bit of early igneous I'd noticed from above, good footing and out from under the cliffs. Then I saw this bit of the planet fall off onto the flyer, quite a sight it was, and after a while it occurred to me the spare aircans were in the flyer, so I leaned on the panic button. But I didn't get any radio reception, that's always happening here during quakes, so I didn't know if the signal was getting through either. And things went on jumping around and pieces of the cliff coming off. Little rocks flying around, and so dusty you couldn't see a meter ahead. I was really beginning to wonder what I'd do for breathing in the small hours, you know, when I saw old Owen buzzing up the Trench in all that dust and junk like a big ugly bat—"

"Want to eat?" said Pugh.

"Of course I want to eat. How'd you come through the quake here, Kaph? No damage? It wasn't a big one actually, was it, what's the seismo say? My trouble was I was in the middle of it. Old Epicenter Alvaro. Felt like Richter fifteen there—total destruction of planet—"

"Sit down," Pugh said. "Eat."

After Martin had eaten a little his spate of talk ran dry. He very soon went off to his cot, still in the remote angle where he had removed it when Pugh complained of his snoring. "Good night, you one-lunged Welshman," he said across the dome.

"Good night."

There was no more out of Martin. Pugh opaqued the dome, turned the lamp down to a yellow glow less than a candle's light, and sat doing nothing, saying nothing, withdrawn.

The silence continued.

"I finished the computations."

Pugh nodded thanks.

"The signal from Martin came through, but I couldn't contact you or him."

Pugh said with effort, "I should not have gone. He had two hours of air left even with only one can. He might have been heading home when I left. This way we were all out of touch with one another. I was scared."

The silence came back, punctuated now by Martin's long, soft snores.

"Do you love Martin?"

Pugh looked up with angry eyes: "Martin is my friend. We've worked together, he's a good man." He stopped. After a while he said, "Yes, I love him. Why did you ask that?"

Kaph said nothing, but he looked at the other man. His face was changed, as if he were glimpsing something he had not seen before; his voice too was changed. "How can you . . . How do you . . ."

But Pugh could not tell him. "I don't know," he said, "it's practice, partly. I don't know. We're each of us alone, to be sure. What can you do but hold your hand out in the dark?"

Kaph's strange gaze dropped, burned out by its own intensity.

"I'm tired," Pugh said. "That was ugly, looking for him

in all that black dust and muck, and mouths opening and
shutting in the ground. . . . I'm going to bed. The ship will
be transmitting to us by six or so." He stood up and
stretched.

"It's a clone," Kaph said. "The other Exploit Team
they're bringing with them."

"Is it then?"

"A twelveclone. They came out with us on the *Passerine*."

Kaph sat in the small yellow aura of the lamp seeming to
look past it at what he feared: the new clone, the multiple
self of which he was not part. A lost piece of a broken set, a
fragment, inexpert at solitude, not knowing even how you
go about giving love to another individual, now he must
face the absolute, closed self-sufficiency of the clone of
twelve; that was a lot to ask of the poor fellow, to be sure.
Pugh put a hand on his shoulder in passing. "The chief
won't ask you to stay here with a clone. You can go home.
Or since you're Far Out maybe you'll come on farther out
with us. We could use you. No hurry deciding. You'll make
out all right."

Pugh's quiet voice trailed off. He stood unbuttoning his
coat, stooped a little with fatigue. Kaph looked at him and
saw the thing he had never seen before, saw him: Owen
Pugh, the other, the stranger who held his hand out in the
dark.

"Good night," Pugh mumbled, crawling into his sleeping
bag and half asleep already, so that he did not hear Kaph
reply after a pause, repeating, across darkness, benediction.

Ursula K. Le Guin (1929–   )
A *Phi Beta Kappa graduate of Radcliffe College, Ursula K.
Le Guin is one of the most honored active science fiction and*

fantasy writers. In addition to three Nebula and four Hugo Awards, she is the recipient of a National Book Award and a Boston Globe–Horn Book Award. Her most famous works include The Left Hand of Darkness (1969), The Lathe of Heaven (1971), and The Dispossessed: An Ambiguous Utopia (1974). A number of her short stories appear in one volume titled The Wind's Twelve Quarters (1975). Ms. Le Guin is also a noted commentator on the science fiction field, and her The Language of the Night: Essays on Fantasy and Science Fiction (1979), edited by Susan Wood, is highly regarded.

PLANT BIOLOGY

ALIEN EARTH
Edmond Hamilton

Chapter 1 SLOWED-DOWN LIFE

The dead man was standing in a little moonlit clearing in the jungle when Farris found him.

He was a small swart man in white cotton, a typical Laos tribesman of this Indo-China hinterland. He stood without support, eyes open, staring unwinkingly ahead, one foot slightly raised. And he was not breathing.

"But he can't be dead!" Farris exclaimed. "Dead men don't stand around in the jungle."

He was interrupted by Piang, his guide. That cocksure little Annamese had been losing his impudent self-sufficiency ever since they had wandered off the trail. And the

motionless, standing dead man had completed his de-
moralization.

Ever since the two of them had stumbled into this grove
of silk-cotton trees and almost run into the dead man,
Piang had been goggling in a scared way at the still unmov-
ing figure. Now he burst out volubly:

"The man is *hunati!* Don't touch him! We must leave
here—we have strayed into a bad part of the jungle!"

Farris didn't budge. He had been a teak-hunter for too
many years to be entirely skeptical of the superstitions of
Southeast Asia. But, on the other hand, he felt a certain
responsibility.

"If this man isn't really dead, then he's in bad shape
somehow and needs help," he declared.

"No, no!" Piang insisted. "He is *hunati!* Let us leave
here quickly!"

Pale with fright, he looked around the moonlit grove.
They were on a low plateau where the jungle was monsoon-
forest rather than rain-forest. The big silk-cotton and ficus
trees were less choked with brush and creepers here, and
they could see along dim forest aisles to gigantic distant
banyans that loomed like dark lords of the silver silence.

Silence. There was too much of it to be quite natural.
They could faintly hear the usual clatter of birds and monkeys from down in the lowland thickets, and the cough of a
tiger echoed from the Laos foothills. But the thick forest
here on the plateau was hushed.

Farris went to the motionless, staring tribesman and
gently touched his thin brown wrist. For a few moments, he
felt no pulse. Then he caught its throb—an incredibly slow
beating.

"About one beat every two minutes," Farris muttered.
"How the devil can he keep living?"

He watched the man's bare chest. It rose—but so slowly that his eye could hardly detect the motion. It remained expanded for minutes. Then, as slowly, it fell again.

He took his pocket-light and flashed it into the tribesman's eyes.

There was no reaction to the light, not at first. Then, slowly, the eyelids crept down and closed, and stayed closed, and finally crept open again.

"A wink—but a hundred times slower than normal!" Farris exclaimed. "Pulse, respiration, reactions—they're all a hundred times slower. The man has either suffered a shock, or been drugged."

Then he noticed something that gave him a little chill.

The tribesman's eyeball seemed to be turning with infinite slowness toward him. And the man's raised foot was a little higher now. As though he were walking—but walking at a pace a hundred times slower than normal.

The thing was eery. There came something more eery. A sound—the sound of a small stick cracking.

Piang exhaled breath in a sound of pure fright, and pointed off into the grove. In the moonlight Farris saw.

There was another tribesman standing a hundred feet away. He, too, was motionless. But his body was bent forward in the attitude of a runner suddenly frozen. And beneath his foot, the stick had cracked.

"They worship the great ones, by the Change!" said the Annamese in a hoarse undertone. "We must not interfere!"

That decided Farris. He had, apparently, stumbled on some sort of weird jungle rite. And he had had too much experience with Asiatic natives to want to blunder into their private religious mysteries.

His business here in easternmost Indo-China was teak-hunting. It would be difficult enough back in this wild hinterland without antagonizing the tribes. These strangely dead-alive men, whatever drug or compulsion they were suffering from, could not be in danger if others were near.

"We'll go on," Farris said shortly.

Piang led hastily down the slope of the forested plateau. He went through the brush like a scared deer, till they hit the trail again.

"This is it—the path to the Government station," he said, in great relief. "We must have lost it back at the ravine. I have not been this far back in Laos many times."

Farris asked, "Piang, what is *hunati?* This Change that you were talking about?"

The guide became instantly less voluble. "It is a rite of worship." He added, with some return of his cocksureness, "These tribesmen are very ignorant. They have not been to mission school, as I have."

"Worship of what?" Farris asked. "The great ones, you said. Who are they?"

Piang shrugged and lied readily. "I do not know. In all the great forest, there are men who can become *hunati,* it is said. How, I do not know."

Farris pondered, as he tramped onward. There had been something uncanny about those tribesmen. It had been almost a suspension of animation—but not quite. Only an incredible slowing down.

What could have caused it? And what, possibly, could be the purpose of it?

"I should think," he said, "that a tiger or snake would make short work of a man in that frozen condition."

Piang shook his head vigorously. "No. A man who is *hunati* is safe—at least, from beasts. No beast would touch him."

Farris wondered. Was that because the extreme motionlessness made the beasts ignore them? He supposed that it was some kind of fear-ridden nature-worship. Such animistic beliefs were common in this part of the world. And it was small wonder, Farris thought a little grimly. Nature, here in the tropical forest, wasn't the smiling goddess of temperate lands. It was something, not to be loved, but to be feared.

He ought to know! He had had two days of the Laos jungle since leaving the upper Mekong, when he had expected that one would take him to the French Government botanic survey station that was his goal.

He brushed stinging winged ants from his sweating neck, and wished that they had stopped at sunset. But the map had showed them but a few miles from the Station. He had not counted on Piang losing the trail. But he should have, for it was only a wretched track that wound along the forested slope of the plateau.

The hundred-foot ficus, dyewood and silk-cotton trees smothered the moonlight. The track twisted constantly to avoid impenetrable bamboo-hells or to ford small streams, and the tangle of creepers and vines had a devilish deftness at tripping one in the dark.

Farris wondered if they had lost their way again. And he wondered, not for the first time, why he had ever left America to go into teak.

"That is the Station," said Piang suddenly, in obvious relief.

Just ahead of them on the jungled slope was a flat ledge. Light shone there, from the windows of a rambling bamboo bungalow.

Farris became conscious of all his accumulated weariness, as he went the last few yards. He wondered whether he could get a decent bed here, and what kind of chap this Berreau might be who had chosen to bury himself in such a Godforsaken post of the botanical survey.

The bamboo house was surrounded by tall, graceful dye-woods. But the moonlight showed a garden around it, enclosed by a low sappan hedge.

A voice from the dark veranda reached Farris and startled him. It startled him because it was a girl's voice, speaking in French.

"Please, Andre! Don't go again! It is madness!"

A man's voice rapped harsh answer, "Lys, tais-toi! Je reviendrai—"

Farris coughed diplomatically and then said up to the darkness of the veranda, "Monsieur Berreau?"

There was a dead silence. Then the door of the house was swung open so that light spilled out on Farris and his guide.

By the light, Farris saw a man of thirty, bareheaded, in whites—a thin, rigid figure. The girl was only a white blur in the gloom.

He climbed the steps. "I suppose you don't get many visitors. My name is Hugh Farris. I have a letter for you, from the Bureau at Saigon."

There was a pause. Then, "If you will come inside, M'sieu Farris—"

In the lamplit, bamboo-walled living room, Farris glanced quickly at the two.

Berreau looked to his experienced eye like a man who had stayed too long in the tropics—his blond handsomeness tarnished by a corroding climate, his eyes too feverishly restless.

"My sister, Lys," he said, as he took the letter Farris handed.

Farris' surprise increased. A wife, he had supposed until now. Why should a girl under thirty bury herself in this wilderness?

He wasn't surprised that she looked unhappy. She might

have been a decently pretty girl, he thought, if she didn't
have that woebegone anxious look.

"Will you have a drink?" she asked him. And then,
glancing with swift anxiety at her brother, "You'll not be
going now, Andre?"

Berreau looked out at the moonlit forest, and a queer,
hungry tautness showed his cheekbones in a way Farris
didn't like. But the Frenchman turned back.

"No, Lys. And drinks, please. Then tell Ahra to care for
his guide."

He read the letter swiftly, as Farris sank with a sigh into
a rattan chair. He looked up from it with troubled eyes.

"So you come for teak?"

Farris nodded. "Only to spot and girdle trees. They have
to stand a few years then before cutting, you know."

Berreau said, "The Commissioner writes that I am to
give you every assistance. He explains the necessity of
opening up new teak cuttings."

He slowly folded the letter. It was obvious, Farris
thought, that the man did not like it, but had to make the
best of orders.

"I shall do everything possible to help," Berreau prom-
ised. "You'll want a native crew, I suppose. I can get one
for you." Then a queer look filmed his eyes. "But there are
some forests here that are impracticable for lumbering. I'll
go into that later."

Farris, feeling every moment more exhausted by the
long tramp, was grateful for the rum and soda Lys handed
him.

"We have a small extra room—I think it will be comfortable," she murmured.

He thanked her. "I could sleep on a log, I'm so tired. My
muscles are as stiff as though I were *hunati* myself."

Berreau's glass dropped with a sudden crash.

Chapter 2 SORCERY OF SCIENCE

Ignoring the shattered glass, the young Frenchman strode quickly toward Farris.

"What do you know of *hunati?*" he asked harshly.

Farris saw with astonishment that the man's hands were shaking.

"I don't know anything except what we saw in the forest. We came upon a man standing in the moonlight who looked dead, and wasn't. He just seemed incredibly slowed down. Piang said he was *hunati*."

A flash crossed Berreau's eyes. He exclaimed, "I knew the Rite would be called! And the others are there—"

He checked himself. It was as though the unaccustomedness of strangers had made him for a moment forget Farris' presence.

Lys' blonde head drooped. She looked away from Farris.

"You were saying?" the American prompted.

But Berreau had tightened up. He chose his words now. "The Laos tribes have some queer beliefs, M'sieu Farris. They're a little hard to understand."

Farris shrugged. "I've seen some queer Asian witchcraft, in my time. But this is unbelievable!"

"It is science, not witchcraft," Berreau corrected. "Primitive science, born long ago and transmitted by tradition. That man you saw in the forest was under the influence of a chemical not found in our pharmacopeia, but none the less potent."

"You mean that these tribesmen have a drug that can slow the life-process to that incredibly slow tempo?" Farris asked skeptically. "One that modern science doesn't know about?"

"Is that so strange? Remember, M'sieu Farris, that a

century ago an old peasant woman in England was curing heart-disease with foxglove, before a physician studied her cure and discovered digitalis."

"But why on earth would even a Laos tribesman want to live so much *slower?*" Farris demanded.

"Because," Berreau answered, "they believe that in that state they can commune with something vastly greater than themselves."

Lys interrupted. "M'sieu Farris must be very weary. And his bed is ready."

Farris saw the nervous fear in her face, and realized that she wanted to end this conversation.

He wondered about Berreau, before he dropped off to sleep. There was something odd about the chap. He had been too excited about this *hunati* business.

Yet that was weird enough to upset anyone, that incredible and uncanny slowing-down of a human being's life-tempo. "To commune with something vastly greater than themselves," Berreau had said.

What gods were so strange that a man must live a hundred times slower than normal, to commune with them?

Next morning, he breakfasted with Lys on the broad veranda. The girl told him that her brother had already gone out.

"He will take you later today to the tribal village down in the valley, to arrange for your workers," she said.

Farris noted the faint unhappiness still in her face. She looked silently at the great, green ocean of forest that stretched away below this plateau on whose slope they were.

"You don't like the forest?" he ventured.

"I hate it," she said. "It smothers one, here."

Why, he asked, didn't she leave? The girl shrugged.

"I shall, soon. It is useless to stay. Andre will not go back with me."

She explained. "He has been here five years too long. When he didn't return to France, I came out to bring him. But he won't go. He has ties here now."

Again, she became abruptly silent. Farris discreetly refrained from asking her what ties she meant. There might be an Annamese woman in the background—though Berreau didn't look that type.

The day settled down to the job of being stickily tropical, and the hot still hours of the morning wore on. Farris, sprawling in a chair and getting a welcome rest, waited for Berreau to return.

He didn't return. And as the afternoon waned, Lys looked more and more worried.

An hour before sunset, she came out onto the veranda, dressed in slacks and jacket.

"I am going down to the village—I'll be back soon," she told Farris.

She was a poor liar. Farris got to his feet. "You're going after your brother. Where is he?"

Distress and doubt struggled in her face. She remained silent.

"Believe me, I want to be a friend," Farris said quietly. "Your brother is mixed up in something here, isn't he?"

She nodded, white-faced. "It's why he wouldn't go back to France with me. He can't bring himself to leave. It's like a horrible fascinating vice."

"What is?"

She shook her head. "I can't tell you. Please wait here."

He watched her leave, and then realized she was not going down the slope but up it—up toward the top of the forested plateau.

He caught up to her in quick strides. "You can't go up into that forest alone, in a blind search for him."

"It's not a blind search. I think I know where he is," Lys whispered. "But you should not go there. The tribesmen wouldn't like it!"

Farris instantly understood. "That big grove up on top of the plateau, where we found the *hunati* natives?"

Her unhappy silence was answer enough. "Go back to the bungalow," he told her. "I'll find him."

She would not do that. Farris shrugged, and started forward. "Then we'll go together."

She hesitated, then came on. They went up the slope of the plateau, through the forest.

The westering sun sent spears and arrows of burning gold through chinks in the vast canopy of foliage under which they walked. The solid green of the forest breathed a rank, hot exhalation. Even the birds and monkeys were stifledly quiet at this hour.

"Is Berreau mixed up in that queer *hunati* rite?" Farris asked.

Lys looked up as though to utter a quick denial, but then dropped her eyes.

"Yes, in a way. His passion for botany got him interested in it. Now he's involved."

Farris was puzzled. "Why should botanical interest draw a man to that crazy drug-rite or whatever it is?"

She wouldn't answer that. She walked in silence until they reached the top of the forested plateau. Then she spoke in a whisper.

"We must be quiet now. It will be bad if we are seen here."

The grove that covered the plateau was pierced by horizontal bars of red sunset light. The great silk-cottons and ficus trees were pillars supporting a vast cathedral-nave of darkening green.

A little way ahead loomed up those huge, monster banyans he had glimpsed before in the moonlight. They dwarfed all the rest, towering bulks that were infinitely ancient and infinitely majestic.

Farris suddenly saw a Laos tribesman, a small brown figure, in the brush ten yards ahead of him. There were two others, farther in the distance. And they were all standing quite still, facing away from him.

They were *hunati*, he knew. In that queer state of sloweddown life, that incredible retardation of the vital processes.

Farris felt a chill. He muttered over his shoulder, "You had better go back down and wait."

"No," she whispered. "There is Andre."

He turned, startled. Then he too saw Berreau.

His blond head bare, his face set and white and masklike, standing frozenly beneath a big wild-fig a hundred feet to the right.

Hunati!

Farris had expected it, but that didn't make it less shocking. It wasn't that the tribesmen mattered less as human beings. It was just that he had talked with a normal Berreau only a few hours before. And now, to see him like this!

Berreau stood in a position ludicrously reminiscent of the old-time "living statues." One foot was slightly raised, his body bent a little forward, his arms raised a little.

Like the frozen tribesmen ahead, Berreau was facing toward the inner recesses of the grove, where the giant banyans loomed.

Farris touched his arm. "Berreau, you have to snap out of this."

"It's no use to speak to him," whispered the girl. "He can't hear."

No, he couldn't hear. He was living at a tempo so low

that no ordinary sound could make sense to his ears. His face was a rigid mask, lips slightly parted to breathe, eyes fixed ahead. Slowly, slowly, the lids crept down and veiled those staring eyes and then crept open again in the infinitely slow wink. Slowly, slowly, his slightly raised left foot moved down toward the ground.

Movement, pulse, breathing—all a hundred times slower than normal. Living, but not in a human way—not in a human way at all.

Lys was not so stunned as Farris was. He realized later that she must have seen her brother like this, before.

"We must take him back to the bungalow, somehow," she murmured. "I can't let him stay out here for many days and nights, again!"

Farris welcomed the small practical problem that took his thoughts for a moment away from this frozen, standing horror.

"We can rig a stretcher, from our jackets," he said. "I'll cut a couple of poles."

The two bamboos, through the sleeves of the two jackets, made a makeshift stretcher which they laid upon the ground.

Farris lifted Berreau. The man's body was rigid, muscles locked in an effort no less strong because it was infinitely slow.

He got the young Frenchman down on the stretcher, and then looked at the girl. "Can you help carry him? Or will you get a native?"

She shook her head. "The tribesmen mustn't know of this. Andre isn't heavy."

He wasn't. He was light as though wasted by fever, though the sickened Farris knew that it wasn't any fever that had done it.

Why should a civilized young botanist go out into the

forest and partake of a filthy primitive drug of some kind
that slowed him down to a frozen stupor? It didn't make
sense.

Lys bore her share of their living burden through the
gathering twilight, in stolid silence. Even when they put
Berreau down at intervals to rest, she did not speak.

It was not until they reached the dark bungalow and had
put him down on his bed, that the girl sank into a chair and
buried her face in her hands.

Farris spoke with a rough encouragement he did not
feel. "Don't get upset. He'll be all right now. I'll soon bring
him out of this."

She shook her head. "No, you must not attempt that! He
must come out of it by himself. And it will take many
days."

The devil it would, Farris thought. He had teak to find,
and he needed Berreau to arrange for workers.

Then the dejection of the girl's small figure got him. He
patted her shoulder.

"All right, I'll help you take care of him. And together,
we'll pound some sense into him and make him go back
home. Now you see about dinner."

She lit a gasoline lamp, and went out. He heard her
calling the servants.

He looked down at Berreau. He felt a little sick, again.
The Frenchman lay, eyes staring toward the ceiling. He
was living, breathing—and yet his retarded life-tempo cut
him off from Farris as effectually as death would.

No, not quite. Slowly, so slowly that he could hardly
detect the movement, Berreau's eyes turned toward Farris'
figure.

Lys came back into the room. She was quiet, but he was
getting to know her better, and he knew by her face that
she was startled.

"The servants are gone! Ahra, and the girls—and your guide. They must have seen us bring Andre in."

Farris understood. "They left because we brought back a man who's *hunati?*"

She nodded. "All the tribespeople fear the rite. It's said there's only a few who belong to it, but they're dreaded."

Farris spared a moment to curse softly the vanished Annamese. "Piang would bolt like a scared rabbit, from something like this. A sweet beginning for my job here."

"Perhaps you had better leave," Lys said uncertainly. Then she added contradictorily, "No, I can't be heroic about it! Please stay!"

"That's for sure," he told her. "I can't go back down river and report that I shirked my job because of—"

He stopped, for she wasn't listening to him. She was looking past him, toward the bed.

Farris swung around. While they two had been talking, Berreau had been moving. Infinitely slowly—but moving.

His feet were on the floor now. He was getting up. His body straightened with a painful, dragging slowness, for many minutes.

Then his right foot began to rise almost imperceptibly from the floor. He was starting to walk, only a hundred times slower than normal.

He was starting to walk toward the door.

Lys' eyes had a yearning pity in them. "He is trying to go back up to the forest. He will try so long as he is *hunati.*"

Farris gently lifted Berreau back to the bed. He felt a cold dampness on his forehead.

What was there up there that drew worshippers in a strange trance of slowed-down life?

Chapter 3   UNHOLY LURE

He turned to the girl and asked, "How long will he stay in this condition?"

"A long time," she answered heavily. "It may take weeks for the *hunati* to wear off."

Farris didn't like the prospect, but there was nothing he could do about it.

"All right, we'll take care of him. You and I."

Lys said, "One of us will have to watch him, all the time. He will keep trying to go back to the forest."

"You've had enough for a while," Farris told her. "I'll watch him tonight."

Farris watched. Not only that night but for many nights. The days went into weeks, and the natives still shunned the house, and he saw nobody except the pale girl and the man who was living in a different way than other humans lived.

Berreau didn't change. He didn't seem to sleep, nor did he seem to need food or drink. His eyes never closed, except in that infinitely slow blinking.

He didn't sleep, and he did not quit moving. He was always moving, only it was in that weird, utterly slow-motion tempo that one could hardly see.

Lys had been right. Berreau wanted to go back to the forest. He might be living a hundred times slower than normal, but he was obviously still conscious in some weird way, and still trying to go back to the hushed, forbidden forest up there where they had found him.

Farris wearied of lifting the statute-like figure back into bed, and with the girl's permission tied Berreau's ankles. It did not make things much better. It was even more upsetting, in a way, to sit in the lamplit bedroom and watch Berreau's slow struggles for freedom.

The dragging slowness of each tiny movement made Farris' nerves twitch to see. He wished he could give Berreau some sedative to keep him asleep, but he did not dare to do that.

He had found, on Berreau's forearm, a tiny incision stained with sticky green. There were scars of other, old incisions near it. Whatever crazy drug had been injected into the man to make him *hunati* was unknown. Farris did not dare try to counteract its effect.

Finally, Farris glanced up one night from his bored perusal of an old *L'Illustration* and then jumped to his feet.

Berreau still lay on the bed, but he had just winked. Had winked with normal quickness, and not that slow, dragging blink.

"Berreau!" Farris said quickly. "Are you all right now? Can you hear me?"

Berreau looked up at him with a level, unfriendly gaze. "I can hear you. May I ask why you meddled?"

It took Farris aback. He had been playing nurse so long that he had unconsciously come to think of the other as a sick man who would be grateful to him. He realized now that Berreau was coldly angry, not grateful.

The Frenchman was untying his ankles. His movements were shaky, his hands trembling, but he stood up normally.

"Well?" he asked.

Farris shrugged. "Your sister was going up there after you. I helped her bring you back. That's all."

Berreau looked a little startled. "Lys did that? But it's a breaking of the Rite! It can mean trouble for her!"

Resentment and raw nerves made Farris suddenly brutal. "Why should you worry about Lys now, when you've made her wretched for months by your dabbling in native wizardries?"

Berreau didn't retort angrily, as he had expected. The young Frenchman answered heavily.

"It's true. I've done that to Lys."

Farris exclaimed, "Berreau, why do you do it? Why this unholy business of going *hunati*, of living a hundred times slower? What can you gain by it?"

The other man looked at him with haggard eyes. "By doing it, I've entered an alien world. A world that exists around us all our lives, but that we never live in or understand at all."

"What world?"

"The world of green leaf and root and branch," Berreau answered. "The world of plant life, which we can never comprehend because of the difference between its life-tempo and our life-tempo."

Farris began dimly to understand. "You mean, this *hunati* change makes you live at the same tempo as plants?"

Berreau nodded. "Yes. And that simple difference in life-tempo is the doorway into an unknown, incredible world."

"But how?"

The Frenchman pointed to the half-healed incision on his bare arm. "The drug does it. A native drug, that slows down metabolism, heart-action, respiration, nerve-messages, everything.

"Chlorophyll is its basis. The green blood of plant-life, the complex chemical that enables plants to take their energy direct from sunlight. The natives prepare it directly from grasses, by some method of their own."

"I shouldn't think," Farris said incredulously, "that chlorophyll could have any effect on an animal organism."

"Your saying that," Berreau retorted, "shows that your biochemical knowledge is out of date. Back in March of 1948, two Chicago chemists engaged in mass production or extraction of chlorophyll, announced that their injection of it into dogs and rats seemed to prolong life greatly by altering the oxidation capacity of the cells.

"Prolong life greatly—yes! But it prolongs it, by slowing it down! A tree lives longer than a man, because it doesn't live so fast. You can make a man live as long—*and as slowly*—as a tree, by injecting the right chlorophyll compound into his blood."

Farris said, "That's what you meant, by saying that primitive peoples sometimes anticipate modern scientific discoveries?"

Berreau nodded. "This chlorophyll *hunati* solution may be an age-old secret. I believe it's always been known to a few among the primitive forest-folk of the world."

He looked somberly past the American. "Tree-worship is as old as the human race. The Sacred Tree of Sumeria, the groves of Dodona, the oaks of the Druids, the tree Ygdrasil of the Norse, even our own Christmas Tree—they all stem from primitive worship of that other, alien kind of life with which we share Earth.

"I think that a few secret worshippers have always known how to prepare the chlorophyll drug that enabled them to attain complete communion with that other kind of life, by living at the same slow rate for a time."

Farris stared. "But how did you get taken into this queer secret worship?"

The other man shrugged. "The worshippers were grateful to me, because I had saved the forests here from possible death."

He walked across to the corner of the room that was fitted as a botanical laboratory, and took down a test-tube. It was filled with dusty, tiny spores of a leprous, gray-green color.

"This is the Burmese Blight, that's withered whole great

forests down south of the Mekong. A deadly thing, to tropical trees. It was starting to work up into this Laos country,
but I showed the tribes how to stop it. The secret *hunati*
sect made me one of them, in reward."

"But I still can't understand why an educated man like
you would want to join such a crazy mumbo-jumbo," Farris said.

"*Dieu*, I'm trying to make you understand why! To show
you that it was my curiosity as a botanist that made me join
the Rite and take the drug!"

Berreau rushed on. "But you can't understand, any more
than Lys could! You can't comprehend the wonder and
strangeness and beauty of living that other kind of life!"

Something in Berreau's white, rapt face, in his haunted
eyes, made Farris' skin crawl. His words seemed momen-
tarily to lift a veil, to make the familiar vaguely strange and
terrifying.

"Berreau, listen! You've got to cut this and leave here at
once."

The Frenchman smiled mirthlessly. "I know. Many
times, I have told myself so. But I do not go. How can I
leave something that is a botanist's heaven?"

Lys had come into the room, was looking wanly at her
brother's face.

"Andre, won't you give it up and go home with me?" she
appealed.

"Or are you too sunken in this uncanny habit to care
whether your sister breaks her heart?" Farris demanded.

Berreau flared. "You're a smug pair! You treat me like a
drug addict, without knowing the wonder of the experience
I've had! I've gone into another world, an alien Earth that
is around us every day of our lives and that we can't even
see. And I'm going back again, and again."

"Use that chlorophyll drug and go *hunati* again?" Farris said grimly.

Berreau nodded defiantly.

"No," said Farris. "You're not. For if you do, we'll just go out there and bring you in again. You'll be quite helpless to prevent us, once you're *hunati*."

The other man raged. "There's a way I can stop you from doing that! Your threats are dangerous!"

"There's no way," Farris said flatly. "Once you've frozen yourself into that slower life-tempo, you're helpless against normal people. And I'm not threatening. I'm trying to save your sanity, man!"

Berreau flung out of the room without answer. Lys looked at the American, with tears glimmering in her eyes.

"Don't worry about it," he reassured her. "He'll get over it, in time."

"I fear not," the girl whispered. "It has become a madness in his brain."

Inwardly, Farris agreed. Whatever the lure of the unknown world that Berreau had entered by that change in life-tempo, it had caught him beyond all redemption.

A chill swept Farris when he thought of it—men out there, living at the same tempo as plants, stepping clear out of the plane of animal life to a strangely different kind of life and world.

The bungalow was oppressively silent that day—the servants gone, Berreau sulking in his laboratory, Lys moving about with misery in her eyes.

But Berreau didn't try to go out, though Farris had been expecting that and had been prepared for a clash. And by evening, Berreau seemed to have got over his sulks. He helped prepare dinner.

He was almost gay, at the meal—a febrile good humor that Farris didn't quite like. By common consent, none of the three spoke of what was uppermost in their minds.

Berreau retired, and Farris told Lys, "Go to bed—you've lost so much sleep lately you're half asleep now. I'll keep watch."

In his own room, Farris found drowsiness assailing him too. He sank back in a chair, fighting the heaviness that weighed down his eyelids.

Then, suddenly, he understood. "Drugged!" he exclaimed, and found his voice little more than a whisper. "Something in the dinner!"

"Yes," said a remote voice. "Yes, Farris."

Berreau had come in. He loomed gigantic to Farris' blurred eyes. He came closer, and Farris saw in his hand a needle that dripped sticky green.

"I'm sorry, Farris." He was rolling up Farris' sleeve, and Farris could not resist. "I'm sorry to do this to you and Lys. But you *would* interfere. And this is the only way I can keep you from bringing me back."

Farris felt the sting of the needle. He felt nothing more, before drugged unconsciousness claimed him.

Chapter 4 INCREDIBLE WORLD

Farris awoke, and for a dazed moment wondered what it was that so bewildered him. Then he realized.

It was the daylight. It came and went, every few minutes. There was the darkness of night in the bedroom, and then a sudden burst of dawn, a little period of brilliant sunlight, and then night again.

It came and went, as he watched numbly, like the slow, steady beating of a great pulse—a systole and diastole of light and darkness.

Days shortened to minutes? But how could that be? And
then, as he awakened fully, he remembered.

"*Hunati!* He injected the chlorophyll drug into my blood-
stream!"

Yes. He was *hunati*, now. Living at a tempo a hundred
times slower than normal.

And that was why day and night seemed a hundred times
faster than normal, to him. He had, already, lived through
several days!

Farris stumbled to his feet. As he did so, he knocked
his pipe from the arm of the chair.

It did not fall to the floor. It just disappeared instantly,
and the next instant was lying on the floor.

"It fell. But it fell so fast I couldn't see it."

Farris felt his brain reel to the impact of the unearthly.
He found that he was trembling violently.

He fought to get a grip on himself. This wasn't witchcraft. It was a secret and devilish science, but it wasn't
supernatural.

He, himself, felt as normal as ever. It was his surroundings, the swift rush of day and night especially, that alone
told him he was changed.

He heard a scream, and stumbled out to the living-room
of the bungalow. Lys came running toward him.

She still wore her jacket and slacks, having obviously
been too worried about her brother to retire completely.
And there was terror in her face.

"What's happened?" she cried. "The light—"

He took her by the shoulders. "Lys, don't lose your
nerve. What's happened is that we're *hunati* now. Your
brother did it—drugged us at dinner, then injected the
chlorophyll compound into us."

"But why?" she cried.

"Don't you see? He was going *hunati* himself again,

going back up to the forest. And we could easily overtake and bring him back, if we remained normal. So he changed us too, to prevent that."

Farris went into Berreau's room. It was as he had expected. The Frenchman was gone.

"I'll go after him," he said tightly. "He's got to come back, for he may have an antidote to that hellish stuff. You wait here."

Lys clung to him. "No! I'd go mad, here by myself, like this."

She was, he saw, on the brink of hysterics. He didn't wonder. The slow, pulsing beat of day and night alone was enough to unseat one's reason.

He acceded. "All right. But wait till I get something."

He went back to Berreau's room and took a big bolo-knife he had seen leaning in a corner. Then he saw something else, something glittering in the pulsing light, on the botanist's laboratory-table.

Farris stuffed that into his pocket. If force couldn't bring Berreau back, the threat of this other thing might influence him.

He and Lys hurried out onto the veranda and down the steps. And then they stopped, appalled.

The great forest that loomed before them was now a nightmare sight. It seethed and stirred with unearthly life—great branches clawing and whipping at each other as they fought for the light, vines writhing through them at incredible speed, a rustling uproar of tossing, living plant-life.

Lys shrank back. "The forest is *alive* now!"

"It's just the same as always," Farris reassured. "It's we who have changed—who are living so slowly now that the plants seem to live faster."

"And Andre is out in that!" Lys shuddered. Then courage came back into her pale face. "But I'm not afraid."

They started up through the forest toward the plateau of giant trees. And now there was an awful unreality about this incredible world.

Farris felt no difference in himself. There was no sensation of slowing down. His own motions and perceptions appeared normal. It was simply that all around him the vegetation had now a savage motility that was animal in its swiftness.

Grasses sprang up beneath his feet, tiny green spears climbing toward the light. Buds swelled, burst, spread their bright petals on the air, breathed out their fragrance—and died.

New leaves leaped joyously up from every twig, lived out their brief and vital moment, withered and fell. The forest was a constantly shifting kaleidoscope of colors, from pale green to yellowed brown, that rippled as the swift tides of growth and death washed over it.

But it was not peaceful or serene, that life of the forest. Before, it had seemed to Farris that the plants of the earth existed in a placid inertia utterly different from the beasts, who must constantly hunt or be hunted. Now he saw how mistaken he had been.

Close by, a tropical nettle crawled up beside a giant fern. Octopus-like, its tendrils flashed around and through the plant. The fern writhed. Its fronds tossed wildly, its stalks strove to be free. But the stinging death conquered it.

Lianas crawled like great serpents among the trees, encircling the trunks, twining themselves swiftly along the branches, striking their hungry parasitic roots into the living bark.

And the trees fought them. Farris could see how the branches lashed and struck against the killer vines. It was like watching a man struggle against the crushing coils of the python.

Very likely. Because the trees, the plants, knew. In their

own strange, alien fashion, they were as sentient as their swifter brothers.

Hunter and hunted. The strangling lianas, the deadly, beautiful orchid that was like a cancer eating a healthy trunk, the leprous, crawling fungi—they were the wolves and the jackals of this leafy world.

Even among the trees, Farris saw, existence was a grim and never-ending struggle. Silk-cotton and bamboo and ficus trees—they too knew pain and fear and the dread of death.

He could hear them. Now, with his aural nerves slowed to an incredible receptivity, he heard the voice of the forest, the true voice that had nothing to do with the familiar sounds of wind in the branches.

The primal voice of birth and death that spoke before ever man appeared on Earth, and would continue to speak after he was gone.

At first he had been conscious only of that vast, rustling uproar. Now he could distinguish separate sounds—the thin screams of grass blades and bamboo-shoots thrusting and surging out of the earth, the lash and groan of enmeshed and dying branches, the laughter of young leaves high in the sky, the stealthy whisper of the coiling vines.

And almost, he could hear thoughts, speaking in his mind. The age-old thoughts of the trees.

Farris felt a freezing dread. He did not want to listen to the thoughts of the trees.

And the slow, steady pulsing of darkness and light went on. Days and nights, rushing with terrible speed over the *hunati*.

Lys, stumbling along the trail beside him, uttered a little cry of terror. A snaky black vine had darted out of the brush at her with cobra swiftness, looping swiftly to encircle her body.

Farris swung his bolo, slashed through the vine. But it struck out again, growing with that appalling speed, its tip groping for him.

He slashed again with sick horror, and pulled the girl onward, on up the side of the plateau.

"I am afraid!" she gasped. "I can hear the thoughts— the thoughts of the forest!"

"It's your own imagination!" he told her. "Don't listen!"

But he too could hear them! Very faintly, like sounds just below the threshold of hearing. It seemed to him that every minute—or every minute-long day—he was able to get more clearly the telepathic impulses of these organisms that lived an undreamed-of life of their own, side by side with man, yet forever barred from him, except when man was *hunati*.

It seemed to him that the temper of the forest had changed, that his slaying of the vine had made it aware of them. Like a crowd aroused to anger, the massed trees around them grew wrathful. A tossing and moaning rose among them.

Branches struck at Farris and the girl, lianas groped with blind heads and snakelike grace toward them. Brush and bramble clawed them spitefully, reaching out thorny arms to rake their flesh. The slender saplings lashed them like leafy whips, the swift-growing bamboo spears sought to block their path, canes clattering together as if in rage.

"It's only in our own minds!" he said to the girl. "Because the forest is living at the same rate as we, we imagine it's aware of us."

He had to believe that, he knew. He had to, because when he quit believing it there was only black madness.

"No!" cried Lys. "No! The forest knows we are here."

Panic fear threatened Farris' self-control, as the mad uproar of the forest increased. He ran, dragging the girl with him, sheltering her with his body from the lashing of the raging forest.

They ran on, deeper into the mighty grove upon the plateau, under the pulsing rush of day and darkness. And now the trees about them were brawling giants, great silk-cotton and ficus that struck crashing blows at each other as their branches fought for clear sky—contending and terrible leafy giants beneath which the two humans were pigmies.

But the lesser forest beneath them still tossed and surged with wrath, still plucked and tore at the two running humans. And still, and clearer, stronger, Farris' reeling mind caught the dim impact of unguessable telepathic impulses.

Then, drowning all those dim and raging thoughts, came vast and dominating impulses of greater majesty, thought-voices deep and strong and alien as the voice of primal Earth.

"Stop them!" they seemed to echo in Farris' mind. "Stop them! Slay them! For they are our enemies!"

Lys uttered a trembling cry. "Andre!"

Farris saw him, then. Saw Berreau ahead, standing in the shadow of the monster banyans there. His arms were upraised toward those looming colossi, as though in worship. Over him towered the leafy giants, dominating all the forest.

"Stop them! Slay them!"

They thundered, now, those majestic thought-voices that Farris' mind could barely hear. He was closer to them— closer—

He knew, then, even though his mind refused to admit the knowledge. Knew whence those mighty voices came, and why Berreau worshipped the banyans.

And surely they were godlike, these green colossi who had lived for ages, whose arms reached skyward and whose aerial roots drooped and stirred and groped like hundreds of hands!

Farris forced that thought violently away. He was a man, of the world of men, and he must not worship alien lords.

Berreau had turned toward them. The man's eyes were hot and raging, and Farris knew even before Berreau spoke that he was no longer altogether sane.

"Go, both of you!" he ordered. "You were fools, to come here after me! You killed as you came through the forest, and the forest knows!"

"Berreau, listen!" Farris appealed. "You've got to go back with us, forget this madness!"

Berreau laughed shrilly. "Is it madness that the Lords even now voice their wrath against you? You hear it in your mind, but you are afraid to listen! Be afraid, Farris! There is reason! You have slain trees, for many years, as you have just slain here—and the forest knows you for a foe."

"Andre!" Lys was sobbing, her face half-buried in her hands.

Farris felt his mind cracking under the impact of the crazy scene. The ceaseless, rushing pulse of light and darkness, the rustling uproar of the seething forest around them, the vines creeping snakelike and branches whipping at them and giant banyans rocking angrily overhead.

"This is the world that man lives in all his life, and never sees or senses!" Berreau was shouting. "I've come into it, again and again. And each time, I've heard more clearly the voices of the Great Ones!

"The oldest and mightiest creatures on our planet! Long ago, men knew that and worshipped them for the wisdom they could teach. Yes, worshipped them as Ygdrasil and the Druid Oak and the Sacred Tree! But modern men have forgotten this other Earth. Except me, Farris—except me! I've found wisdom in this world such as you never dreamed. And your stupid blindness is not going to drag me out of it!"

Farris realized then that it was too late to reason with Berreau. The man had come too often and too far into this other Earth that was as alien to humanity as though it lay across the universe.

It was because he had feared that, that he had brought the little thing in his jacket pocket. The one thing with which he might force Berreau to obey.

Farris took it out of his pocket. He held it up so that the other could see it.

"You know what it is, Berreau! And you know what I can do with it, if you force me to!"

Wild dread leaped into Berreau's eyes as he recognized that glittering little vial from his own laboratory.

"The Burmese Blight! You wouldn't, Farris! You wouldn't turn that loose *here!*"

"I will!" Farris said hoarsely. "I will, unless you come out of here with us, now!"

Raging hate and fear were in Berreau's eyes as he stared at that innocent corked glass vial of gray-green dust.

He said thickly, "For this, I will kill!"

Lys screamed. Black lianas had crept upon her as she stood with her face hidden in her hands. They had writhed around her legs like twining serpents, they were pulling her down.

The forest seemed to roar with triumph. Vine and branch and bramble and creeper surged toward them. Dimly thunderous throbbed the strange telepathic voices.

"Slay them!" said the trees.

Farris leaped into that coiling mass of vines, his bolo

slashing. He cut loose the twining lianas that held the girl, sliced fiercely at the branches that whipped wildly at them.

Then, from behind, Berreau's savage blow on his elbow knocked the bolo from his hand.

"I told you not to kill, Farris! I told you!"

"Slay them!" pulsed the alien thought.

Berreau spoke, his eyes not leaving Farris. "Run, Lys. Leave the forest. This—murderer must die."

He lunged as he spoke, and there was death in his white face and clutching hands.

Farris was knocked back, against one of the giant banyan trunks. They rolled, grappling. And already the vines were sliding around them—looping and enmeshing them, tightening upon them!

It was then that the forest shrieked.

A cry telepathic and auditory at the same time—and dreadful. An utterance of alien agony beyond anything human.

Berreau's hands fell away from Farris. The Frenchman, enmeshed with him by the coiling vines, looked up in horror.

Then Farris saw what had happened. The little vial, the vial of the blight, had smashed against the banyan trunk as Berreau charged.

And that little splash of gray-green mould was rushing through the forest faster than flame! The blight, the gray-green killer from far away, propagating itself with appalling rapidity! "*Dieu!*" screamed Berreau. "*Non—non—*"

Even normally, a blight seems to spread swiftly. And to Farris and the other two, slowed down as they were, this blight was a raging cold fire of death.

It flashed up trunks and limbs and aerial roots of the

majestic banyans, eating leaf and spore and bud. It ran triumphantly across the ground, over vine and grass and shrub, bursting up other trees, leaping along the airy bridges of lianas.

And it leaped among the vines that enmeshed the two men! In mad death-agonies the creepers writhed and tightened.

Farris felt the musty mould in his mouth and nostrils, felt the constriction of steel cables crushing the life from him. The world seemed to darken—

Then a steel blade hissed and flashed, and the pressure loosened. Lys' voice was in his ears, Lys' hand trying to drag him from the dying, tightening creepers that she had partly slashed through. He wrenched free. "My brother!" she gasped.

With the bolo he sliced clumsily through the mass of dying writhing snake-vines that still enmeshed Berreau.

Berreau's face appeared, as he tore away the slashed creepers. It was dark purple, rigid, his eyes staring and dead. The tightening vines had caught him around the throat, strangling him.

Lys knelt beside him, crying wildly. But Farris dragged her to her feet.

"We have to get out of here! He's dead—but I'll carry his body!"

"No, leave it," she sobbed. "Leave it here, in the forest."

Dead eyes, looking up at the death of the alien world of life into which he had now crossed, forever! Yes, it was fitting.

Farris' heart quailed as he stumbled away with Lys through the forest that was rocking and raging in its death-throes.

Far away around them, the gray-green death was leaping

on. And fainter, fainter, came the strange telepathic cries that he would never be sure he had really heard.

"We die, brothers! We die!"

And then, when it seemed to Farris that sanity must give way beneath the weight of alien agony, there came a sudden change.

The pulsing rush of alternate day and night lengthened in tempo. Each period of light and darkness was longer now, and longer—

Out of a period of dizzying semi-consciousness, Farris came back to awareness. They were standing unsteadily in the blighted forest, in bright sunlight.

And they were no longer *hunati*.

The chlorophyll drug had spent its force in their bodies, and they had come back to the normal tempo of human life.

Lys looked up dazedly, at the forest that now seemed static, peaceful, immobile—and in which the gray-green blight now crept so slowly they could not see it move.

"The same forest, and it's still writhing in death!" Farris said huskily. "But now that we're living at normal speed again, we can't see it!"

"Please, let us go!" choked the girl. "Away from here, at once!"

It took but an hour to return to the bungalow and pack what they could carry, before they took the trail toward the Mekong.

Sunset saw them out of the blighted area of the forest, well on their way toward the river.

"Will it kill all the forest?" whispered the girl.

"No. The forest will fight back, come back, conquer the blight, in time. A long time, by our reckoning—years, decades. But to *them*, that fierce struggle is raging on even now."

And as they walked on, it seemed to Farris that still in his mind there pulsed faintly from far behind that alien, throbbing cry.

"We die, brothers!"

He did not look back. But he knew that he would not come back to this or any other forest, and that his profession was ended, and that he would never kill a tree again.

Edmond Hamilton (1904–77)

Edmond Hamilton was one of the great pioneers of American magazine science fiction, publishing his first story in Amazing in 1928. During the early part of his long career he was known as "World Wrecker Hamilton" because many of his stories featured battles between planetary systems. During the early 1940's he wrote most of the stories in the famous Captain Future series. His wife was the noted science fiction writer Leigh Brackett, who edited The Best of Edmond Hamilton (1977).

ECOLOGY

GRANDPA
James H. Schmitz

A green-winged downy thing as big as a hen fluttered along the hillside to a point directly above Cord's head and hovered there, twenty feet above him. Cord, a fifteen-year-old human being, leaned back against a skipboat parked on the equator of a world that had known human beings for only the past four Earth-years, and eyed the thing speculatively. The thing was, in the free and easy terminology of the Sutang Colonial Team, a swamp bug. Concealed in the downy fur behind the bug's head was a second, smaller, semi-parasitical thing, classed as a bug rider.

The bug itself looked like a new species to Cord. Its parasite might or might not turn out to be another unknown. Cord was a natural research man; his first glimpse of the odd flying team had sent endless curiosities thrilling through him. How did that particular phenomenon tick, and *why*? What fascinating things, once you'd learned about it, could you get it to *do*?

Normally, he was hampered by circumstances in carrying out any such investigation. Junior colonial students like Cord were expected to confine their curiosity to the pattern of research set up by the station to which they were attached. Cord's inclination towards independent experiments had got him into disfavour with his immediate superiors before this.

He sent a casual glance in the direction of the Yoger Bay Colonial Station behind him. No signs of human activity about that low, fortress-like bulk in the hill. Its central lock was still closed. In fifteen minutes, it was scheduled to be opened to let out the Planetary Regent, who was inspecting the Yoger Bay Station and its principal activities today.

Fifteen minutes was time enough to find out something about the new bug, Cord decided.

But he'd have to collect it first.

He slid out one of the two handguns holstered at his side. This one was his own property: a Vanadian projectile weapon. Cord thumbed it to position for anaesthetic small-game missiles and brought the hovering swamp bug down, drilled neatly and microscopically through the head.

As the bug hit the ground, the rider left its back. A tiny scarlet demon, round and bouncy as a rubber ball, it shot towards Cord in three long hops, mouth wide to sink home inch-long, venom-dripping fangs. Rather breathlessly, Cord triggered the gun again and knocked it out in mid-leap. A new species, all right! Most bug riders were harmless plant-eaters, mere suckers of vegetable juice—

"*Cord!*" A feminine voice.

Cord swore softly. He hadn't heard the central lock click open. She must have come around from the other side of the station.

"Hello, Grayan!" he shouted innocently without looking round. "Come and see what I've got! New species!"

Grayan Mahoney, a slender, black-haired girl two years older than himself, came trotting down the hillside towards him. She was Sutang's star colonial student, and the station manager, Nirmond, indicated from time to time that she was a fine example for Cord to pattern his own behaviour on. In spite of that, she and Cord were good friends.

"Cord, you idiot," she scowled as she came up. "Stop playing the collector! If the Regent came out now, you'd be sunk. Nirmond's been telling her about you!"

"Telling her what?" Cord asked, startled.

"For one thing," Grayan reported, "that you don't keep up on your assigned work."

"Golly!" gulped Cord, dismayed.

"Golly is right! I keep warning you!"

"What'll I do?"

"Start acting as if you had good sense mainly." Grayan grinned suddenly. "But if you mess up our tour of the Bay Farms today you'll be off the Team for good!"

She turned to go. "You might as well put the skipboat back; we're not using it. Nirmond's driving us down to the edge of the bay in a treadcar, and we'll take a raft from there."

Leaving his newly bagged specimens to revive by themselves and flutter off again, Cord hurriedly flew the skipboat around the station and rolled it back into its stall.

Three rafts lay moored just offshore in the marshy cove at the edge of which Nirmond had stopped the treadcar.

They looked somewhat like exceptionally broad-brimmed, well-worn sugarloaf hats floating out there, green and leathery. Or like lily pads twenty-five feet across, with the upper section of a big, grey-green pineapple growing from the centre of each. Plant animals of some sort. Sutang was too new to have had its phyla sorted out into anything remotely like an orderly classification. The rafts were a local oddity which had been investigated and could be regarded as harmless and moderately useful. Their usefulness lay in the fact that they were employed as a rather slow means of transportation about the shallow, swampy waters of the Yoger Bay. That was as far as the Team's interest in them went at present.

The Regent stood up from the back seat of the car, where she was sitting next to Cord. There were only four in the party; Grayan was up front with Nirmond.

"Are those our vehicles?" The Regent sounded amused.

Nirmond grinned. "Don't underestimate them, Dane! They could become an important economic factor in this region in time. But, as a matter of fact, these three are smaller than I like to use." He was peering about the reedy edges of the cove. "There's a regular monster parked here usually—"

Grayan turned to Cord. "Maybe Cord knows where Grandpa is hiding."

It was well meant, but Cord had been hoping nobody would ask him about Grandpa. Now they all looked at him.

"Oh, you want Grandpa?" he said, somewhat flustered. "Well, I left him . . . I mean I saw him a couple of weeks ago about a mile south from here—"

Nirmond grunted and told the Regent, "The rafts tend to stay wherever they're left, providing it's shallow and muddy. They use a hair-root system to draw chemicals and microscopic nourishment directly from the bottom of the bay. Well—Grayan, would you like to drive us there?"

Cord settled back unhappily as the treadcar lurched into motion. Nirmond suspected he'd used Grandpa for one of his unauthorized tours of the area, and Nirmond was quite right.

"I understand you're an expert with these rafts, Cord," Dane said from beside him. "Grayan told me we couldn't find a better steersman, or pilot, or whatever you call it, for our trip today."

"I can handle them," Cord said, perspiring. "They don't give you any trouble!" He didn't feel he'd made a good impression on the Regent so far. Dane was a young, hand-some-looking woman with an easy way of talking and laughing, but she wasn't the head of the Sutang Colonial Team for nothing.

"There's one big advantage our beasties have over a skipboat, too," Nirmond remarked from the front seat. "You don't have to worry about a snapper trying to climb on board with you!" He went on to describe the stinging ribbon-tentacles the rafts spread around them under water to discourage creatures that might make a meal off their tender underparts. The snappers and two or three other active and aggressive species of the bay hadn't yet learned it was foolish to attack armed human beings in a boat, but they would skitter hurriedly out of the path of a leisurely perambulating raft.

Cord was happy to be ignored for the moment. The Regent, Nirmond, and Grayan were all Earth people, which was true of most of the members of the Team; and Earth people made him uncomfortable, particularly in groups. Vanadia, his own home world, had barely graduated from the status of Earth colony itself, which might explain the difference.

The treadcar swung around and stopped, and Grayan stood up in the front seat, pointing. "That's Grandpa, over there!"

Dane also stood up and whistled softly, apparently impressed by Grandpa's fifty-foot spread. Cord looked around in surprise. He was pretty sure this was several hundred yards from the spot where he'd left the big raft two weeks ago; and, as Nirmond said, they didn't usually move about by themselves.

Puzzled, he followed the others down a narrow path to the water, hemmed in by tree-sized reeds. Now and then he got a glimpse of Grandpa's swimming platform, the rim of which just touched the shore. Then the path opened out, and he saw the whole raft lying in sunlit, shallow water; and he stopped short, startled.

Nirmond was about to step up on the platform, ahead of Dane.

"Wait!" Cord shouted. His voice sounded squeaky with alarm. "Stop!"

He came running forward.

"What's the matter, Cord?" Nirmond's voice was quiet and urgent.

"Don't get on that raft—it's changed!" Cord's voice sounded wobbly, even to himself. "Maybe it's not even Grandpa—"

He saw he was wrong on the last point before he'd finished the sentence. Scattered along the rim of the raft were discoloured spots left by a variety of heat-guns, one of which had been his own. It was the way you goaded the sluggish and mindless things into motion. Cord pointed at the cone-shaped central projection. "There—his head! He's sprouting!"

Grandpa's head, as befitted his birth, was almost twelve feet high and equally wide. It was armour-plated like the

back of a saurian to keep off plant suckers, but two weeks
ago it had been an otherwise featureless knob, like those on
all other rafts. Now scores of long, kinky, leafless vines had
grown out from all surfaces of the cone, like green wires.
Some were drawn up like tightly coiled springs, others
trailed limply to the platform and over it. The top of the
cone was dotted with angry red buds, rather like pimples,
which hadn't been there before either. Grandpa looked un-
healthy.

"Well," Nirmond said, "so it is. Sprouting!" Grayan
made a choked sound. Nirmond glanced at Cord as if puzzled. "Is that all that was bothering you, Cord?"

"Well, sure!" Cord began excitedly. He had caught the
significance of the word "all"; his hackles were still up, and
he was shaking. "None of them ever—"

Then he stopped. He could tell by their faces that they
hadn't got it. Or, rather, that they'd got it all right but
simply weren't going to let it change their plans. The rafts
were classified as harmless, according to the Regulations.
Until proved otherwise, they would continue to be regarded as harmless. You didn't waste time quibbling with
the Regulations—even if you were the Planetary Regent.
You didn't feel you had the time to waste.

He tried again. "Look—" he began. What he wanted to
tell them was that Grandpa with one unknown factor
added wasn't Grandpa any more. He was an unpredictable,
oversized life form, to be investigated with cautious thor-
oughness till you knew what the unknown factor meant. He
stared at them helplessly.

Dane turned to Nirmond. "Perhaps you'd better check,"
she said. She didn't add, "to reassure the boy!" but that was
what she meant.

Cord felt himself flushing. But there was nothing he
could say or do now except watch Nirmond walk steadily

across the platform. Grandpa shivered slightly a few times, but the rafts always did that when someone first stepped on them. The station manager stopped before one of the kinky sprouts, touched it and then gave it a tug. He reached up and poked at the lowest of the bud-like growths. "Odd-looking things!" he called back. He gave Cord another glance. "Well, everything seems harmless enough, Cord. Coming aboard, everyone?"

It was like dreaming a dream in which you yelled and yelled at people and couldn't make them hear you! Cord stepped up stiff-legged on the platform behind Dane and Grayan. He knew exactly what would have happened if he'd hesitated even a moment. One of them would have said in a friendly voice, careful not to let it sound contemptuous: "You don't have to come along if you don't want to, Cord!"

Grayan had unholstered her heat-gun and was ready to start Grandpa moving out into the channels of the Yoger Bay.

Cord hauled out his own heat-gun and said roughly, "I was to do that!"

"All right, Cord." She gave him a brief, impersonal smile and stood aside.

They were so infuriatingly polite!

For a while, Cord almost hoped that something awesome and catastrophic would happen promptly to teach the Team people a lesson. But nothing did. As always, Grandpa shook himself vaguely and experimentally when he felt the heat on one edge of the platform and then decided to withdraw from it, all of which was standard procedure. Under the water, out of sight, were the raft's working sections: short, thick leaf-structures shaped like paddles and designed to work as such, along with the slimy nettle-streamers which kept the vegetarians of the Yoger Bay away, and a jungle of hair roots through which Grandpa sucked nourishment from the mud and the sluggish waters of the bay and with which he also anchored himself.

The paddles started churning, the platform quivered, the hair roots were hauled out of the mud; and Grandpa was on his ponderous way.

Cord switched off the heat, reholstered his gun, and stood up. Once in motion, the rafts tended to keep travelling unhurriedly for quite a while. To stop them, you gave them a touch of heat along their leading edge; and they could be turned in any direction by using the gun lightly on the opposite side of the platform. It was simple enough.

Cord didn't look at the others. He was still burning inside. He watched the reed beds move past and open out, giving him glimpses of the misty, yellow and green and blue expanses of the brackish bay ahead. Behind the mist, to the west, were the Yoger Straits, tricky and ugly water when the tides were running; and beyond the Straits lay the open sea, the great Zlanti Deep, which was another world entirely and one of which he hadn't seen much as yet.

Grayan called from beside Dane, "What's the best route from here into the farms, Cord?"

"The big channel to the right," he answered. He added somewhat sullenly, "We're headed for it!"

Grayan came over to him. "The Regent doesn't want to see all of it," she said, lowering her voice. "The algae and plankton beds first. Then as much of the mutated grains as we can show her in about three hours. Steer for the ones that have been doing best, and you'll keep Nirmond happy!"

She gave him a conspiratorial wink. Cord looked after her uncertainly. You couldn't tell from her behaviour that anything was wrong. Maybe—

He had a flare of hope. It was hard not to like the Team people, even when they were being rock-headed about their

Regulations. Anyway, the day wasn't over yet. He might still redeem himself in the Regent's opinion.

Cord had a sudden cheerful, if improbable, vision of some bay monster plunging up on the raft with snapping jaws; and of himself alertly blowing out what passed for the monster's brains before anyone else—Nirmond, in particular—was even aware of the threat. The bay monsters shunned Grandpa, of course, but there might be ways of tempting one of them.

So far, Cord realized, he'd been letting his feelings control him. It was time to start thinking!

Grandpa first. So he'd sprouted—green vines and red buds, purpose unknown, but with no change observable in his behaviour-patterns otherwise. He was the biggest raft in this end of the bay, though all of them had been growing steadily in the two years since Cord had first seen one. Sutang's seasons changed slowly; its year was somewhat more than five Earth-years long. The first Team members to land here hadn't yet seen a full year pass.

Grandpa, then, was showing a seasonal change. The other rafts, not quite so far developed, would be reacting similarly a little later. Plant animals—they might be blossoming, preparing to propagate.

"Grayan," he called, "how do the rafts get started? When they're small, I mean."

"Nobody knows yet," she said. "We were just talking about it. About half of the coastal marsh-fauna of the continent seems to go through a preliminary larval stage in the sea." She nodded at the red buds on the raft's cone. "It looks as if Grandpa is going to produce flowers and let the wind or tide take the seeds out through the Straits."

It made sense. It also knocked out Cord's still half-held hope that the change in Grandpa might turn out to be drastic enough, in some way, to justify his reluctance to get

on board. Cord studied Grandpa's armoured head carefully
once more—unwilling to give up that hope entirely. There
were a series of vertical gummy black slits between the
armour plates, which hadn't been in evidence two weeks
ago either. It looked as if Grandpa were beginning to come
apart at the seams. Which might indicate that the rafts, big
as they grew to be, didn't outlive a full seasonal cycle, but
came to flower at about this time of Sutang's year, and
died. However, it was a safe bet that Grandpa wasn't going
to collapse into senile decay before they completed their
trip today.

Cord gave up on Grandpa. The other notion returned to
him—perhaps he *could* coax an obliging bay monster into
action that would show the Regent he was no sissy!

Because the monsters were there all right.

Kneeling at the edge of the platform and peering down
into the wine-coloured, clear water of the deep channel
they were moving through, Cord could see a fair selection
of them at almost any moment.

Some five or six snappers, for one thing. Like big, flattened crayfish, chocolate-brown mostly, with green and red
spots on their carapaced backs. In some areas they were so
thick you'd wonder what they found to live on, except that
they ate almost anything, down to chewing up the mud in
which they squatted. However, they preferred their food in
large chunks and alive, which was one reason you didn't go
swimming in the bay. They would attack a boat on occasion; but the excited manner in which the ones he saw were
scuttling off towards the edges of the channel showed they
wanted nothing to do with a big moving raft.

Dotted across the bottom were two-foot round holes
which looked vacant at the moment. Normally, Cord knew,
there would be a head filling each of those holes. The heads
consisted mainly of triple sets of jaws, held open patiently

like so many traps to grab at anything that came within range of the long wormlike bodies behind the heads. But Grandpa's passage, waving his stingers like transparent pennants through the water, had scared the worms out of sight, too.

Otherwise, mostly schools of small stuff—and then a flash of wicked scarlet, off to the left behind the raft, darting out from the reeds, turning its needle-nose into their wake.

Cord watched it without moving. He knew that creature, though it was rare in the bay and hadn't been classified. Swift, vicious—alert enough to snap swamp bugs out of the air as they fluttered across the surface. And he'd tantalized one with fishing tackle once into leaping up on a moored raft, where it had flung itself about furiously until he was able to shoot it.

"What fantastic creatures!" Dane's voice just behind him.

"Yellowheads," said Nirmond. "They've got a high utility rating. Keep down the bugs."

Cord stood up casually. It was no time for tricks! The reed bed to their right was thick with Yellowheads, a colony of them. Vaguely froggy things, man-sized and better. Of all the creatures he'd discovered in the bay, Cord liked them least. The flabby, sack-like bodies clung with four thin limbs to the upper section of the twenty-foot reeds that lined the channel. They hardly ever moved, but their huge bulging eyes seemed to take in everything that went on about them. Every so often, a downy swamp bug came close enough; and a Yellowhead would open its vertical, enormous, tooth-lined slash of a mouth, extend the whole front of its face like a bellows in a flashing strike; and the bug would be gone. They might be useful, but Cord hated them.

"Ten years from now we should know what the cycle of

coastal life is like," Nirmond said. "When we set up the Yoger Bay Station there were no Yellowheads here. They came the following year. Still with traces of the oceanic larval form; but the metamorphosis was almost complete. About twelve inches long—"

Dane remarked that the same pattern was duplicated endlessly elsewhere. The Regent was inspecting the Yellowhead colony with field glasses; she put them down now, looked at Cord, and smiled. "How far to the farms?"

"About twenty minutes."

"The key," Nirmond said, "seems to be the Zlanti Basin. It must be almost a soup of life in spring."

"It is," nodded Dane, who had been here in Sutang's spring, four Earth-years ago. "It's beginning to look as if the Basin alone might justify colonization. The question is still"—she gestured towards the Yellowheads—"how do creatures like that get there?"

They walked off towards the other side of the raft, arguing about ocean currents. Cord might have followed. But something splashed back of them, off to the left and not too far back. He stayed, watching.

After a moment, he saw the big Yellowhead. It had slipped down from its reedy perch, which was what had caused the splash. Almost submerged at the water line, it stared after the raft with huge, pale-green eyes. To Cord, it seemed to look directly at him. In that moment, he knew for the first time why he didn't like Yellowheads. There was something very like intelligence in that look, an alien calculation. In creatures like that, intelligence seemed out of place. What use could they have for it?

A little shiver went over him when it sank completely under the water and he realized it intended to swim after the raft. But it was mostly excitement. He had never seen a

Yellowhead come down out of the reeds before. The obliging monster he'd been looking for might be presenting itself
in an unexpected way.

Half a minute later, he watched it again, swimming
awkwardly far down. It had no immediate intention of
boarding, at any rate. Cord saw it come into the area of the
raft's trailing stingers. It manœuvred its way between them,
with curiously human swimming motions, and went out of
sight under the platform.

He stood up, wondering what it meant. The Yellowhead
had appeared to know about the stingers; there had been
an air of purpose in every move of its approach. He was
tempted to tell the others about it, but there was the moment of triumph he could have if it suddenly came slob-
bering up over the edge of the platform and he nailed it
before their eyes.

It was almost time anyway to turn the raft in towards the
farms. If nothing happened before then—

He watched. Almost five minutes, but no sign of the
Yellowhead. Still wondering, a little uneasy, he gave
Grandpa a calculated needling of heat.

After a moment, he repeated it. Then he drew a deep
breath and forgot all about the Yellowhead.

"Nirmond!" he called sharply.

The three of them were standing near the centre of the
platform, next to the big armoured cone, looking ahead at
the farms. They glanced around.

"What's the matter now, Cord?"

Cord couldn't say it for a moment. He was suddenly,
terribly scared again. Something *had* gone wrong!

"The raft won't turn!" he told them.

"Give it a real burn this time!" Nirmond said.

Cord glanced up at him. Nirmond, standing a few steps
in front of Dane and Grayan as if he wanted to protect

them, had begun to look a little strained, and no wonder. Cord already had pressed the gun to three different points on the platform; but Grandpa appeared to have developed a sudden anaesthesia for heat. They kept moving out steadily towards the centre of the bay.

Now Cord held his breath, switched the heat on full, and let Grandpa have it. A six-inch patch on the platform blistered up instantly, turned brown, then black—

Grandpa stopped dead. Just like that.

"That's right! Keep burn—" Nirmond didn't finish his order.

A giant shudder. Cord staggered back towards the water. Then the whole edge of the raft came curling up behind him and went down again, smacking the bay with a sound like a cannon shot. He flew forward off his feet, hit the platform face down, and flattened himself against it. It swelled up beneath him. Two more enormous slaps and joltings. Then quiet. He looked round for the others.

He lay within twelve feet of the central cone. Some twenty or thirty of the mysterious new vines the cone had sprouted were stretched stiffly towards him now, like so many thin green fingers. They couldn't quite reach him. The nearest tip was still ten inches from his shoes.

But Grandpa had caught the others, all three of them. They were tumbled together at the foot of the cone, wrapped in a stiff network of green vegetable ropes, and they didn't move.

Cord drew his feet up cautiously, prepared for another earthquake reaction. But nothing happened. Then he discovered that Grandpa was back in motion on his previous course. The heat-gun had vanished. Gently, he took out the Vanadian gun.

A voice, thin and pain-filled, spoke to him from one of the three huddled bodies.

"Cord? It didn't get you?" It was the Regent.

"No," he said, keeping his voice low. He realized suddenly he'd simply assumed they were all dead. Now he felt sick and shaky.

"What are you doing?"

Cord looked at Grandpa's big, armour-plated head with a certain hunger. The cones were hollowed out inside, the station's lab had decided their chief function was to keep enough air trapped under the rafts to float them. But in that central section was also the organ that controlled Grandpa's overall reactions.

He said softly, "I have a gun and twelve heavy-duty explosive bullets. Two of them will blow that cone apart."

"No good, Cord!" the pain-racked voice told him. "If the thing sinks, we'll die anyway. You have anaesthetic charges for that gun of yours?"

He stared at her back. "Yes."

"Give Nirmond and the girl a shot each, before you do anything else. Directly into the spine, if you can. But don't come any closer—"

Somehow, Cord couldn't argue with that voice. He stood up carefully. The gun made two soft spitting sounds.

"All right," he said hoarsely. "What do I do now?"

Dane was silent a moment. "I'm sorry, Cord, I can't tell you that. I'll tell you what I can—"

She paused for some seconds again.

"This thing didn't try to kill us, Cord. It could have easily. It's incredibly strong. I saw it break Nirmond's legs. But as soon as we stopped moving, it just held us. They were both unconscious then—

"You've got that to go on. It was trying to pitch you within reach of its vines or tendrils, or whatever they are, too, wasn't it?"

"I think so," Cord said shakily. That was what had happened, of course; and at any moment Grandpa might try again.

"Now it's feeding us some sort of anaesthetic of its own through those vines. Tiny thorns. A sort of numbness—" Dane's voice trailed off a moment. Then she said clearly, "Look, Cord—it seems we're food it's storing up! You get that?"

"Yes," he said.

"Seeding time for the rafts. There are analogues. Live food for its seed probably; not for the raft. One couldn't have counted on that. Cord?"

"Yes, I'm here."

"I want," said Dane, "to stay awake as long as I can. But there's really just one other thing—this raft's going somewhere, to some particularly favourable location. And that might be very near shore. You might make it in then; otherwise it's up to you. But keep your head and wait for a chance. No heroics, understand?"

"Sure, I understand," Cord told her. He realized then that he was talking reassuringly, as if it wasn't the Planetary Regent but someone like Grayan.

"Nirmond's the worst," Dane said. "The girl was knocked unconscious at once. If it weren't for my arm—but, if we can get help in five hours or so, everything should be all right. Let me know if anything happens, Cord."

"I will," Cord said gently again. Then he sighted his gun carefully at a point between Dane's shoulder-blades, and the anaesthetic chamber made its soft, spitting sound once more. Dane's taut body relaxed slowly, and that was all.

There was no point Cord could see in letting her stay awake; because they weren't going anywhere near shore. The reed beds and the channels were already behind them, and Grandpa hadn't changed direction by the fraction of a degree. He was moving out into the open bay—and he was picking up company!

So far, Cord could count seven big rafts within two miles of them; and on the three that were closest he could make out a sprouting of new green vines. All of them were travelling in a straight direction; and the common point they were all headed for appeared to be the roaring centre of the Yoger Straits, now some three miles away!

Behind the Straits, the cold Zlanti Deep—the rolling fogs, and the open sea! It might be seeding time for the rafts, but it looked as if they weren't going to distribute their seeds in the bay. . . .

Cord was a fine swimmer. He had a gun and he had a knife; in spite of what Dane had said, he might have stood a chance among the killers of the bay. But it would be a very small chance, at best. And it wasn't, he thought, as if there weren't still other possibilities. He was going to keep his head.

Except by accident, of course, nobody was going to come looking for them in time to do any good. If anyone did look, it would be around the Bay Farms. There were a number of rafts moored there; and it would be assumed they'd used one of them. Now and then something unexpected happened and somebody simply vanished; by the time it was figured out just what had happened on this occasion, it would be much too late.

Neither was anybody likely to notice within the next few hours that the rafts had started migrating out of the swamps through the Yoger Straits. There was a small weather-station a little inland, on the north side of the Straits, which used a helicopter occasionally. It was about as improbable, Cord decided dismally, that they'd use it in the right spot just now as it would be for a jet transport to happen to come in low enough to spot them.

The fact that it was up to him, as the Regent had said, sank in a little more after that!

Simply because he was going to try it sooner or later, he carried out an experiment next that he knew couldn't work. He opened the gun's anaesthetic chamber and counted out fifty pellets—rather hurriedly because he didn't particularly want to think of what he might be using them for eventually. There were around three hundred charges left in the chamber, then; and in the next few minutes Cord carefully planted a third of them in Grandpa's head.

He stopped after that. A whale might have showed signs of somnolence under a lesser load. Grandpa paddled on undisturbed. Perhaps he had become a little numb in spots, but his cells weren't equipped to distribute the soporific effect of that type of drug.

There wasn't anything else Cord could think of doing before they reached the Straits. At the rate they were moving, he calculated that would happen in something less than an hour; and if they did pass through the Straits he was going to risk a swim. He didn't think Dane would have disapproved, under the circumstances. If the raft simply carried them all out into the foggy vastness of the Zlanti Deep, there would be no practical chance of survival left at all.

Meanwhile, Grandpa was definitely picking up speed. And there were other changes going on—minor ones, but still a little awe-inspiring to Cord. The pimply-looking red buds that dotted the upper part of the cone were opening out gradually. From the centre of most of them protruded something like a thin, wet, scarlet worm: a worm that twisted weakly, extended itself by an inch or so, rested, and twisted again, and stretched up a little farther, groping into the air. The vertical black slits between the armour plates looked deeper and wider than they had been even some minutes ago; a dark, thick liquid dripped slowly from several of them.

In other circumstances Cord knew he would have been fascinated by these developments in Grandpa. As it was, they drew his suspicious attention only because he didn't know what they meant.

Then something quite horrible happened suddenly. Grayan started moaning loudly and terribly and twisted almost completely around. Afterwards, Cord knew it hadn't been a second before he stopped her struggles and the sounds together with another anaesthetic pellet; but the vines had tightened their grip on her first, not flexibly but like the digging, bony, green talons of some monstrous bird of prey.

White and sweating, Cord put his gun down slowly while the vines relaxed again. Grayan didn't seem to have suffered any additional harm; and she would certainly have been the first to point out that his murderous rage might have been as intelligently directed against a machine. But for some moments Cord continued to luxuriate furiously in the thought that, at any instant he chose, he could still turn the raft very quickly into a ripped and exploded mess of sinking vegetation.

Instead, and more sensibly, he gave both Dane and Nirmond another shot, to prevent a similar occurrence with them. The contents of two such pellets, he knew, would keep any human being torpid for at least four hours.

Cord withdrew his mind hastily from the direction it was turning into; but it wouldn't stay withdrawn. The thought kept coming up again, until at last he had to recognize it.

Five shots would leave the three of them completely unconscious, whatever else might happen to them, until they either died from other causes or were given a counteracting agent.

Shocked, he told himself he couldn't do it. It was exactly like killing them.

But then, quite steadily, he found himself raising the gun once more, to bring the total charge for each of the three Team people up to five.

Barely thirty minutes later, he watched a raft as big as the one he rode go sliding into the foaming white waters of the Straits a few hundred yards ahead, and dart off abruptly at an angle, caught by one of the swirling currents. It pitched and spun, made some headway, and was swept aside again. And then it righted itself once more. Not like some blindly animated vegetable, Cord thought, but like a creature that struggled with intelligent purpose to maintain its chosen direction.

At least, they seemed practically unsinkable. . . .

Knife in hand, he flattened himself against the platform as the Straits roared just ahead. When the platform jolted and tilted up beneath him, he rammed the knife all the way into it and hung on. Cold water rushed suddenly over him, and Grandpa shuddered like a labouring engine. In the middle of it all, Cord had the horrified notion that the raft might release its unconscious human prisoners in its struggle with the Straits. But he underestimated Grandpa in that. Grandpa also hung on.

Abruptly, it was over. They were riding a long swell, and there were three other rafts not far away. The Straits had swept them together, but they seemed to have no interest in one another's company. As Cord stood up shakily and began to strip off his clothes, they were visibly drawing apart again. The platform of one of them was half-submerged; it must have lost too much of the air that held it afloat and, like a small ship, it was foundering.

From this point, it was only a two-mile swim to the shore north of the Straits, and another mile inland from there to the Straits Head Station. He didn't know about the current; but the distance didn't seem too much, and he couldn't bring himself to leave knife and gun behind. The bay creatures loved warmth and mud; they didn't venture beyond the Straits. But Zlanti Deep bred its own killers, though they weren't often observed so close to shore.

Things were beginning to look rather hopeful.

Thin, crying voices drifted overhead, like the voices of curious cats, as Cord knotted his clothes into a tight bundle, shoes inside. He looked up. There were four of them circling there; magnified sea-going swamp bugs, each carrying an unseen rider. Probably harmless scavengers—but the ten-foot wingspread was impressive. Uneasily, Cord remembered the venomously carnivorous rider he'd left lying beside the station.

One of them dipped lazily and came sliding down towards him. It soared overhead and came back, to hover about the raft's cone.

The bug rider that directed the mindless flier hadn't been interested in him at all! Grandpa was baiting it!

Cord stared in fascination. The top of the cone was alive now with a softly wriggling mass of the scarlet, worm-like extrusions that had started sprouting before the raft left the bay. Presumably, they looked enticingly edible to the bug rider.

The flier settled with an airy fluttering and touched the cone. Like a trap springing shut, the green vines flashed up and around it, crumpling the brittle wings, almost vanishing into the long, soft body!

Barely a second later, Grandpa made another catch, this

one from the sea itself. Cord had a fleeting glimpse of something like a small, rubbery seal that flung itself out of the water upon the edge of the raft, with a suggestion of desperate haste—and was flipped on instantly against the cone where the vines clamped it down beside the flier's body.

It wasn't the enormous ease with which the unexpected kill was accomplished that left Cord standing there, completely shocked. It was the shattering of his hopes to swim ashore from here. Fifty yards away, the creature from which the rubbery thing had been fleeing showed briefly on the surface, as it turned away from the raft; and that glance was all he needed. The ivory-white body and gaping jaws were similar enough to those of the sharks of Earth to indicate the pursuer's nature. The important difference was that, wherever the White Hunters of the Zlanti Deep went, they went by the thousands.

Stunned by that incredible piece of bad luck, still clutching his bundled clothes, Cord stared towards shore. Knowing what to look for, he could spot the tell-tale rollings of the surface now—the long, ivory gleams that flashed through the swells and vanished again. Shoals of smaller things burst into the air in sprays of glittering desperation, and fell back.

He would have been snapped up like a drowning fly before he'd covered a twentieth of that distance!

Grandpa was beginning to eat.

Each of the dark slits down the sides of the cone was a mouth. So far only one of them was in operating condition, and the raft wasn't able to open that one very wide as yet. The first morsel had been fed into it, however: the bug rider the vines had plucked out of the flier's downy neck fur. It took Grandpa several minutes to work it out of sight, small as it was. But it was a start.

Cord didn't feel quite sane any more. He sat there,

clutching his bundle of clothes and only vaguely aware of
the fact that he was shivering steadily under the cold spray
that touched him now and then, while he followed Grandpa's activities attentively. He decided it would be at least
some hours before one of that black set of mouths grew
flexible and vigorous enough to dispose of a human being.
Under the circumstances, it couldn't make much difference
to the other human beings here; but the moment Grandpa
reached for the first of them would also be the moment he
finally blew the raft to pieces. The White Hunters were
cleaner eaters, at any rate; and that was about the extent to
which he could still control what was going to happen.

Meanwhile, there was the very faint chance that the
weather station's helicopter might spot them.

Meanwhile also, in a weary and horrified fascination, he
kept debating the mystery of what could have produced
such a nightmarish change in the rafts. He could guess
where they were going by now; there were scattered strings
of them stretching back to the Straits or roughly parallel to
their own course, and the direction was that of the plank-
ton-swarming pool of the Zlanti Basin, a thousand miles to
the north. Given time, even mobile lily pads like the rafts
had been could make that trip for the benefit of their seed-
lings. But nothing in their structure explained the sudden
change into alert and capable carnivores.

He watched the rubbery little seal-thing being hauled up
to a mouth. The vines broke its neck; and the mouth took it
in up to the shoulders and then went on working patiently
at what was still a trifle too large a bite. Meanwhile, there
were more thin cat-cries overhead; and a few minutes later,
two more sea-bugs were trapped almost simultaneously and
added to the larder. Grandpa dropped the dead sea-thing
and fed himself another bug rider. The second rider left its
mount with a sudden hop, sank its teeth viciously into one

of the vines that caught it again, and was promptly battered to death against the platform.

Cord felt a resurge of unreasoning hatred against Grandpa. Killing a bug was about equal to cutting a branch from a tree; they had almost no life-awareness. But the rider had aroused his partisanship because of its appearance of intelligent action—and it was in fact closer to the human scale in that feature than to the monstrous life form that had, mechanically, but quite successfully, trapped both it and the human beings. Then his thoughts drifted again; and he found himself speculating vaguely on the curious symbiosis in which the nerve systems of two creatures as dissimilar as the bugs and their riders could be linked so closely that they functioned as one organism.

Suddenly an expression of vast and stunned surprise appeared on his face.

Why—now he *knew!*

Cord stood up hurriedly, shaking with excitement, the whole plan complete in his mind. And a dozen long vines snaked instantly in the direction of his sudden motion and groped for him, taut and stretching. They couldn't reach him, but their savagely alert reaction froze Cord briefly where he was. The platform was shuddering under his feet, as if in irritation at his inaccessibility; but it couldn't be tilted up suddenly here to throw him within the grasp of the vines, as it could around the edges.

Still, it was a warning! Cord sidled gingerly around the cone till he had gained the position he wanted, which was on the forward half of the raft. And then he waited. Waited long minutes, quite motionless, until his heart stopped pounding and the irregular angry shivering of the surface of the raft-thing died away, and the last vine tendril had stopped its blind groping. It might help a lot if, for a second or two after he next started moving, Grandpa wasn't too aware of his exact whereabouts!

He looked back once to check how far they had gone by now beyond the Straits Head Station. It couldn't, he decided, be even an hour behind them. Which was close enough, by the most pessimistic count—if everything else worked out all right! He didn't try to think out in detail what that "everything else" could include, because there were factors that simply couldn't be calculated in advance. And he had an uneasy feeling that speculating too vividly about them might make him almost incapable of carrying out his plan.

At last, moving carefully, Cord took the knife in his left hand but left the gun holstered. He raised the tightly knotted bundle of clothes slowly over his head, balanced in his right hand. With a long, smooth motion he tossed the bundle back across the cone, almost to the opposite edge of the platform.

It hit with a soggy thump. Almost immediately, the whole far edge of the raft buckled and flapped up to toss the strange object to the reaching vines.

Simultaneously, Cord was racing forward. For a moment, his attempt to divert Grandpa's attention seemed completely successful—then he was pitched to his knees as the platform came up.

He was within eight feet of the edge. As it slapped down again, he drew himself desperately forward.

An instant later, he was knifing down through cold, clear water, just ahead of the raft, then twisting and coming up again.

The raft was passing over him. Clouds of tiny sea creatures scattered through its dark jungle of feeding roots. Cord jerked back from a broad, wavering streak of glassy greenness, which was a stinger, and felt a burning jolt on his side, which meant he'd been touched lightly by another. He bumped on blindly through the slimy black tangles of hair roots that covered the bottom of the raft; then green half-light passed over him, and he burst up into the central bubble under the cone.

Half-light and foul, hot air. Water slapped around him, dragging him away again—nothing to hang on to here! Then above him, to his right, moulded against the interior curve of the cone as if it had grown there from the start, the frog-like, man-sized shape of the Yellowhead.

The raft rider!

Cord reached up, caught Grandpa's symbiotic partner and guide by a flabby hind-leg, pulled himself half out of the water, and struck twice with the knife, fast, while the pale-green eyes were still opening.

He'd thought the Yellowhead might need a second or so to detach itself from its host, as the bug riders usually did, before it tried to defend itself. This one merely turned its head; the mouth slashed down and clamped on Cord's left arm above the elbow. His right hand sank the knife through one staring eye, and the Yellowhead jerked away, pulling the knife from his grasp.

Sliding down, he wrapped both hands around the slimy leg and hauled with all his weight. For a moment more, the Yellowhead hung on. Then the countless neural extensions that connected it now with the raft came free in a succession of sucking, tearing sounds; and Cord and the Yellowhead splashed into the water together.

Black tangle of roots again—and two more electric burns suddenly across his back and legs! Strangling, Cord let go. Below him, for a moment, a body was turning over and over with oddly human motions; then a solid wall of water thrust him up and aside, as something big and white struck the turning body and went on.

Cord broke the surface twelve feet behind the raft. And that would have been that, if Grandpa hadn't already been slowing down.

After two tries, he floundered back up on the platform and lay there gasping and coughing awhile. There were no indications that his presence was resented now. A few lax vine-tips twitched uneasily, as if trying to remember previous functions, when he came limping up presently to make sure his three companions were still breathing; but Cord never noticed that.

They were still breathing; and he knew better than to waste time trying to help them himself. He took Grayan's heat-gun from its holster. Grandpa had come to a full stop.

Cord hadn't had time to become completely sane again, or he might have worried now whether Grandpa, violently sundered from his controlling partner, was still capable of motion on his own. Instead, he determined the approximate direction of the Straits Head Station, selected a corresponding spot on the platform, and gave Grandpa a light tap of heat.

Nothing happened immediately. Cord sighed patiently and stepped up the heat a little.

Grandpa shuddered gently. Cord stood up.

Slowly and hesitatingly at first, then with steadfast—though now again brainless—purpose, Grandpa began paddling back towards the Straits Head Station.

James H. Schmitz (1911–81)
James H. Schmitz was best known to science fiction readers as the creator of "Telzey Amberdon," a teenage girl with telepathic powers who was featured in his novels The Universe Against Her *(1964), and* The Lion Game *(1973). Telzey was one of the*

first female series characters in science fiction, and she still has a large following. Mr. Schmitz excelled in the portrayal of exotic aliens, and other notable books by him include The Witches of Karres (1966), The Demon Breed (1968), and A Pride of Monsters (1970).

NOTES

ISAAC ASIMOV

ORIGIN   KEEP OUT by Fredric Brown

Considering the vast difference between life and non-life, it makes sense to wonder how the two came into being.

Did the two come into being separately? Already distinct? Did only one come into being at the start, and was the other added somehow? Was the universe alive at first and did it gradually die? Was it dead at first and did it gradually come alive?

The general assumption, preceding the days of science, was that life and non-life came into being separately, through the creative act of something greater than either. There are innumerable myths detailing the creation of the universe and of life by a "supernatural being," that is, some being not subject to the laws of nature as evidenced in the universe about us.

Many millions of people firmly believe one or another of these myths, but there is no scientific evidence for any of them.

Scientific evidence, painfully gathered over the last three centuries, would make it seem the universe was non-living to begin with and that somehow, here on Earth, life arose out of non-living material.

How strange! Life is so different from non-life. What is the essential spark of life and how was it first inserted into non-living things? Can we possibly find an answer without being forced to call upon the supernatural?

One way of doing this is to suppose that it is a matter of organization. Life is a chemical system that is far more organized than non-life is, and there exists the possibility of chemical change in the direction of greater organization, driven by some energy source such as solar radiation or volcanic heat.

In other words, the chemicals in the newly formed Earth grew gradually more complicated and more intricately interrelated through energy-driven chemical change. Eventually, chemicals were produced that could reproduce themselves, and at that point we might speak of "life."

Even after that point, with life-property added, the reproduction was never perfect; there was always the possibility of accidental or random change, which we call *mutation*. Every once in a while, such a mutation would produce a changed form of life that could take advantage of some aspect of the change to make a new and better, or at any rate *different*, adjustment to its environment. In this way, a new species might get its start.

Humanity has now reached the point where it can fiddle with the material in the chromosomes of the cells, with the nucleic acids that make up the chromosomes. These nucleic acids reproduce themselves and produce the mutations. Scientists now have the capacity to modify the behavior and properties of simple forms of life such as bacteria. Someday they might be able to adjust human chromosomes to remove inborn deficiencies and, eventually, to produce new species.

Brown's "Keep Out" takes up this question. His "daptine" is not perhaps the direction in which science is actually moving these days, but the question of what happens *after* a new species is established will persist, whatever the actual method of establishment. And Brown's answer to that question is all too realistic according to what we observe of human nature here on Earth.

EVOLUTION
STUDENT BODY by Floyd L. Wallace
A SOUND OF THUNDER by Ray Bradbury

The word *evolution* comes from a Latin term meaning "unrolling." It is like the unrolling of a scroll, a continuous tale of gradual change.

According to most myths of origin, life was created ready-made in various species. This is the tale of the Book of Genesis in the Bible. There is, however, an incredible weight of evidence from geology, physiology, anatomy, and biochemistry that this is not so. Instead, species have more or less slowly evolved from earlier species.

There are two basic drives behind biological evolution.

First, there are *mutations*. These produce an element of random change that is the raw material of evolution.

Second, there is *natural selection*. Those mutations

which result in organisms that, in one way or another, fit more efficiently into their environment have a better chance of surviving and reproducing than those mutations which do not. For that reason, some mutations survive and flourish while others die out.

Hence, the story of biological evolution seems to be a striving for ever greater complexity of body organization, efficiency of fit to the environment, or both. There seems to be a continuous trail from the simplest forms of life to the most complex that exist today, albeit there are many, many dead ends and retreats.

I said that evolution is a more or less slow process. How more or less? Until recently the general feeling was that the process was exceedingly slow; that it took millions of years to produce a new species. Some evolutionists are now suggesting "punctuated evolution." They propose that species remain stable for many millions of years, but that under special conditions, which arise now and then, change is comparatively rapid, and a new species might arise in a hundred thousand years or so. And, of course, if conscious guidance is introduced, changes might be more rapid still. Human beings have guided the matings of their domestic animals and produced new strains, though not yet new species, very rapidly indeed.

What if we encountered a world where, for some reason, the rate of evolution was *extremely* rapid? What problems would that pose? This is the question taken up in Wallace's "Student Body."

Again, consider the random nature of mutations. This is something that is disquieting to most people. Can mere randomness result in the production of the human species? Of course, it is not *mere* randomness, it is randomness guided by natural selection; but is such a guide, itself blind and unilluminated by intelligence, sufficient?

If, indeed, evolution has progressed randomly and without conscious guidance, then is it sheer dumb luck that we are here? Any one of uncounted millions of quirks might have taken place in evolutionary history that would have resulted in our *not* being here.

Probably no one has illustrated this point more dramatically than Bradbury in "A Sound of Thunder" (my own personal nomination for his best story). If we learn how to travel in time, we may have to watch every step we take. Literally!

LIFE CYCLE INVARIANT by John R. Pierce

Part of life is death.

In one sense, life is immortal. Every molecule of nucleic acid in the body of any organism now alive was replicated from another which was replicated from still another which was replicated from yet another and so on back to the very origin of life. All nucleic acids now in existence form part of an unbroken chain that has endured for at least 3 billion years. In theory, particular nucleic acid molecules may have survived for eons, even though the odds against that are astronomical.

If, however, we leave single molecules aside and consider organisms made up of many cells, in turn made up of many molecules, all forms of life, however long-lived, eventually die.

Human beings are better off than most. The average mammal has a heart that beats a billion times or so before death comes. The larger the mammal, the slower the heartbeat, and the longer the life. A shrew scarcely lives longer than a year, while an elephant may live up to 70 years, and some large whales possibly up to 90. Yet human beings, far smaller than elephants and whales, can live up to as much as 115 years, and have hearts that can beat up to *four* billion times before giving out.

Remarkable! And we don't know why!

But even human beings die eventually, and we must recognize such deaths as necessary for the greater good of the species.

For one thing, there is only so much room on Earth and, for that matter, in the universe. If no one died, while new births continued, the Earth would rapidly be filled; and, in a remarkably few thousand years, so would the universe (assuming we could devise means for transferring human beings freely to planets surrounding other stars).

Nevertheless, people dream of immortality, and we might suspect that if the price of immortality were an end to children, many people might accept that. They might opt for life for one generation at the cost of non-life for all future generations.

That is not just selfishness; it is death for the species. Children have not only young brains, they have *new* brains: brains and bodies containing new combinations of nucleic acids. They have the power to produce new things, to reason, to create, to solve, as the old were not able to. They introduce new mutations that may lead to further evolution.

In short, death for the individual implies change—plus new and better life—for the species. In reverse, immortality for the individual means changelessness for the species, the same minds, running in the same ruts; and stultification and death for the species.

In a way, you can bring this home to the individual by putting it on a personal basis. We change constantly as we live, and with age we deteriorate. If we avoid accident and disease and approach the ultimate decay of old age, the deterioration reaches a point where we find it a relief to die and rest.

The alternative? No deterioration! No change! But is that better? See what Pierce has to say in "Invariant."

CELL BIOLOGY
THE EXTERMINATOR by A. Hyatt Verrill

Far back in the history of life, the first cells were formed. It is uncertain whether there was an era previously in which life consisted of mere molecules of nucleic acids and proteins, but if so, the formation of a cell represented a major breakthrough in the history of life.

The cell is a pinched-off microscopic section of the ocean, surrounded and protected by a semipermeable membrane—one through which some molecules could penetrate and others could not. Food, the molecules used by the life-form to construct more of itself, or to be dismantled into energy, could penetrate and be preserved inside. Waste material could be pushed out of the cell. Within the cell was a concentration of the material involved in life, packed together for ease of manipulation and chemical change, secure, protected.

The cell was infinitely more successful—had to be—than naked living molecules would be, for those molecules would have to search the ocean for what they needed, a molecule at a time, with no way of gathering and concentrating them. The result was that once cells appeared, precellular material was outclassed and disappeared.

Today all life, with one exception, is cellular in nature. The exception is the viruses, and even they cannot reproduce except as parasites on cells. What's more, viruses may not be remnants of ancient pre-cellular life, but may have evolved, degeneratively, from cells.

A large cell like that of a paramecium is more advanced than a small cell like that of bacteria. A large cell can divide its substance into different specializations, can develop *organelles*, small sub-cellular regions that digest food, or produce energy, or construct protein, or protect the nucleic acid blueprints that run the show.

Yet there is a limit to how large cells can become. The cell works throughout its volume, but it can absorb food and eject waste only through its surface membrane. The volume of a cell increases as the cube of its linear measurement, the surface as the square. Double a cell in all its dimensions, and its inner material increases eight times in quantity, but its surface only four times in area. The working of the membrane has to become twice as efficient. On the whole, the membrane runs out of efficiency, and cells must either stay very small, or become very flat or long to increase the surface (and, in so doing, gain weaknesses).

How, then, can large organisms evolve? The answer is to leave the cells small but to join them together, to develop specializations not within the cell but among cells and groups of cells. In short, there came the *multicellular organism*, some time over 600 million years ago. Today we have whales that are up to 150 tons in mass and that contain up to 100,000,000,000,000,000,000 cells, all of which are within immediate reach of a complex blood stream that is an efficient ocean substitute. Every one of those cells has an "ocean-side" location and can make use of its membrane.

Somehow we always look back to those cells. Something inside us tells us those cells are fundamental to life; that we ourselves are cells in bunches, but cells just the same. Science fiction writers can dramatize that, as in Verrill's "The Exterminator."

GENETICS

TOMORROW'S CHILDREN by Poul Anderson
MARY AND JOE by Naomi Mitchison

About 1900, biologists realized that there were objects within cells that were responsible for the recognizable characteristics of organisms. They also realized that these objects were able to transmit those characteristics to the new cells into which an old cell divided—and to children from parents. Those objects were called *genes*, from a Greek word meaning "to give birth to."

We now know the chemicals that make up the genes are *deoxyribonucleic acid*, usually abbreviated *DNA*. Nevertheless, the study of the manner in which physical characteristics are transmitted and modified is the science of *genetics*, from "gene."

DNA molecules replicate themselves in a complex manner that biologists have worked out only in the last thirty years; and it is not surprising that occasionally the replication is imperfect. (The surprise is that it is perfect so often.) The result is that a DNA molecule is occasionally produced that is not quite like its "parent," and the result of *that* is a mutation.

In general, mutations tend to be relatively few, unimportant, or both, and natural selection sees to it that most are eliminated, or are held down to manageable numbers. What, however, if the number of mutations are increased?

This can be done. Anything that, so to speak, "nudges" the DNA molecule while it replicates itself is quite likely to produce a mistake—just as you would err if your elbow was nudged while you were trying to do something that requires considerable care, such as threading a needle.

Many things will serve as a "nudge": heat, certain chemicals, cosmic rays, and other penetrating radiation. It so happens that, in the twentieth century, human beings learned to work with hard radiation. In the second half of the century, particularly, there arose the possibility of nuclear fission, either as bombs or as power sources, which could, either deliberately or accidentally, vastly increase the amount of radiation in the environment.

Would the rate of mutation then go up? If so, what then? Anderson took up this problem in "Tomorrow's Children," not long after the nuclear bomb became a reality.

In the passage of genes from parents to children, sperm cells and egg cells are involved. Each parent has twenty-three pairs of chromosomes (which are long strings of genes), and each sperm cell or egg cell has a half-set, one chromosome of each pair. When a sperm cell fertilizes an egg cell, the resultant *fertilized ovum* has twenty-three pairs of chromosomes again, one of each pair from the father and one from the mother. The child is genetically different from either parent.

Suppose, though, the nucleus of the fertilized egg (which contains the chromosomes) is removed and replaced by an ordinary nucleus that contains a complete set from a male, or from a female. The fertilized ovum can then evolve to produce a human being who is genetically identical to the person supplying the nucleus. That is a *clone*, and, in recent years, clones have offered a number of plot possibilities to science fiction writers—witness Mitchison's "Mary and Joe."

PHYSIOLOGY
SEA CHANGE by Thomas N. Scortia

All forms of multicellular life are made up of cells of roughly the same size and structure, containing roughly the same kind of chemicals. To be sure, plant cells contain chloroplasts, which, in turn, contain chlorophyll, which, in turn, makes possible the use of sunlight to convert carbon dioxide and water into carbohydrates. Animal cells lack chloroplasts, a difference of crucial nature, but even so, the similarities among cells are far greater than the differences.

Yet even tiny differences suffice. The fertilized ovum of a porcupine, of a human being, of a starfish are surprisingly alike to the eye and even to chemical analysis, and yet there is no danger that two porcupines will give birth to a starfish, or vice versa.

What's more, built out of these very similar raw materials, different species possess remarkable and differing abilities. Their physiologies (the way in which the various parts of their bodies function together) differ, and fit their different ways of life.

For instance, we cannot dive under water very far, but a sperm whale can dive half a mile deep and remain under water for over an hour. Somehow it can store oxygen, and somehow it can avoid having the ocean pressure hurt it or drive nitrogen into solution in its blood stream (all of which the human body cannot do). When the sperm whale zooms upward again, the lowered pressure does not release the nitrogen as bubbles in its blood stream and kill it.

A giraffe can have its head eighteen feet in the air and yet its heart can drive the blood up through the long neck, against the pull of gravity, and supply the brain with all the blood it needs. A very high blood pressure is required for this, yet the giraffe flourishes. What's more, when the giraffe drinks, it lowers its head to the level of the pool; down, down, through eighteen feet; yet the blood stream, which must change from a long travel upward against gravity to a long travel downward with it (and vice versa when the head is raised again), manages to adjust.

On the whole, human beings lack very unusual capacities. They are generalized animals, who can do a large number of different things, mostly badly. We cannot run like horses, or leap like kangaroos, or dive like whales, or swim like seals, but we can do each of these things after a fashion.

The fact that we don't possess these unusual abilities is good. The more specialized a creature is, the more of itself is sacrificed to that one ability, and the fewer its options are. The more specialized it is, the less it has to make choices among many actions, since it can do so few, and the less intelligent it need be. It is because we are generalized that we have had to develop intelligence to choose among our many possibilities.

And because of our intelligence, we have developed machines that outdo the specialized animals. In our machines, we can fly faster than swifts, race faster than antelopes, dive deeper than whales, lift more than elephants, see farther than eagles, kill better than tigers.

But what if human beings must someday adapt themselves to something never faced by life-forms before? What if they must adapt themselves to space? Scortia considers that in "Sea Change."

ANATOMY
CAUGHT IN THE ORGAN DRAFT by Robert Silverberg

Our cells are combined into tissues of various sorts—connective tissue, adipose tissue, muscle tissue, nerve tissue, and others—and different kinds of tissue are combined to form an organ, a part of the body designed to do a particular job. We're very familiar with some of the organs. We all know about the heart that pumps the blood through the circulatory system; the kidneys that filter wastes out of the blood; the stomach that stores food for a while and helps digest it; the lungs devised for the intake of oxygen; the liver, our general chemical factory to store sugar, form bile, and detoxify poisons. We could continue—the eyes, the tongue, the thyroid gland, and so on.

Each organ performs its function, always convenient, sometimes absolutely vital.

If the heart fails, it doesn't matter that every other part of the body is in perfect, tiptop working order. The whole body dies.

Ditto, ditto, if the kidneys fail, if the lungs fail, if a vital blood vessel ruptures. Even if an organ is not essential to life, existence without it could be seriously handicapped. If the eyes go, for instance, or if a leg must be removed, a person will have great problems.

And yet none of these organs is you. If a limb is amputated, the essential you still exists. However much you are handicapped, you keep all your memories, all your emotions, all your likes and dislikes, all your little ways and quirks and prejudices, all your personality, all your you. Your friends accept the continuity of you despite these failures of parts.

The only organ that is essentially you is your brain.

One must envy an automobile, in a way. When an automobile part goes, someone gets a duplicate part. The failed part is removed, the new part is inserted, and off goes the car, "good as new." One can imagine a car being replaced, bit by bit, until nothing that was in it when first bought is still there, and since it doesn't have a brain, it will be accepted always as the same car.

To be sure, human parts can continue to trundle along, after a fashion, even after a hundred years of continual use, and that is true of no car (or any human machine) ever devised. We should be grateful for that, and yet, when a heart starts failing, who among us would not long for another heart off the shelf—a fresh young heart, tested, approved, and stamped by a government inspector?

Unfortunately, those hearts belong to other bodies. But what if a body dies for some other reason, leaving the heart intact and in fine working order—but doomed to death, unless quickly scooped out and put to a useful repair purpose?

We can do that. There have been numerous cases of heart transplants, kidney transplants, liver transplants, and corneal transplants.

We can't help but look at that sort of thing with approval, for we tend to visualize ourselves as potential receivers of transplants and if we need something vital, we would want it available. For every receiver, however, there is a donor, and it is that point Silverberg takes up in "Caught in the Organ Draft."

REPRODUCTION
NINE LIVES by Ursula K. Le Guin

In an earlier note, I mentioned cloning. That is not really so new and startling a conception. *Clone* is the Greek word for "twig," and it is easy to reproduce a plant by sticking part of it into the ground and letting it take root, or by grafting a twig onto the branch of another tree, even one of a different species.

Cloning is a term that can be used for any form of asexual reproduction, where the new organism has all the genetic equipment of the old; where there is no sperm-egg combination that fuses half the equipment of the mother with half the equipment of the father to form a new individual not entirely like either.

Simple animals—sponges, flatworms, starfish—can be torn into pieces and each piece will grow and reconstruct an entire organism, all with the same genetic equipment.

Sometimes a fertilized ovum of an advanced species— even a human being—can divide in two, and the two half-ova can, for some reason, fall apart. Each will then develop on its own and the result will be identical twins, each with the same genetic equipment. This happens, on the average, in 1 out of about 85 human births. Each such twin is a clone of the other.

Among complex animals, however, barring such incidents at the very beginning of development, cloning does not take place, and reproduction is purely sexual. You cannot get a new bull by planting a bull's leg in the ground, or even by taking a freshly removed bull's leg and by keeping its circulation carefully going. For that matter, the bull cannot grow a new leg if one is removed.

Nevertheless, biologists have succeeded in inducing a form of asexual reproduction in animals that does not take place in nature. It is done by microsurgery. The nucleus of an ovum is removed, and another nucleus is substituted. If the ovum then proceeds to develop, the resulting clone is a genetic duplicate of the adult that contributed the nucleus. It is an identical twin of the donor.

Of course, in this case, the twin may be thirty years

younger than the donor, which is not very "identical."
However, suppose a donor donates a dozen nuclei, which
are placed in a dozen ova. The result will be twelve identical twins, all the same age.

This sort of thing has been done on cold-blooded animals such as frogs, and, in principle, it should therefore
work on mammals as well. Mammalian cloning has some
practical difficulties in the way, however. First, mammalian
ova are particularly small and fragile, and operating on
them requires great delicacy and precision, so that the
chances of success are greatly diminished. Second, in the
case of mammals, the ova are within the body and not quite
as easy to get at as, for instance, those of frogs, which
deposit eggs in the water. Nevertheless, mammals, and even
human beings, can be cloned, if delicate procedures are
worked out, and there seems no doubt that someday it will
be done, if biologists put their minds to it.

And what will cloned human beings be like? Will they be
just one more set of identical twins, triplets, quadruplets,
and so on? Probably yes. Each will be a distinct personality
despite identical genetic equipment. But science fiction
writers like to speculate. What if not? And it is with that
that Le Guin's "Nine Lives" deals.

PLANT BIOLOGY
ALIEN EARTH by Edmond Hamilton

Through most of history, plants were not considered to be
alive. They did not live; they merely vegetated. After all,
they did not move, they did not eat, they made no sound.
They seemed to exist merely for the purpose of serving as
food for animals.

In the Bible, in fact, when the dry land was created on
the third day, God at once had plants appear on it. It

seemed to be merely an attribute of the land. The word *life* is not used in connection with them. It is only on the fifth day, when animals are first produced that the word is used: "And God said, Let the waters bring forth abundantly the moving creature that hath life . . ." (Genesis 1:20).

Animals are moving creatures, plants are not.

After the animal world is created (including man), God says, to the man and, presumably, to animal life in general: ". . . Behold, I have given you every herb bearing seed . . . and every tree . . . yielding seed; to you it shall be for meat" (Genesis 1:29).

Though this seems to classify animals as alive and plants as food, plants are every bit as alive as animals. In the 1830's, it was discovered that plants, like animals, are made up of cells containing protoplasm. Further studies made it appear that the chemical nature of plant cells and animal cells were much alike; that both plants and animals made use of proteins and nucleic acids, along with chemical reaction systems that were similar in both.

In fact, if the chemistry of plants and that of animals are compared, the balance would seem to lie with the plants. First, plants have chlorophyll, which makes it possible for them to use the energy of sunlight to store chemical energy and build up their tissues. Animals don't have chlorophyll and must live, parasitically, on this plant talent. Second, plants have the ability to manufacture cellulose, a strong and chemically resistant supporting material, an ability animals do not have. Third, plants can manufacture from simple substances all the complex chemicals they need for life, without exception. Animals need to find some complex structures ready-made in their diet and would die without them. (We call those complex structures *vitamins*.)

And yet plants are a simpler form of life than animals are in a number of ways. They lack the more complicated tissues that animals have; they have neither muscles nor nerves. They do not move because (on land, at least) they must have roots to obtain water, and the roots anchor them in place.

Still, they move after a fashion. They do grow. They bend their stems slowly in such a way as to face the sun; their roots bend in such a way as to grow toward water. Some plants have leaves that close when touched.

The motion is there, but it is slow, for it makes use of such things as liquid turgor or differential growth, rather than the quickness of contracting muscle fibers. If plants are viewed by time-lapse photography, with individual photographs taken at considerable intervals, in series, and the whole run through a motion picture projector, the motion is speeded up and the plants take on obvious life. The same might be accomplished if we slowed our own perceptions, and Hamilton makes that point in "Alien Earth."

ECOLOGY   GRANDPA by James H. Schmitz

We tend to think of living things as individuals or, at most, as species. Human beings are human beings, cats are cats, chipmunks are chipmunks, and so on. They are items in a long list of living things—separate items. Hence, if something bad happens to chipmunks, that's for chipmunks to worry about.

Not so. If "no man is an island," so much more so is no species. There is no species that lives in isolation; every species depends in one way or another on other species, which in turn depend on others, and so on until every species on Earth is tied together in a complex pattern. What's more, all species are also dependent on various facets of the inanimate environment, and affect the inanimate environment as well.

There is a tree on Mauritius Island that is headed for extinction since no new shoots have taken root in three centuries. The seeds could sprout only after they had been softened up by passing through the digestive tract of the dodo—and the dodo has been extinct for three centuries.

There are corals that form reefs in the tropics that are homes for countless species of sea creatures. There are plants that require no living food but are absolutely dependent on insects, sometimes on one particular kind of insect, for their fertilization. Without the insects they would die out, like the tree on Mauritius without the dodo.

Cattle eat grass, but would die of starvation without the microorganisms in their digestive tract, for it is the microorganisms, not the cattle, that can digest the grass. Termites eat wood (that is the one thing the average person knows about termites), but they cannot digest wood. They, too, depend upon microorganisms.

This pattern of interdependence is an ecological balance, and ecology is the study of the pattern of specie as a whole.

We need such studies desperately, for never before in Earth's history has a single species of large animals so increased in numbers, so spread over the world generally, so drastically changed the environment, so encouraged the growth of species it favors, so wildly slaughtered or simply crowded out species it does not want or toward which it is indifferent, as is the case with human beings now.

We do not yet know enough to be able to estimate the damage we are doing to life on Earth generally, and to ourselves in particular (for we, too, depend on the smooth working of the ecological balance). If it appears, eventually, that the balance has been sufficiently upset to produce vast undesirable changes on Earth, it may, by the time this becomes apparent, be too late to correct the trouble.

Ecology is a science that is of great importance to the

science fiction writer, too. Almost always, in describing a distant world, mention is made of various life-forms upon it without any effort being made to tie it into a plausible pattern. In short, extraterrestrial life is often considered, but extraterrestrial ecology almost never. This is understandable. Ecology is not a very well developed branch of biology, and it is a complex study that is not easy to understand. Nevertheless, we get an interesting glimpse of another world's ecology in Schmitz's "Grandpa."